#1 RIVAL

USA *Today* Bestselling Author

T. GEPHART

#1 Rival
Published by T Gephart
Copyright 2018 T Gephart

ISBN-13: 978–0-6480231–4-2
ISBN-10: 0–6480231–4-1

Cover by:
Hang Le

Editing by:
Nichole Strauss, Insight Editing Services

Interior Design & Formatting by:
Christine Borgford, Type A Formatting

#1
RIVAL

DEDICATION

To my Brothers,
In our darkest moments, we had each other.

CHAPTER #1

I HATED HIM.

My distaste for Roman Pierce wasn't new, but as I stared across the table—my eyes drilling into him—the feelings of hostility bubbled inside of me. The heat traveled up my neck as my skin flushed, his stupid perfect smile edging wider as he glared back at me smugly.

"Don't you have anything better to do?" My venom-laced words jutting out from my clenched jaw. "Like a paralegal or something? Or have you worked your way through them already?"

He laughed, throwing his head back with genuine amusement before his eyes settled back onto me. "You have a very unhealthy interest in my private life, Harper. Maybe if you put that energy into your own, you might crack a smile once in a while."

"I smile, Pierce. But *only* when there is something worth smiling about," I fired back, my knuckles whitening as I gripped the arm of the chair. "Which right now seems to be in short supply."

No one could push my buttons like he could.

No. One.

It was his sport, his hobby, his favorite pastime. All of which could have been avoided if he'd been a half decent person with an ability to be friendly.

But he wasn't.

Something I found out the day we'd met.

Roman and I were two of the five junior associates at Moss, Byrne & Carter. He'd graduated from Yale, while I'd gained my entry into the bar after my time at Princeton. Both of us had been working at other firms when we'd been headhunted by Daniel Moss. He wanted fresh blood, and I was done treading water and being a glorified secretary. His offer had been too good to refuse.

But while I had been excited to be part of a vibrant team, anxious to cut my teeth on something juicy and work closely with someone who was rumored to be brilliant. Roman didn't seem to share the same thoughts.

Sure, I'll admit that when he'd first walked into the room, I'd been momentarily blinded by his exceptional good looks. He was hard to miss at six-four (a little more than a foot taller than me), blond, with clear blue eyes. That wasn't even taking into account how amazing he seemed to fill out his tailored suit.

It looked expensive, definitely designer.

But he'd taken one look at me, and my warm smile, and told me he didn't need any more friends. And while I was willing to overlook his rudeness—chalking it up to possible nerves—he'd gone out of his way to make my time a living hell.

Oh, and that line he'd given me about not needing any more friends had been total bullshit too. He was more than happy to go out and have beer with some of the other associates, just not me.

It didn't help that we were both being mentored by Daniel Moss himself, meaning almost every day I had to see him, work with him and put up with his snide remarks.

Every opportunity he had to challenge me or my work, he did. Which meant I had no choice but to do the same. I didn't want to appear weak or submissive in front of one of the greatest legal minds in California. Not a chance. So, instead of working as a team, it was a daily grudge match, neither of us willing to concede in an effort to out "lawyer" each other.

"Ahhh, I see you're both here." Daniel strode in, unbuttoning his jacket. "Hope you've been playing nice."

Daniel Moss knew of our rivalry, hell, I was almost positive he got off on it. He watched our heated discussions like a proud parent, more often than not, encouraging them. So it came as no surprise that Roman and I were already in a staring match and the morning had just begun.

"Of course, Daniel." The asshole AKA Roman anchored his hand behind his neck as his smug grin widened. "Harper was just telling me how much I made her smile."

How much he made me smile? I'd rather have my spleen removed than have to look at his stupid face.

Even if he was insanely gorgeous.

Which just made it worse because he didn't deserve to be that attractive. His devastating good looks wasted on an arrogant prick.

My jaw tightened, the words barely able to come out as I matched his obnoxious grin. "Yes, that's right. Pierce is finally going to see the Wizard and ask him for a brain." I clutched my hands to my chest in mock pride.

"You should join me." He laughed, my taunt barely leaving a mark. "We can get him to give you a sense of humor."

"Sounds good, *Roman*." I said his name like it was a dirty word. "I'm sure it was your stellar sense of humor that got the client an extra twenty five thousand on the settlement yesterday. No, wait." I tapped my finger on my chin, squinting my eyes like I was deep in thought. "That's right, it was me."

Daniel's lips thinned to a tight line as he sat down in his leather chair. His palms rested on two matching folders that lay in front of him on the glass boardroom table. "While I enjoy your morning skirmishes, we have work to do. A new case. Here you go." He pushed the folders toward us, one stopping in front of me while the other was saved from going over the edge by Roman's large, steady hand.

Excellent, my excitement spiked at the thought of a new challenge. While I preferred working alone, the team assignments pushed me harder. Nothing like having a six-foot-four know-it-all breathing down your neck to light a fire under your ass. And I not so secretly loved that he'd have a perfect view when I wiped the floor with him. I didn't even care what the case was; I'd outshine him in a traffic infringement if I had to.

"A divorce?" Roman was the first to speak, his liquid blue eyes filling with confusion. "Since when do we handle family law?"

Dumb move.

I'd been so preoccupied with Roman and our *competition* that I had yet to read the file. That was a rookie mistake and one I hadn't made in a while. Damn him, I cursed under my breath as I quickly opened the folder and tried to speed-read the particulars of the case. I hated being at a disadvantage, even more so when it gave Roman the upper hand.

"Since the petitioner is Jana Cane," Daniel announced as my eyes skimmed over the brief.

This wasn't just any divorce. This was huge.

"Oh. Wow." The words escaped my lips as my eyes stayed glued to the page.

"That name supposed to mean something?" Roman's voice lacked the excitement mine had, clearly not so clued up as I'd first thought.

I didn't even try to pretend how thrilled I was that I knew more about the client than he did, the smile spreading across my lips widening as I cleared my throat.

"Jana Cane is the CEO and founder of Cane Cosmetics." I

lifted my chin proudly as I looked at him in those stupid, gorgeous blue eyes. "Not only has she developed a line of make up that looks and feels great, but the pharmaceutical arm of her company is developing a line which delivers topical medicine through her product. I'm not just talking anti-aging treatments, but actually treating skin infections and burns." I neglected to mention that her eye cream had been my saving grace for the last few years, a girl needed to have some secrets.

"Sounds like Roman might need some of the miracle cream." Daniel laughed, folding his arms across his chest. "It's not like you not to be on top of things." His head tipped toward my adversary, goading him further.

"I'm sorry, my area of expertise is the *law*, doesn't leave me a lot of time to flick through copies of *Vogue*," he said with no apology in his voice. "But it looks like Harper has that covered for us." His mouth twitched into a taunting grin.

Anger spiked in me as heat traveled up the back of my neck.

God, I hated him. He couldn't just accept I knew more about our client than he did, no, he had to go throw in some backhanded compliment. Maybe he needed to ask the Wizard for a heart as well, because from what I'd seen, he was seriously lacking one.

"Actually, it was *Forbes* not *Vogue*." I forced the smile even though I could feel myself grinding my teeth. "The article didn't have any pictures, so I can understand how you missed it. I can give you a condensed version if you want. Maybe draw you a diagram so it's easier to understand and there aren't so many words to confuse you."

Ha, take that you cocky bastard. The smile I had originally needed to fake now genuine as I grinned with a sense of victory.

Daniel didn't bother interjecting, knowing from experience it was easier to let us go. It was our process, and one that had raised productivity of the firm. So, other than looking slightly bored and a little annoyed, he raised his eyebrow, waiting for Roman's response we both knew was coming.

He didn't flinch, my return serve barely leaving a mark as he sat there smirking. "I appreciate the effort, Harper, but I'm sure her financials and her business details are listed in the brief. Let's worry less about your ability to make a flip chart and more about the huge settlement her ex-husband is probably demanding. That is why I'm assuming she hired us, right?" He shot me a quick wink before returning his gaze to Daniel.

I don't know how he did it.

No matter what I threw at him, it was like he was made of Teflon—nothing stuck. Nothing. He probably could be caught red-handed screwing a secretary in the copying room, and he'd still manage to put a positive spin on it and land a promotion. Wowing the senior partners with tales of the extra training he was providing or some other bullshit. And if I didn't hate him so much, I would be in awe. It's what made him a brilliant lawyer, and lethal in a courtroom. Not that I'd ever admit it to him. No, I wouldn't give him the satisfaction.

Gah. Screw him, his talent and good looks. I silently hoped he gained fifty pounds and got a receding hairline sometime in the future.

"Ironically, it's not the settlement Jana is concerned with." Daniel's brow rose as he blew out a breath. "Against my advice, she is willing to give him the house and a sizeable payout. There aren't any children involved, but she even agreed to more than reasonable spousal support as well."

Silence filled the room as both Roman and I looked to Daniel. He too was the master of disguising his emotions. And had we not spent more time with him in the past year than his own wife, it would have been next to impossible to know he was silently seething. But there it was, the slight tick of his jaw, hiding the displeasure

I knew was bubbling just underneath the surface.

"What's he have on her?" Roman asked, knowing the only way someone would be willing to give money away for a quickie divorce was if the other party had something that could possibly be damaging. "I know a guy, he could dig up some dirt on him. Affairs, gambling addiction—give me a week and he'll deliver. Everyone has something to hide."

With Jana, her brand was her livelihood. Her husband was reported to be a dope-smoking slacker, who had gone from one dead-end job to another until she hit the big time. Which meant his claim to her fortune would be easily refuted.

"You *know* a guy?" Unable to hide my surprise, I turned to Roman, wondering if he'd been watching re-runs of the *Soprano's*. "You going to offer to kneecap the soon to be ex-husband too or is your *guy* going to take care of it."

"Now, now, Harper. I would *never* do something like that." Roman shot me a wink. "I've taken an oath to uphold the law, which I *always* do."

Yeah, I wasn't feeling especially confident considering his assurance came with a wink. I had no doubt Roman would play dirty if he felt justified. Not turn into a full-blooded vigilante, but from everything I'd seen, he didn't like to lose. Which made two of us. Except, I wasn't sure how far I would bend the rules. I had a hunch the asshole sitting across from me was going to be instrumental in my self-discovery.

"He doesn't have anything, yet." Daniel interrupted my mental to-and-fro, pulling our attention back to the case. "But he and his lawyer will have something soon. Your job," his hand gestured to the two of us, "is to stop the fall-out before it happens."

"Wait." I held up my hand confused by the whole scenario. "You're saying there's dirt on Jana that we know and he doesn't? If she is ready to go through with a quick divorce, let's move ahead *before* he finds out. Once the paper has been signed, it won't matter."

"It's not that easy." Roman's eyes moved from his file back to Daniel, his poker face displaying zero expression. "Because if it was, you wouldn't need us."

And judging by Daniel's tight smile, Roman was right. "She is filing a patent, a big one. We're talking multi-million dollars in expected revenue once it hits the market, and it will make the current divorce settlement look like loose change. The paperwork will be filed in the next month, any longer than that and she risks information leaking out." The air whistled as he blew out from between his teeth. "She says they were separated before she'd started to develop it, but she has no proof."

"Which means that, while the marriage had ended, they were still living under the same roof. And let me guess, no prenup," I responded before I'd even had a chance to process the information fully.

Shit. This was not good on two counts.

One, without a prenup and a very clear date on when they commenced their separation, it was going to be difficult to argue the patent, and the income that came with it, wasn't communal property. And the other—and most important—I hated that Roman's smug grin indicated he wasn't sharing in the same sense of concern.

"We establish a new timeline," he responded, like I'd been worried for no reason at all and the solution was so easy. "One that puts the dissolution of the marriage *before* our client started working on the patent. We do that and it doesn't matter if he was living with her or not. *Fredrick v Carrick*, 1984."

God, I hated him.

So freaking cool and confident, whipping out precedent like he had the Yale law library committed to memory. Pity, he was wrong in this instance. His argument was completely flawed and unusable, it was a shame I was going to have to demonstrate that for the second time in the meeting so far. If I didn't enjoy it so much, I might have been sorry. But I wasn't. Sucker. "Ah yes, except that in *Fredrick v Carrick* neither of them could afford the divorce. That isn't the case here."

Take that, Pierce. How dumb do you have to be to compare two rich people—well, one rich person and their parasitic leech—against two people who in 1984 were barely surviving on food stamps? Maybe the product he used to slick back his gorgeous blond hair had melted his brain. That could be the only explanation.

"Actually, it's *exactly* the case here." His smile didn't waver as his eyes locked on mine. "If the amount of wealth is sizeable, then it's not exactly as easy as splitting a couple grand in their bank account. So, yes, it *is* relevant."

Screw him and his freaking slicked back hair, his example was shaky at best.

"Defense will argue she had means therefore she could have left. She at any time could have moved to a hotel room or an apartment." While I didn't believe Jana was to blame here, I had a fairly good idea how the opposing counsel would play this.

"And leave him in the house *she* was paying for? Ha, come on, Harper. Would you let some man you couldn't stand stay in the house you worked hard for? Doubtful. I maintain that she was the rightful owner of the house even if his name was on the title." His voice rose, confidence echoing out of every word. "The fact she is giving it to him now is out of the generosity of her heart. She was sad, depressed, wanted to maintain a wholesome image, didn't have time or the mental energy to move out—pick one. Mental anguish clouds judgment, and the cash made her isolated. How could she confess to her rich, professional friends that she was living a lie? So instead, she decided to play along with the charade until it was no longer tenable."

"Wow, you got all of that just from reading the file?" I rolled my eyes, the sarcasm thick in my voice. "Why even bother to interview her at all? I mean, you know everything, right?"

"It's not about *knowing*, it's about *proving*. And when I establish that the marriage was over, regardless of them sharing a roof, she will have her amended date. One that puts him out of reach of a claim on the new patent."

"Excellent, Roman, sounds like someone paid attention in law school. You can take point. Lauren, you're his back up. I want you both to go through the files and give me something solid by nine a.m. tomorrow in time for Jana Cane, who will be in my office by ten. So, if you have any plans tonight, cancel them."

Perfect. Just freaking perfect. Not only had Daniel given *him* the lead—me relegated to second chair—but I was going to have to spend all day and who knew how much of the night, with Roman's conceited, ego-inflated ass. Not to mention that I *did* have plans. It was the first date I'd agreed to in weeks, and I was looking forward to spending a night in the company of someone whose existence I didn't despise.

"Great." I forced the smile, the words tight against my clenched jaw. "We won't let you down."

As much as I hated all of it—Roman, having to change my plans, and falling short on impressing Daniel—I loved my job more. And I would do whatever I had to in order to succeed.

Even if it meant spending time with assholes who needed personality transplants.

"I know you won't." Daniel straightened his jacket as he stood. "It's why the two of you are earning more than any other junior associate has in the history of this firm. So get to work." His parting words serving as a goodbye as he strode to the door and left us there.

"Don't look so thrilled, Harper." Roman laughed, his enjoyment over the situation annoying me further. "We both know you had nothing better to do tonight."

Ugh. I hated him.

Hated him.

"I *did* have plans," I sneered at him, annoyed it was barely ten a.m. and already he was getting under my skin. I was better than this, and yet, I couldn't stop myself as he turned and looked at me with interest.

"Let me guess?" His weighted stare made me feel uncomfortable, his gaze fixed on me. He stopped, narrowing his eyes as if he was trying to look inside my head. "You and your cat have a standing date. You sit in yoga pants, order take-out, watch television and then take Buzzfeed quizzes about which character you'd be on *Game of Thrones*." He smiled with such satisfaction it made my skin heat.

Hated. Him.

"I think you're confusing *your* plans for the evening with mine. I actually had a date. You know, with a real person. And someone I don't have to pay or who doesn't require inflation."

He threw his head back and laughed, his voice bouncing off the walls as he took a minute to compose himself. "First you accuse me of screwing paralegals and now I need to *pay* women to date me. So which is it, Harper? Am I a whore or a desperate deviant?" His lips twitched as he waited for me to answer.

Why couldn't he be like any reasonable man? Taken the insult or flung another my way. Instead he seemed to remember everything I'd ever said to him and kept it in his back pocket, throwing it out at just the right time to make me feel stupid.

"You can be both." I met his eye, refusing to back down. "Neither is mutually exclusive."

He stood, his tall muscular body coming to full height as he strode slowly to where I was sitting. "That's weak and you know it." His hot breath tickled my ear as he lowered his head, bringing his lips closer to my ear. "But it's interesting how much thought you give my sex life."

I swallowed, not willing to admit exactly how much I thought about him and sex. The truth was, if he didn't open that know-it-all mouth of his and I didn't know him—or if I'd had amnesia and could wipe out what I did—I would be *more* than just interested.

Everything about him was sex personified. He belonged on the cover of a magazine, or in the movies—head to toe oozing some unquantifiable levels of attraction. But it was going to take more than just an amazing face to forget he was an arrogant, self-centered and cocky asshole.

A Praying Mantis had the right idea, mating and then eating the male. It sure would simplify the morning after.

"Don't flatter yourself, Roman. I don't care about anything in your life." I lied through my teeth. "So, if you're done posturing maybe we can get started. A judge isn't going to just take your word for it on when the marriage ended. You're going to need proof."

"Oh, I'll get my proof, Harper." His body leaned forward, a sexy waft of cologne invading my nose. "I don't intend to come out of this any other way than on top."

The case.

He meant the *case*, I reminded myself even though his grin suggested otherwise.

"Funny. That's where I like to be too."

And unlike him, I wasn't sure in what context I meant that statement.

CHAPTER 2

HOURS.

It had taken me literally hours combing through the Cane file trying to establish a feasible timeline. Roman had found receipts for two personal trips Jana had taken on her own prior to the official separation date, but we needed more. Basically, we had to prove they'd been living separate lives for two years, rather than just the last twelve months. Our job made harder by a shared bank account that would make Sawyer Cane's lawyers get a hard-on.

My feet had started to hurt as I paced in my heels, the noise from surrounding offices quieting as people went home for the evening. But instead of me grabbing my handbag and checking out like they were, I was stuck in the large glass box that served as one of the boardrooms.

The black marker tapped at my lips as I stared at the large whiteboard in front of me. I was a visual person and worked better when things were laid out so I could see them. It also didn't hurt that the squeak of the marker against the surface of the board drove Roman insane, and that I had perfected just the right angle for maximum squeak.

"Why don't you take them off?" Roman's voice echoed from

behind me.

"Excuse me?" I turned around, glaring at him as he casually loosened his tie.

"The shoes." He pointed down at my feet. "It's obvious they're pissing you off, and it's not like there's anyone around left to see."

A quick scan through the glass revealed that we were probably the only ones left. The light from our boardroom spilled into an otherwise dark hall.

"Not that I need your permission, but I'd prefer to leave them on." I turned back to my board, twisting my long brown hair into a knot at the base of my neck. I'd always wanted bouncy, curly hair, but instead I was gifted with a mane of thick, straight strands. And right now, their weight on my scalp was annoying me as much as my feet *and* Roman.

"Why? To prove a point?" He barked out a laugh as I ignored him, my marker squeaking down another date. "Just pretend I didn't say anything and take off the damn shoes."

"No." I turned, my eyes hitting his chest, his body closer than it had been a minute ago. "Because I don't want to."

My refusal hadn't been solely because it had been his suggestion, although I'll admit, that was a consideration too. It was because, in addition to my lack of light and bouncy locks, I had also come up short in the height department. And I do mean *literally*.

At a stretch, I was five-foot-three, which meant in order to not look like I was still in high school, I needed an extra couple of inches.

Ha, wasn't *that* a disappointment I'd faced on more than one occasion. And in this instance, I wasn't just talking about my height.

"Fine." Roman reached across to my hand and uncurled my fingers, the marker that had been housed there, taken from my grasp. "But if you write one more thing on that board, it's not going to be your sore feet that are going to be an issue."

"Touchy. Maybe you should take off *your* shoes." I folded my arms across my chest as I watched him stride back to the table. The offending marker was tossed aside, his hand reaching for his phone.

"I'm ordering dinner, what do you want?" He fingered the glass as he waited for my reply.

"Shit. What time is it?" I looked around wondering where I'd put my phone, the wall clock obscured by the whiteboard.

I assumed it was late but didn't know exactly how late. Six o'clock? Six thirty? It wouldn't be later than seven surely. I was supposed to meet Gavin at seven thirty; it had totally escaped my mind to call him and cancel. Hopefully I could catch him before he left. It was still short notice, but at least I could save him the trip.

"Eight thirty, why?" Roman deadpanned.

"Crap. I need to make a call."

Great, now I was one of those women who stood men up in bars and gave them lame-ass excuses like I'd lost track of the time. It didn't help that *lost track of time* was the truth.

"Oh, that's right." He snapped his fingers, a grin spreading across his lips. "Your *date*."

I didn't miss the inflection on the word, nor the sarcasm. And while he had assumed my plans had been fictional or exaggerated—I didn't own or even like cats—they had been with a living, breathing human who hadn't deserved my rudeness.

"Not that it is any of your business," I snapped, irrationally feeling like part of this had been his doing. "But I did have an actual date. He is a nice guy too."

Unlike the man I was currently with, Gavin was a decent man. He wasn't boastful, was more comfortable in jeans and a T-shirt, and worked in tech support for a data recovery firm in Pasadena. And while I had met him on a dating website—save the eye roll, there is literally nowhere in the city where you can meet a decent guy these days—we had sort of clicked. He was one of the few guys I'd met in the last couple of years who hadn't run for the hills the minute I mentioned I was a lawyer. And tonight we were supposed to be meeting face-to-face for the first time.

"Sure he is." Roman looked amused as he lost interest in his phone and our dinner order and turned his attention to me. "Does he know you weren't into him and using him to pass the time?"

"What?" I stopped fumbling with my phone, my eyes snapping up to meet his. "You have no idea what you are talking about."

I glared at him. Even for Roman this was a new low.

"Really?" He laughed, tilting his head to the side as he folded his arms across his chest. "You had a date with some *nice guy* who you barely give a second thought to except when *I* bring up dinner. I'd say the precedent has already been set, and not in his favor."

"It's new, we're just getting to know each other." I had no idea why I felt the need to defend myself, but I did.

He was so wrong.

So wrong.

I had been distracted.

Too busy trying to dig us out of an impossible hole when it had been him who implied to Daniel it was going to be a walk in the park. He should be thanking me, getting down on his knees and showing all kind of gratitude that I didn't fight him on what deep down I knew was a bad idea.

But does he do that? Nooooooo. Instead, he speculates on my personal relationships, which he knows nothing about.

"You are wrong." I said it out loud for the first time even though it had been echoing around my head. "I *am* interested."

And damn him and his oozy confident smile. I wanted to take his tie that hung loose around his neck and choke him with it. That would end all his stupid and inaccurate speculation.

"Please, save yourself the time." He continued to laugh as he straightened. "If you'd given two shits about Mr. Nice Guy, you would have picked up the phone the minute you knew we had to work late. And if he were in there with at least half a chance, you wouldn't have scheduled a date on a Monday. Who even does that?"

Anger spiked inside of me. "You know what, Roman. Screw you."

It wasn't a good comeback. And if the smile on his face was anything to go by, he knew he'd won the round. It was dumb, so childish, and I should have just ignored him. Instead, I let his words eat at me like they always did.

Why? Why did I care what he thought? He was a nobody. He had literally zero impact on my life other than I had to tolerate him at work. And yet, here I was, tossing schoolyard taunts at him because I couldn't think of anything better to say.

Damn him.

DAMN. HIM.

"Great. Screw me? Wow, Harper." He clapped, leaning back on his heels. "You should remember that for our closing statement. Passionate pleas always impress the jury. In other news, you haven't said one thing that convinces me I'm wrong. And you know what, it doesn't even matter. Don't prove me wrong; it's not about me. But be honest with yourself. Now, what do you want for dinner? I'm hungry." He picked up his phone and waved it in the air.

I couldn't believe him.

He was a machine, incapable of any human emotion and/or empathy. Completely cold. A shell. And now he wanted me to sit and eat dinner with him? I didn't even know where to begin with it. And more infuriating than all of that, I was absolutely livid I hadn't just told him to mind his own business and that he knew he had gotten to me.

Slowly the breath escaped my lips as I tried to control my temper. He *wanted* me to keep going. It gave him a sick satisfaction, and I wasn't giving him any more than I already had.

"Whatever you want." I picked up my phone, affixing a smile

to my lips as I moved to the door. "I'm not very hungry anyway, and I need to make this call." I walked out the door before he could say another word.

Cursing under my breath, I walked down the hall to my small office. Calling it an office was seriously overstating, it was more like a closet with a desk. But at least I was no longer in a bullpen, the "office" affording me privacy when I needed it, especially for a time like now.

Gavin's number hadn't even been entered into my phone yet, me needing to pull out a notebook I'd scribbled it on before I could dial it. It was so late, I wasn't even sure he was going to accept the call.

"Hello?" Gavin answered after only the second ring.

"Hey, Gavin, it's Lauren." My fingers rubbed nervously at my forehead. "I am so sorry. I'm still at work and . . ." I looked around realizing Roman was right. I should have called the minute I knew I would have to work late. And maybe I was so mad at him *because* he was right. Nice-guy Gavin hadn't been a priority. "I'm sorry."

"Hey, it happens. Lawyer hours, right?" He laughed, maintaining the good-guy persona even though he would have been justified to drop it. "You want to try for some other time?"

No. I should have said.

You are a nice guy who would probably make a great boyfriend. But there's no spark and I know I picked you because you are safe. Also something I should have said.

"It's just a really crazy time at work right now, and I don't know when it's going to stop."

It was a half-truth. A brush off, which was kinder than the other alternatives.

"Well, okay then." I could hear the disappointment in his voice. "You know my number if you change your mind."

"Yes, of course." I nodded, knowing I wouldn't be calling him.

"And sorry again about tonight."

"It's fine. Goodnight."

Nice until the end, he waited for me to say my goodbye before he hung up. Defeated, tired and hungry—I'd lied when I'd told Roman I wasn't—I sunk into my office chair and let my head drop into my hands. I just needed a minute before I suited up in armor again and went out there and ripped his head off.

Like a Praying Mantis.

Except, there would be no sex.

Taking one final breath, I pushed myself out of my seat and walked back to the boardroom.

Roman was sitting, the fabric of his business shirt stretched across his broad shoulders as he hunched over the table reading a file. There were two glasses of amber liquid in tumblers to his side that hadn't been there before.

"I ordered pizza," he said without looking up. "And I raided Daniel's desk, found a bottle of Glenlivet. Don't get too excited, it's only a twelve-year-old. Who knew he was such a cheap bastard? At least it's a single malt." Blue eyes met mine as he picked up the glass and brought it to his smiling lips.

What the hell?

I had to wonder if he hadn't necked half the bottle while I was gone. It was like he had completely forgotten the previous conversation, the one where he'd been rude and presumptuous, and was now talking about scotch like it was the most natural thing in the world.

He was infuriating.

"Glare at me all you want, Harper." He took another sip. "But maybe you can multitask while you look at the property title I found. Seems Ms. Cane had an investment apartment in her port-folio that's been vacant for three years. Property taxes are all up to date and the notation from the realtor indicated that it isn't to be leased. Ms. Cane likes to have a workspace away from her office. I'm sure if I questioned her about it, she's probably spent a night or two there too. It's enough to establish the separation was earlier than reported. At least with the supporting evidence we've got."

"And you know about the office how?" I temporarily shelved my annoyance and anger, curious how he'd come to be the all-seeing, all-knowing oracle of all things Jana Cane, considering he hadn't even know her name twenty-four hours ago.

"I found the title and called the realtor." He laughed. "Those sons-of-bitches will take calls any time if they think there is a buck in it. They're worse than us. And I happen to know Vanessa." He lowered his glass. "She was most helpful in providing information."

He didn't need to tell me *how* he knew her either. His stupid grin was all I needed to surmise they had probably fucked. I'm sure she probably showed him a condo, and then he screwed her up against the glass as they admired the beautiful view. Asshole.

"I'm sure she was helpful." I strolled over to the table and took a seat opposite him. "Well, that seems like a win for us." I took a sip from my glass, the scotch hot as it traveled down my throat.

"No *thank you, Roman?*" He picked up his drink, hiding his grin behind the rim of the glass. "I'd have thought you would have been more appreciative."

"Well, considering moving the timeline was *your* theory, it was *your* own ass you were saving." Not that I would have allowed us to fail. Of course I wouldn't have. And he knew that, which was why he had boldly made claims. "And you don't get a thanks for doing your job, Roman. It's called a paycheck." I took another sip, the warmness of the liquor spreading through my body as I relaxed into my chair.

"I believe it was both our asses I saved." He tipped his head to me. "Unless I misheard when Daniel told you to be my back up."

"You can just leave my ass out of it."

I didn't want him talking or even thinking about my ass. Or any part of me, which I realized was hypocritical since I had—in the past—thought about his ass. Not that he knew that. And *that* would be changing. Any thoughts about him and his body from here on out would not be entertained.

He didn't respond, instead choosing to look at me silently, which was worse. I hated that I never seemed to know what he was thinking, but he'd always managed to know my thoughts.

"Stop acting creepy." I rolled my eyes when he didn't respond. "And that pizza you ordered better not have been pepperoni." My attempt to try to turn the conversation to something more neutral wasn't great, but I was off my game tonight.

"Half pepperoni, half cheese." He didn't shift his gaze. "I'm not sure what your problem is with pepperoni, but it's unnatural."

"Your processed meat is unnatural and will probably be the reason you keel over from a heart attack before you're forty." I couldn't help but grin. Not that I wanted him to die, I wasn't a monster. But the idea that even Roman would have to deal with middle age like the rest of us was reassuring, and his diet wouldn't continue to be so forgiving.

"Wow, you almost sounded concerned." He swallowed what was left in his glass before letting out a throaty laugh. "The grin gave you away though, you might want to work on that for court."

"Yeah, you're right." I shook my head wondering if he'd taken classes to become such a conceited ass. "No need to be concerned at all, you have no heart."

"In that, you would be correct." He didn't even try and deny it, almost enjoying the sentiment. "It might serve you well to lose yours also."

Never. I could be ambitious and smart, and still be compassionate. It didn't have to be a choice.

It was something my father had warned me about when I had

chosen law. He didn't have a college education, and was still working as a delivery driver, but he and my mom were happy. And wanted me to be the same. *Keep your heart, Lauren. Don't let them turn you into stone*, he'd said and I promised him I would. But I hadn't had nearly enough scotch to have that conversation with Roman, and I'd never tell him something about me he would see as a weakness.

"Yo." Charlie the security guard knocked on the door with pizza boxes in hand. "You order two pizzas?"

"Sure did." Roman pushed away from the table and walked to where Charlie was standing at the door. He opened the lid of the first, inspecting the pizza before taking the box. "Other one is for you. Figured you and the boys might be hungry."

"Gee, thanks Roman." Charlie smiled, believing the pizza was an act of kindness. "You're awesome. Anything I can do for you, let me know."

And there it was, the ulterior motive I knew existed.

"Will do." Roman nodded as he walked back to the table.

Meanwhile, Charlie scurried off with his unexpected bounty and a debt to Roman Pierce that came at a cost of a large pepperoni. I assumed it was pepperoni as I'm sure he wanted to share his future coronary with the masses.

"What?" He eyed me suspiciously as he lowered the box to the table.

"You're always working something, aren't you?" I flipped open the lid and took a slice.

"I have no idea what you are talking about." He shook his head, helping himself to the pizza.

Whether he admitted it or not, I was well aware of his MO. There was nothing random about him. He was cool and calculated, and was slowly building a cache of favors owed. Ones he would cash in when he needed them. I had yet to be included into his servitude of gratitude, and I wasn't sure if I should be thankful or offended.

"Sure, sure. Nothing going on here." I rolled my eyes wondering if he thought I was stupid or blind. "Let's wrap up the rest of these details. I want to get home sometime tonight."

"Good." He didn't press, taking a bite from the heart attack covered crust as he retook his seat. "Let's go over this timeline again."

CHAPTER #3

IT WAS LATE by the time I got back to the apartment my sister and I shared. She was an ER nurse and worked erratic shifts and I . . . well, I had my own crazy hours too.

"Hey Lo, have you eaten?" Morgan yawned from underneath the comforter on the couch. "There's some meatloaf in the fridge if you're hungry."

"Thanks, but I ate at the office." I kicked off my shoes like I had been dying to do hours ago and joined her under the comforter. "How do you work an entire shift and still manage to cook dinner? You're making me feel inadequate."

"Cooking is a stress reliever. The food doesn't demand anything and if I screw up, nobody dies." She grinned, the political drama on the television ignored as she turned her attention to me. "How was work?"

"Ugh, don't ask," I groaned not wanting to talk about Roman or the hours I'd spent imagining his perfect face under the heels I'd refused to take off.

"You know, if you ever decide to kill him, at least you can be your own defense. Will save me the effort of trying to drum up the legal fees." Morgan grinned knowing better than anyone how much I hated him.

"Trust me, it's nothing I haven't already thought of myself." I chuckled, grabbing the remote and notching up the volume.

At thirty-one, Morgan was three years older than me and breathtakingly beautiful. She had dark auburn curls that floated just above her shoulders and deep emerald green eyes that shone with sincerity. And she was tall. Not inappropriately gigantic, but a graceful five-foot-seven. She looked exactly like our mother. They even shared the same temperament, both kind and patient, with a drive to help people.

Mom worked at the same non-profit organization she had since she left college. They helped find jobs for the homeless and the marginalized. And thirty-five years ago, my dad brought in a buddy of his who had fallen on some hard times. The way he tells the story, the minute he saw my mom he was knocked off his feet and asked her to marry him that day. Of course, she said no, but agreed to a date. And then finally after four years of proposing, she finally said yes. So, with two kindhearted and loving parents, it was no surprise their first-born was basically a saint. I on the other hand, was not.

While I'd inherited our dad's thick, straight hair, dark brown eyes and darker complexion, that was where our similarities ended. He edged closer to six-two, rarely rose his voice, and I could count on one hand the amount of times he'd lost his temper. And had we not shared the hair/skin/eye color combo, I would have sworn I was adopted. But I wasn't, I was just different.

It's not that I didn't want to help people, or make a difference, because I did. But I wanted to make money too. I wanted the power, the prestige, the respect, and the success. I also wanted the chase, the thrill of the kill, and I didn't feel guilty about it. The law allowed me to do that, especially working somewhere like Moss, Byrne & Carter. And if I played my cards right, I would become a named partner or go out on my own. I just hadn't decided which yet.

"Hey, when are you going out with that guy you met online?" Morgan asked breaking the comfortable silence we shared as we watched mindless television. "Garry?"

"Gavin," I corrected her, amazed that with everything she had on her mind, she'd remembered. I told you she was a saint. "And it was supposed to be tonight, but I stood him up."

"Lauren." Her ability to show disappointment in a single word—usually my name—unparalleled.

"It wasn't intentional, I swear." My hands rose in defense. "We have a tough case at work and I lost track of time. It was probably for the best anyway, I'm sure he had unrealistic expectations of us spending time together and going on weekend getaways or something."

"Lo, that's what usually happens in relationships." She laughed. "Spending time together, some people even like it so much they move into the same apartment." She gasped in mock horror.

"Well, lucky for you we dodged that bullet." My shoulder nudged hers playfully. "Who is going to sit on the couch and eat all your wonderful cooking if I leave? Nope, I wouldn't do that to you."

"Did you ever think that maybe I haven't found Mr. Right because I am too worried about leaving you?" She shoved me back, her grin widening.

"Sure," I mused, knowing Morgan's lack of relationship was because she had even less free time than I did. "You going to have a happily ever after with yesterday's gunshot wound or maybe it was last week's builder who stupidly shot a nail right through his hand? Not sure how you would choose though, so many possibilities for everlasting love." I batted my eyes at her, my hands clasped tight under my chin.

"Yeah, yeah, wiseass. Let's agree we both suck at dating. But I, unlike someone," her pointed look unnecessary, "at least call when I can't make it."

"You are also nicer than me," I scoffed. "And I *did* call, it was just late."

She sighed. "Poor Garry."

"Gavin."

"Him too." A giggle escaped her lips as she shuffled out from under the comforter. "I'm going to bed. I have two more day shifts before I switch to nights. I want to enjoy a regular sleep pattern while the going's good."

"I'll be heading to bed soon too." The fatigue creeping up on me the longer I sat. "It's been a long day and tomorrow is probably going to be just as long."

"Lo, if you ever need to talk, you know I'm here for you, right?" She hesitated, her hip resting against the doorframe.

"I know, and the same goes for you too." I smiled, knowing that while I wasn't as nurturing as the rest of my family, I loved them just as fiercely.

She nodded, her wordless acknowledgement enough as she moved down the hall to her bedroom and shut the door.

And if I had any sense at all I wouldn't wait and do the same. Except that I didn't. Instead, I let the thoughts of the day roll around in my head as my eyelids started to droop. Like always, my last thought of the day was always the same.

Roman Pierce.

And how I was going to annihilate him.

CHAPTER #4

NOT THAT I was willing to admit it last night, but Roman's find on the investment property was good. It wasn't a smoking gun by any means, but if what he said was true and she did spend time "away" from the family home, it would definitely give us a better position.

Both Roman and I had been at the office since eight. He was going over a series of questions he'd compiled, while I was doing research into Mr. Cane's lawyers.

Lehman, Atkins and Lowe were vermin. Career divorce attorneys with a tendency to drag out cases to increase billing hours. And they did not like to settle. If Jana gave them an easy out, they would become suspicious and argue the generous settlement purely to prove a point. I had never gone up against them, but their reputation was clear. Maybe Roman's idea for changing the timeline hadn't been so brilliant after all.

"What date would you say your marriage was over?" Roman sat across from Jana Cane as he asked his first question.

Daniel was seated at the head of the table while I sat beside Roman with my own set of questions.

"It was New Year's Eve, two years ago." Her voice didn't waver.

She was dressed in a navy pantsuit with her blond hair pulled back into a tight bun. Nothing about her suggested how much money she was worth, but the way she held herself radiated power. "I had suggested we try couples counseling, but Sawyer didn't want to. Said there was nothing wrong with him and if I was unhappy then I needed to work on it myself."

"And did you see a professional—a counselor or a psychologist?" Roman asked, scribbling his notes as he waited for her to speak.

"Yes, I did." Jana didn't hesitate, keeping her voice unemotional. "But I realized the issues that needed fixing were a two-person deal and there was only one of us in therapy. Which is why I decided that I wanted out."

"And did you communicate your desire to end the marriage to Mr. Cane?" His brow rose, the pen in his hand still.

"Yes, I did. I told him I wanted a divorce. He said fine and continued to play on his video game. I asked him to move out repeatedly, but he refused."

While Roman continued his line of questioning—how many times were the requests made, were there any witnesses, were there any instances in writing—I couldn't help but wonder. What if, instead of trying the easy way out and hand her ex-husband a whole bunch of money he didn't deserve, if we shut him and his defense down instead.

"Stop." It came out of my mouth before I had a chance to rethink it.

"Excuse me?" Roman turned, his voice just as sharp as his look.

"Look, Ms. Cane, I know you want this done quickly and painlessly." I didn't bother addressing Roman or Daniel who were both looking at me like I'd spontaneously caught fire. "But you can't do this. You said it yourself, he wasn't interested in saving the marriage. He wasn't interested in you or your company. What he was interested in was your income. He doesn't get the house, he gets a settlement and minimal spousal support, and we can argue down his percentage of future income on past products, but he gets nothing on new developments." The words came rushing out, unable to be stopped once I'd started.

"Ms. Harper, I'd like a moment with you outside if I could." Roman's lips were thinned into a tight smile, but there was nothing warm about it. He was beyond pissed, and he was going to tell me about it too.

"Sure. Please excuse us." I nodded to Jana who, by some miracle, didn't flinch. If she was concerned by the power play, she didn't show it.

Roman quietly pushed back from the table, waiting for me to stand before following me out. His smile didn't falter, and neither did his stride as we walked down the hall to where our offices were.

He didn't speak, probably assuming we'd go into his considering he'd asked for the private conversation. But I preferred mine, so screw him.

"What the fuck are you doing?" I'd barely gotten the door closed when the words came out of his mouth. "We discussed the strategy last night, we're doing this my way. I am taking the lead, you don't fucking change the game now."

"Oh, that's very mature, Roman. You going to take your ball and go home?" My hands anchored on my hips as I stood my ground. "He wants her money, clearly that's all he cares about. You think for one second that when he or his lawyers find out about the patent they are just going to roll over because you said they split up earlier?"

"It's not about what I fucking said, it's about what he is legally entitled to. Which won't be any part of the patent and that is what our client wants."

Usually when I challenged him, he laughed it off and then went about proving me wrong. He didn't show emotion, like his feelings were in a vacuum. But as he stood before me, his muscles coiled, that mask he seemed to have tied down had lifted at the edges.

"She's hurt and wants it over, her judgment is clouded, even Daniel thinks so. I'm telling you settling is the wrong move," I tried to reason, knowing that if he could just see it my way he would agree. "We need to be aggressive, that's why she came here in the first place."

He moved closer, watching to see if I took a step back as his large frame loomed above me. "Funny how you didn't mention any of this yesterday, or last night. Instead, you preferred to undermine me in front of the client today."

And there it was.

The real reason on why he was so pissed.

Because God forbid anyone see that Roman fucking Pierce wasn't the best, even if he was wrong.

"Because we hadn't interviewed her last night." I refused to budge, holding my ground as I continued. "Today, when you were asking questions and hearing her answers, it changed things. We cannot settle and this isn't personal."

He let out a laugh, completely devoid of humor, as he looked me in the eyes. "You think I'm taking this personally? Please, you're the one throwing away a case. We were asked to negotiate, to get it done quickly and quietly. Not wage a fucking war." His voice dropped, his eyes boring into mine. "Is that what you want, Harper? A war?"

I'm not sure if he was talking about Jana or us, and in both instances, I wasn't going to let it go.

"If that's what it takes."

We were so close, our eyes locked in a stare down that neither of us was ready to drop as heat traveled up my spine and radiated across my chest. I didn't know if I was hot from anger or if some sick part of me was turned on by all of it.

By him.

And this.

There was an intensity that seemed to exist, especially when the two of us argued, and in that moment I wasn't sure if I was supposed to kiss him or punch him in the balls. Maybe both. And I couldn't tell you which would have given me the most satisfaction.

This was not good.

Not. Good.

A slight grin edged at his lips, his eyes darkening as his mood seemed to shift from pissed off to intrigued. Like he couldn't quite believe I had it in me. Or, he had been reading my mind and was preparing for a possible strike to the groin.

"Okay then, we'll do it your way." He took a step back, surprising me with his compliance.

"Really?" I didn't have time to hide my surprise, the word squeaking out of me.

I'll admit, apart from being shocked he'd agreed, I was a little disappointed. The idea of getting down and dirty with him was kind of hot. Down and dirty in the legal sense, of course. There was no way he'd be into the other stuff. I wasn't even sure he found me attractive. And why in the hell I even cared about that when we had a client waiting for us in a boardroom was beyond me.

"Yes, really." His voice was laced with amusement as he leaned back on his heels, his menacing grin widening.

"I have to say, Roman, I didn't think you would be so . . ." I searched for the word, "okay with this." And more to the point, why was I questioning it? Why had I not nodded and then walked myself back to our client and started our new plan of attack?

"Oh, you think I was agreeing with you?" He shook his head as a chuckle made its way up his throat. "No, I stand behind everything I said. You are making a huge mistake, Harper."

In the twelve months we'd know each other, he had never used my first name. I wasn't even sure he knew it was Lauren, preferring to call me Harper like I was a cadet in basic training. And if it had been reserved just for me, I would have shoved his *Harper* right down his throat, but he called all the lawyers by their last name. Except for the partners, of course. And the paralegals and the secretaries were exempt too. But then I assumed he was trying to sleep with most of them so it didn't fit with his agenda—whatever that agenda was.

So, the fact I was annoyed as hell at my last name coming out of his mouth right now made no sense.

It seemed to be the morning for it.

Being pissed off, and things not making sense.

"You said we'd do it my way." I was sure I hadn't hallucinated that part of the conversation. I distinctly remembered my shock that he'd given in so easily. "You don't get to turn it around now and say I misheard."

"No, you heard me correctly, but you clearly didn't understand what I meant." He could barely contain his grin. "I asked you if you wanted a war, you said if that's what it took. So we're doing it your way. You present your defense and I'll present mine, and whichever the client picks will be the way we go."

Speechless.

My mouth opened and closed a few times as I struggled to find words.

Nope.

He made an exaggerated display of checking his watch. "Oh, and she's been waiting awhile, so we should get back and plead our cases, don't you think."

"I haven't had time to prepare my case. You had all of yesterday." I stopped short of saying it wasn't fair because that would sound too childish, but it was exactly what I was thinking.

"Well then, you better think on your feet." He tipped his head toward the door. "Maybe appeal to her sense of sisterhood. Girl power, that kind of thing." He raised his eyebrow and continued to mock me.

"Game on, Pierce." I didn't bother waiting for him to move, shoving him aside as I marched to the door and flung it open.

I also didn't wait, heading back to the boardroom with quick, confident strides, feeling the sense of power surging through my veins.

When I entered, Daniel was going over assets with Jana and most likely apologizing for our hasty exit. He would want to speak to both of us at some point too, but that was a concern for another time. Right now, I needed to talk fast and think faster and turn this around somehow.

"Glad you could rejoin us." Daniel might not have been hostile, but he didn't sound *glad* either. "I trust the two of you are ready to proceed." The warning loud and clear as Roman and I retook our seats.

"Yes. We wanted to present Ms. Cane two lines of defense," I said, knowing the minute Roman started talking he would try and bewitch her with his sexy self-confidence. He might have encouraged me to try and use the *sisterhood* as a means of swaying her, but he would be bringing his own big guns. And *charming* was not something that was in short supply.

"So, if you will allow me to start." I waited for Jana to nod before continuing. "Here is why I believe settling would be a mistake and what should be our plan moving forward."

I didn't leave room for interpretation, spelling it out as clear as I could that an aggressive approach would be what we needed and why.

Both Jana and Daniel listened intently as I built my case on the fly while Roman sat in silence, his fingers tented in front of him, with the urge to say something probably eating him alive.

He waited.

Waited until I was finished, and I could almost taste the victory.

And it was at exactly that moment that he calmly opened his folder and double-barreled his counter argument like he was presenting new found evidence for an innocent man on death row.

"Well, they are both compelling arguments." Jana adjusted her jacket as she looked to Daniel. "I'm going to need some time to process it."

"Of course, Ms. Cane." Daniel nodded. "Take the afternoon and I'll get my secretary, Stephanie, to schedule a meeting for tomorrow."

She lifted herself gracefully out of her chair, shaking Daniel's hand first before moving to Roman's and mine as she thanked us for our time. Daniel escorted her out while Roman and I managed to keep the fake smiles in place.

"You honestly think you can get him to agree to your terms." She stopped at the door, looking back to me. "And he will have no claim on the patent?"

"Yes, I do."

CHAPTER #5

"SHE WON'T AGREE." He was the first to talk, unbuttoning his suit jacket as he sat down. "You think you have it in the bag, but she is going to go home, think about the risk and what she could lose if we go your way. She isn't a gambler, Harper, and that was your mistake." He leaned back smugly, not the slightest bit concerned I had basically kicked his ass before and I would do it again.

"Why, because she is a woman?" My back straightened, ready to show him exactly what a woman could do.

"No, because she is scared to lose." His eyes stayed on mine. "Fear doesn't play out well in a courtroom which is exactly where this is heading. She's scared shitless and if she wasn't, she wouldn't have asked for the reassurance at the door. She isn't sure about you, but she *knows* I can deliver what she asked. And that's why tomorrow she is going to stay with her original agreement of a quick and quiet divorce." He simmered with the confidence he always seemed to possess.

"Yeah, well we'll just have to wait and see then, won't we?" I crossed my arms, not willing to concede that he'd won.

There was no way to know yet and her body language gave nothing away. And as for Roman's bullshit observation, that didn't prove anything. He just wanted to rattle my cage a little, make me think he had already won, but the truth was he knew nothing.

"You want to make it interesting?" His hands anchored at the back of his neck as he spun around on his chair to face me.

"Seriously? You want to gamble over whether or not she will gamble?"

The irony was not lost on me.

"Do you have any fun at all?" he deadpanned. "Like *anything* that could mildly be perceived as a good time?"

"Shut up and tell me what you had in mind." I still hadn't agreed to it, but part of me was curious.

"Winner gets to pick the loser's next case." His eyebrow arched, drawing me in. "And the loser *takes it*, relinquishing complete control."

The way his lips moved around those words was ridiculously erotic, and I could only blame the high emotions of the morning for my confused aroused state.

"What do you say, Harper?" He toyed with me further, his mouth twisting around my name seductively. "You game?"

It was hard to swallow, the air seeming to be thicker as I breathed, and I couldn't make myself say no.

I didn't want to say no.

But giving him that kind of dominion over me wasn't wise. Especially when I didn't know his intentions.

Of course, all of that only mattered if I lost.

Which I wouldn't.

"Tania Pearson needs help with the L Corp merger," I said before I could stop myself.

He'd be buried in litigation for weeks, maybe even months. Stuck in corporate hell with forensic accountants and a team of brown-suit-wearing Wall Street guys. Chances were good he'd probably have to fly to New York. Out of sight, out of mind, and more importantly, out of my way.

"It has *your* name all over it."

"Oh yeah?" He didn't look concerned, almost as if he welcomed the challenge. "Well, ITP wants to acquire a fiber optics company. Happy scouting."

Wow, he was a lot kinder with his case suggestion than I had been, still we didn't have time for me to question his motives or wonder if he was getting soft. Besides, all of that only came into to play if Jana went with his strategy, so there was no point thinking about something that wasn't going to happen.

We shook on the deal, Daniel walking back in with a face full of fury. "I'm not sure if this was some bullshit role-play or if you two have lost your damn minds. But if you lose Jana Cane as a client, you're both going to get knocked down to filing claims against market stalls selling counterfeit goods. And I assure you, it is not as interesting as it sounds."

And by the look of Daniel's flaring nostrils it wasn't a threat, more a promise, if one or the two of us screwed up what should have been a slam-dunk.

"We've got it handled." Roman oozed with his trademark composure. "Just want to make sure our client has the best options available."

"You might be able to pull that with her, Roman, but I'm not buying it," Daniel warned, meeting Roman's eyes before turning back to me. "Whatever she decides tomorrow, you will both play nice and wrap this up. We get her divorce in the can and we sign her as an ongoing client. And we already know what kind of money is on the table."

"We're not going to blow this," I added, meaning every word.

"Good." Daniel's hands sunk into his pants pockets, not looking any more reassured than when he walked in. "Now, because of your *excellent* work today, I'm going to reward you. The two of you get to take the rest of the day to knockout both angles. I know how much you love spending time together. Enjoy."

He didn't wait for a response, walking out the doorway and leaving us alone in the boardroom.

"You got another date?" Roman baited, ignoring we had unofficially been put on notice by our boss who was a named partner. "You might want to call him now, get the disappointment out of the way."

"What about you?" I glared, wondering why he enjoyed pushing my buttons as much as he did. Surely he had bigger things to worry about. His job for one. "Tuesday nights." I tapped my lip pretending to be deep in thought. "Isn't that your regular hook up with Carla? Or is she Friday nights? And Rebecca is Tuesday. I get them confused—they all look the same."

I hated that I knew their names and the frequency of which he seemed to entertain his female "companions." All in the name of knowing your adversary, information was useful. And *that* was the only reason I knew.

He laughed, not bothering to deny it. "Carla. And she knows that my work comes first. I'm sure she'll find some other way to fill her evening. But I'll let her know you were concerned. Maybe the two of you can have lunch sometime, talk about how wonderful I am."

Ugh. *Excuse me while I go throw up. Who even thinks like that, let alone says it out loud?*

"Don't flatter yourself, Roman." I waved him off trying to get my gag reflex under control. "If I had anything to say about you, I'm positive you wouldn't want her or anyone else hearing it."

"Rule number one, Harper." He leaned in closer, so close every breath I took came with an inhale of his infectious cologne. "Don't assume you know what I want."

He was too close, and I didn't hate it.

No.

Of course I hated it.

I hated him. Every part of him. And that was why I took a step back.

"Your rules won't mean shit if we don't get to work." I moved to the safety of the table and sat down. "I'm not getting demoted because of you." The file on the table getting my full attention.

He didn't answer, keeping his usually well-timed comebacks to himself as he took a seat beside me. I felt his stare on me but ignored it, ignored *him* as I reread the same paragraph three times and it still didn't make sense.

It was too quiet in the room. Everything too still. And while I had worked with him hundreds of times side by side, today it was making my skin itch.

"Something wrong, Harper?"

I didn't lift my head or acknowledge him, keeping my focus on the page in front of me. "Shut up and start researching."

I wasn't sure if he was done playing or he was bored already, but either way he did what I asked and opened his own file. Thankfully, he kept his mouth shut and his invasive glances to himself.

We fell into a similar routine as the day before. While I spared him my torture by whiteboard, we did discuss my suggestion and put together a game plan. Well, two game plans. We still weren't sure which way Jana was leaning.

And by the time we lifted our heads from the files and our conversation, the floor was virtually empty. Again, we were almost alone.

"You think one of the other partners has better scotch?" I yawned, not convinced we'd be done before midnight. Sleeping under a desk looked like a very real possibility.

"Byrne drinks Kentucky Bourbon but keeps it under lock and key. I could probably pick the lock, but the old bastard is so paranoid he probably has his office under constant video surveillance," he answered without hesitation, throwing out the information like it was common knowledge. "And Carter is a recovering alcoholic."

My eyes darted around, checking to make sure we were alone as I lowered my voice. Even in private, the conversation felt wrong. "How do you know all this?"

His eyes twinkled in delight, his lips curling at the edges. "Did I just impress you?"

"Just answer the question." I ignored his because it wasn't the first time he'd impressed me, I was just usually better at hiding it.

"Well," he swung around in his chair, "Carter is easy. His five-year sobriety coin is sitting on his desk. He has a nervous habit of flipping it between his fingers whenever he's working on a tough case."

It was funny how I'd been in Desmond Carter's office so many times and never noticed. Not that I had a habit of walking into a room and taking a mental snapshot on the off chance I had to recreate it for a crime scene later. I wondered how much else I didn't notice or if Roman just had incredible observation skills. And he was right, I was very impressed.

"And Byrne's wife is from Tennessee." He continued when I didn't speak. "Every month he gets a package with a bottle of Special Reserve Bourbon from a small but old distillery from the small town she grew up in. She hates the west coast, hates L.A even more. So, if I was to guess, she is trying to subliminally convince him to move. The smooth swallow of a good bourbon will probably get a man thinking about those pretty green rolling hills, sitting in a rocking chair while he watches the sun set. Or she's trying to give him liver disease so he finds himself in an early grave and she inherits his money. Either way she gets to go home better than when she left it." He laughed, seeming to be unconcerned for the possible untimely death of one of the senior partners.

"You investigated them?" It was asked as a question, but I already knew the answer. While the coin on the desk was easy enough to notice—or maybe not, considering I'd completely missed it—the details on Carter's personal life weren't.

He shrugged. "Don't look so shocked. I want to know who I work for. Their weaknesses, whether or not their firms were propped up on solid foundations or if the name was the best thing going for them."

"Let me guess, your guy?" The earlier mention of the investigator making a little more sense. I wondered who else he'd "looked into."

"Partly, and I highly recommend it." He leaned closer, his gaze more attentive than I would have liked. "But a lot is observation, just keeping your eyes open. You'd be surprised what people hide, even those you think you know."

"I have nothing to hide." I straightened, mentally cataloging everything that could be remotely bad in my past.

Ambition had meant keeping my head down and studying. Therefore, my past hadn't been filled with scandal or shadiness. There was nothing even close to be worth worrying about.

His phone buzzed, the illuminating screen and vibration stopping whatever he was going to say as he brought it to his ear.

"Roman," he answered, his name in place of a regular hello.

"Hmm, I see." He kept his eyes on me as the person on the other end of the line spoke. "Okay. Sure. Thanks." His words coming out sharp and clipped while his face betrayed nothing. "Bye."

"Bad news?" I asked, unable to pretend I wasn't curious about the call.

"Here's an idea." He closed his file, completely avoiding the question. "Let's go find a bar and I'll buy you a drink. And for the record, I'm not cheap."

I didn't need it on record, one look at his wardrobe and I

could tell he liked the finer things. Expensive suits, nice ties and there was his watch. Not flashy Rolex, but it didn't look he'd got it at Wal-Mart either.

"Are you trying to distract me?" Or spike my drink so I'd forget what he'd told me. It hadn't escaped my attention the offer of a drink was after a secretive phone call and after he'd admitted he'd investigated the senior partners.

"When I'm trying to distract a woman, she won't know it." He grinned, continuing to distractingly not be distractive. "I'm tired and I'm thirsty. Besides, none of this is going to matter anyway." He waved his hands over the other files strew across the boardroom table. "Tomorrow Jana is going to walk in and tell Daniel we're going with my plan, so we're just wasting a perfectly good night."

"That's not what's going to happen." I shook my head, refusing to accept he'd already won. "But your enthusiasm should be commended. Good for you."

"Suit yourself." He shrugged, rising out of his chair and buttoning up his jacket. "But I'm done for the night."

"You're leaving?" My eyes bulged wide in disbelief.

Roman was cocky but never irresponsible. Not with work anyway. So, while he might be confident on what tomorrow's decision was going to be, he wouldn't risk being underprepared. Would he? Unless this was some ploy to make me underprepared so Jana would have no choice but to choose him.

"Sure am. So, you can come with me and get that drink, or not." He waited, resting his arm on the back of the chair. "Your way, my way—tomorrow's outcome isn't being changed by anything we do tonight."

He was right about that.

Chances were Jana had already made her choice, but there was something about tonight that made me unsettled.

Roman had never asked me out for a drink.

Never.

We'd been out together at a bar after work, but there were always other people around. Other associates, work people, it had never been the two of us. *He didn't need any more friends,* remember? So, while the invitation was unexpected and an obvious diversion, I couldn't deny I was curious.

Roman in the wild was something I'd never seen before. It wasn't something that was easy to turn down either.

That's why the idea was tempting, so I could get some secret insight like he seemed to have on everyone else. Something that could potentially be useful further down the line. Information was good. Practical. Wanting to say yes had nothing to do with the fact he was an attractive, smart man who would never ask a woman like me on a real date.

It wasn't that I was being self-critical. I knew I was smart, and while I wasn't a candidate for *Sport's Illustrated,* I wasn't hideous either. But Roman had a very definite type. The women he was interested in were always beautiful, and while I could probably qualify for this on a good day, I came up lacking on his other criteria.

Like big breasted.

Nope, even on a good day I was average, and I was totally okay with that. Big boobs were more trouble than they were worth from what I'd seen, and I was fine with my adequate bust size.

But most importantly, almost every woman I'd seen Roman with had been tall. Towering super models who gave gravity a run for its money—with the aforementioned big boobs surely throwing their balance off. Even in heels, height was a stretch for me. Unless I was in a room full of preschoolers, and then it *might* be a possibility. But in the world of Roman Pierce, I one hundred percent did not fit the definition of anyone he would date.

Which was why I had to go.

Because that made sense.

"I'll go." I stood up, throwing caution and clearly common sense to the wind as I agreed to *go get a drink* with him. "Let me just get these files back together."

"Leave the files." He put his hand down on the mess of papers, any effort to clean them up stopped by his massive palm. "Get your stuff and let's get out of here."

"O-kay." I didn't bother to argue, leaving everything where it was. "I'll be back in a minute."

I moved out of the boardroom to my office at the end of the hall. He might have ignored my question about the phone call, but who or whatever it was had definitely got under his skin. Grabbing my purse, I shut my office door behind me and walked back toward the boardroom to find him waiting out in the hall.

"We'll take my car." He didn't ask, more dictated what we were going to do.

"Mine is parked downstairs too." I stopped short of telling him that riding in the car together was not going to happen. Not when I had no idea what was going through his mind. "Just tell me which bar you want to go to, and I'll meet you there. Then I can just drive home."

He looked at me for a second, almost like he was going to argue. "Heart and Vine."

"Okay, I just want to get something else before I leave, I'll see you down there."

I was lying of course; I just needed an excuse to stall. It would be too awkward to ride the elevator with him, walk to our cars and then drive to the bar. Not sure why exactly, but it felt weird and considering the whole scenario felt strange, I wasn't going to add any more.

"Fine." Again he didn't argue. "See you there."

And with a nod he left.

Well, the evening just took a turn for the unexpected; my only hope was that it was a good thing.

CHAPTER #6

I WAS SURPRISED to find a vacant parking spot when I got to the bar. Even though it was a weeknight, like most bars in L.A., Heart and Vine was packed.

I felt slightly overdressed wearing a pencil skirt and jacket, so as I slipped out of the car seat, I pulled off my jacket and unbuttoned my blouse a little. Not enough to be sexy, just so I didn't look like I was in there to serve anyone a subpoena.

A quick adjustment of my hair, pulling it out of the ponytail and letting it fall loose, I de-corporate-fied myself. Well, as I much as I could using the side mirror of my car and working with what I had. It wasn't that I was trying to impress him either, but the effort made me feel less self-conscious.

So without giving it any more thought, I locked my car and made my way inside.

The venue was unremarkable. Lots of polished wood with a long bar at the back and small round tables cluttering the edges of the room, allowing drinkers to talk and sit. The ambiance was more old school, lacking the shine of a new, hip and happening place, which was surprising for some reason. In the few occasions we'd shared a drink—outside of our late night desk drinking—he'd seemed to favor more higher brow establishments while this was more 90's flannel Nirvana.

It was easy to spot Roman when I walked in. He was sitting at the bar with a beer in front of him while a bunch of women giggled nervously at his side.

Cue my lack of surprise.

He didn't look interested in the conversation, his eyes floating across the room until they met mine. Then he said something to his lady friends and their giggling stopped, watching me as I walked over.

"Ladies, it seems my friend has arrived. It's been nice talking to you." He gave them a sexy smile that made one of them moan but they didn't linger, dispersing like a pack of roaches after the light had been turned on.

I wondered if that was what it was like for him whenever he went out? Buzzards circling a carcass, just wanting to make their move. I'd accused him of being a horse's ass on more than one occasion so I could totally see it, the thought making me smile as he watched me intently.

"I thought we were having scotch." I nodded to the beer, taking the newly vacated stool beside him. "You promised me you weren't cheap."

"I'm not." He took the bottle into his hands and lifted it off the bar. "The beer was just my starter, I'll have a scotch with dinner."

"Dinner?"

Whoa. *Dinner?* I had already established—at least in my own mind—that this wasn't a date. It was a drink. Now we were at the bar and he'd changed the parameters by introducing food, which made it more date-like. I wasn't sure if the new development was welcomed or not. I didn't like surprises, especially from people I didn't quite trust.

"I'm sure it didn't escape your attention that we didn't eat."

He brought the bottle of beer to his lips and took a slow mouthful. "Drinking without food consumption would be irresponsible, especially since both of us are driving. Given your size and weight." His eyes traveled up and down my body. "It wouldn't take a lot to put you over the legal limit. And considering you turned down my offer to drive you, I doubt you are going to let me do that later when you are at risk for a DUI. So, dinner. They're holding a table for us, let's go." He took another mouthful and moved off the barstool waiting for me to do the same.

"You constantly talk like you're trying to secure a verdict, you know that." I rolled my eyes, my time sitting at the bar short lived as I joined him on my feet.

He placed his hand on the small of my back as he prompted me to walk. "People usually just do what I say the first time. And I could say the same for you. You're argumentative."

"Occupational hazard," I declared proudly as I moved in the direction he indicated.

There was an odd sense of awareness as we walked through the crowd. Like there were eyes on us, watching our every move. Almost as if they were wondering what we were doing together, something I still hadn't worked out. Or maybe it was because Roman looked like he could be someone famous and they were trying to guess which celebrity he was. I could have saved them the time, while the man was gorgeous, being an asshole didn't qualify you for stardom. Unless he was leading a double life and shot catalogues for Hugo Boss in his spare time. It would explain all the fancy suits. Maybe I needed to hire a "guy" and do some investigating of my own.

"This is us." His head tipped to the small round table with a reserved sign on it. There were menus already in place as he pulled out one of the two chairs and waited for me to sit down.

"Wow, you have all the moves don't you?" I shook my head as

I took my seat. "Please tell me I'm not taking poor Carla's place. I'm not in the mood for showy confrontations with any of your girlfriends."

Considering we'd made plans less than an hour ago, I found the reserved table suspicious. But it would make sense if he had a standing date that it would be easy to "sub" me in.

How very convenient for him.

Asshole.

"You sure you want to know the answer to that?" He looked amused as he took his seat opposite me.

"Sure, why not." I shrugged, almost positive I knew the answer. It wasn't that my feelings were hurt, I was just surprised he was so transparent.

"I don't take Carla anywhere. I fuck Carla, and then I leave," he said with almost no emotion.

I smiled, refusing to be embarrassed when he didn't seem to be. "Well, I guess that's efficient."

"What about you?" His eyes seared me as he looked at me from across the table.

My skin tingled at the intimate suggestion. "I'm sure she's a nice girl, but not interested in fucking Carla."

He laughed, seeming to be amused by the answer as he shook his head. "I meant, are we going to have any *showy confrontations* after yesterday's failed date? How many times has he texted you?"

Gulp.

I hated that he knew things. Things he had no business knowing. And maybe Gavin had sent me a few texts, but they were only friendly how-are-you-doing messages. Just being friendly and decent, not because he wanted anything from me. Not that Roman would know anything about that.

"You guys ready to order?"

I was saved from answering the question by a pretty waitress.

Her smile was on Roman as she moved the pencil to her lips and bit the end in what I assumed was flirting. Seriously, was no one immune?

"Two eighteen-year-old Macallans, neat." He ignored Miss Flirty Pencil-in-my-lips as he ordered our drinks without asking, his eyes turning over the menu before adding. "And a Philly cheesesteak with fries."

"Ummm." Panic fluttered across poor Miss Flirty's face as she leaned in. "I'm not sure we have Macallan." She seemed to take it personal, like she was disappointed at not being able to get Roman what he wanted.

"You do." He blinded her with his effortless smile, the poor girl not standing a chance. Even if they didn't have it behind the bar, there wasn't a doubt she'd probably commit armed robbery just to get it for him. "I've had it here before."

"Oh, okay." She smiled, not bothering to write it down and committing his order to memory like she'd been given the Ten Commandments by Moses himself. "And for you?" Her smile less bright and cheery as she directed her attention to me, my existence no doubt putting a damper on her fantasy.

"I'll have the chicken club," I responded after a quick scan of the food on offer. It was standard bar food but since sitting down I was feeling hungry. "Thank you." I grinned as I handed her back my menu.

"No problem." Her voice was laced with faux sweetness as she turned back to Roman. "Anything else before I go?"

I rolled my eyes, wondering if the showy confrontation wasn't going to come in the form of our waitress. No wonder he didn't go on "dates." Especially if this was what it was like every time he went out.

"No, thank you." He gave her a tight smile signaling she was free to go, her ass swaying like she was going to dislocate a hip as she walked away from the table.

"So, your date." Roman slid straight back into the conversation, the break not enough apparently to shift his focus. "How did he take it?"

"He was fine, completely understanding," I answered, knowing there was no point dodging the question. Roman clearly wasn't going to let it go and hopefully now we could drop it and move on. Besides, there was no need to lie. Gavin had been great about the whole thing.

He rolled his eyes. "I'm sure. And was he understanding when you told him you weren't interested?"

I swallowed, wondering if as part of his investigations if he hadn't tapped my phone. "Tell me, Roman." I refused to give into him anymore than I had already. "If I'm not here as a Carla proxy, who were you intending to meet here tonight? Unless you managed to call and get a table between the time I left you at the office and here."

"Actually, that's exactly what happened," he said, not breaking eye contact. "I called from the car. I know the owner of the bar, he's a friend of my brother and owed me a favor."

"You have a brother?" I leaned in closer, my eyes widening in surprise.

It was the first personal bit of information he'd ever shared. And while the fact he had a sibling wasn't shocking in itself, part of me had believed he had been abandoned at birth and raised by a pack of coyotes or something.

"I have a few." His lack of a committed response intriguing me even more.

"A few." It was my turn to pursue the hardline, my pulse spiking as I delved deeper. "Like two or three? Or are you talking a reality show size numbers? Wait." I held my hands up, wondering if he hadn't been brought up in a weird cult, which would totally explain his prickly behavior. "We are talking blood relations, right? *Brother* isn't some code for something else, is it?"

"You think I'm in some sort of gang, Harper?" He looked amused, saying nothing to disprove any of my theories.

"Honestly, it seems unlikely." Unless the gang was a white-collar syndicate and then it made all kind of sense. "But if you were, you aren't going to admit it to me, are you?" I'd be obligated to report his illegal activities to the bar and turn him in.

"No, I wouldn't." His lips edged into a sexy smile. "But if it makes you feel better, we share DNA."

The waitress returned, showing how talented she was carrying a tray of our food while maintaining her hip-swing. She'd also applied a fresh coat of shimmery lip gloss, her tongue sliding across her sparkling pink lips as she placed Roman's plate in front of him.

To his credit, he didn't look up, her performance going unnoticed as she delivered my food and our drinks. She slinked back away without the acknowledgment she'd obviously been after.

"So, where do you fit in the *band of brothers*?" He might have been coy about giving me specifics, but I wasn't done with my interrogation yet.

"Second oldest." He again gave me as little as possible.

"Ah, which means there's at least four of you." I nodded, his brow rising at my deduction "See, if there were less than three, you'd have a specific birth order. Oldest, middle or youngest. When there are four or more, then unless you are the *oldest*, or *youngest*—which you aren't—the *middle* category becomes redundant. So, there's at least four of you." My reasoning was solid, and whether he wanted to admit it or not, I knew I was right.

"There are five," he conceded, looking impressed that I'd been close.

"Holy shit," I choked out, the idea of five versions of Roman roaming the Earth, terrifying. "*Five?* Five of *you?*"

He waved dismissively, picking up his Philly cheesesteak and bringing it to his mouth. "Relax, my brothers are nothing like me."

"Are they nicer?" It slipped out, my mind still reeling he was one of five boys. He hadn't mentioned any sisters, but he hadn't ruled them out either. Maybe I'd nixed the cult idea too soon.

"They like to think so." He laughed, yet to take a bite of the sandwich in his hands. "Can we eat yet, or do you want to continue with the cross examination?"

"Sorry, I'm just . . ." *Shocked, surprised, utterly confused* how he could have at least four—we still didn't have a final number—siblings and I'd assumed he'd been an only child. "Glad you felt you could share that with me."

Roman was a vault, so any information he shared was intentional. Why he'd chosen tonight to let down his guard, I still wasn't sure, but I'd hoped it was because even though we weren't friends, he respected me.

"I have a sister," I offered, feeling he'd earned the mutual exchange. "Morgan is older by three years, she's a nurse," I added, giving him a lot more than he'd given me.

Not that I cared, most people I worked with knew about the sister I shared an apartment with, some had even met her. Roman had been the only one who hadn't seemed the slightest bit interested in my personal life.

"I know. She works at Ronald Reagan UCLA." He lowered his sandwich, my mouth dropping open before he added, "I saw her uniform when she came in last month."

I nodded, not needing to tell him because he probably already knew. "Yes, she works in the E.R."

"Good to know." He winked. "If the *gang* ever needs medical attention, I know who to call."

We were in unchartered territory.

Regular conversation.

Being pleasant.

I had been sitting with him for almost an hour and hadn't contemplated a random act of violence since before we left the office. I hadn't insulted him in a while either, and I didn't want to.

It was almost as if he was *human*.

Maybe this was the turning point, and he'd finally, for whatever reason, let me in. And while I loved our mental sparing, it would be nice to have a *real* partnership. Someone who would *have* my back rather than someone who wanted to drive a knife into it.

"Thanks for asking me out." I smiled, a warmth spreading through my body as I looked down at my food. "It was good to get out of the office."

"Just don't tell anyone at work." He leaned across the table and whispered, "We don't want to ruin my reputation of being an asshole."

"Your secret is safe with me," I whispered back.

We enjoyed dinner while making small talk.

Correction.

I made small talk.

He contributed a little here and there but for the most part he just listened. It was really nice actually, when he wasn't channeling the demon know-it-all he seemed to be in the office. He was still cagey about his brothers—no sisters, I got that out of him—and other than telling me they all lived in L.A., he didn't say much at all. His youngest brother Alex was still in college, and the oldest, Eric was in some kind of "business."

Both Roman and his brother, Eric, had helped the owner of Heart and Vine when it was close to going under. So I assumed Eric was possibly an investment banker or a strategist of some kind. But I didn't press, enjoying the flow of easy conversation between us.

My pulse raced with an unexpected thrill. I was wandering around in an area that had previously been deemed off-limits and I wasn't about to leave just yet.

CHAPTER #7

BY THE TIME dinner had finished, hours had passed and our *one* scotch had turned into two, with the constant tension in my shoulders whenever I was around him all but vanishing.

"You sure you're okay to drive?" He helped me out of my seat after he'd paid the check. I had offered to pay half, but he turned me down saying it had been his treat.

"Yeah, I'm fine." My fingers wrapped around his arm; it was the first time I'd ever touched him other than his hand. My skin prickled with excitement and I liked the way it felt. It was slightly confusing but I couldn't make myself stop, wanting to keep the contact and the new—albeit uncertain—connection. "The drinks were a couple of hours apart. I'm well under the limit."

"Fine, then let me walk you out to your car."

He wasn't being overly touchy-feely, but he was definitely being sweet. His hand pressed against my back as he guided me out into the parking lot, his strides matching mine.

"Thank you for tonight." I leaned against the side of my car, looking up at him in the moonlight and having the unbelievable urge to kiss him. Insanity buzzed through my body as the night air crackled and maybe he was feeling a little something too.

I'd always thought he was attractive but never in a million years considered acting on it. Well, not acting on it in real life—dreams didn't count. And I had always assumed that he had never seen me as anything other than a colleague—more likely a rival—but maybe he was bored playing with beautiful, tall women with mediocre intelligence.

"Roman." My hands moved up the front of his jacket, the firm muscles underneath rippling against my fingertips. It felt illicit and dangerous, but I couldn't making my hands stop, loving the element of uncertainty that came with it.

Sexy didn't even come close. I'd had a glimpse of that fine body last September during the company fun run and that had given me fantasy material for months. Being able to touch him was something I didn't think was ever going to be possible.

"Harper." He didn't move, letting my hands glide up and down the delicious expanse of his chest as his jaw tightened. "I should go."

"Yes, you should." I lifted my chin, not really sure what the hell I was doing as I gripped his jacket tighter.

While I didn't hate him anymore, making out with him wasn't a good idea either. We still had to work together and office romances usually ended badly. Maybe that scotch was stronger than I thought, or maybe shiny-lip-pop-and-lock had sprinkled some kind of aphrodisiac in our food, hoping to get lucky. Sadly it hadn't worked out that way for her, but I wasn't about to look a gift horse in the mouth.

"What are you doing, Harper?" His gazed move from my eyes to my lips as he brought his mouth closer, hovering just out of reach.

In a moment of recklessness I did the unthinkable.

"The evidence is right in front of you, counselor." I swallowed, a knot tightening in my lower gut as feelings of desire spread across my skin. "And I'd always thought you were a closer."

Turns out, I was right.

His mouth came crushing down on mine, and the space between us became nonexistent as his large frame pressed against me. He decided against words, letting his tongue and lips get familiar with mine as his hands dropped to my ass and pulled me closer to him.

It was insane.

Insane, frenzied and probably stupid, but as I lost myself in that kiss, I didn't care. Heat unfurled in my body as a rush of excitement tingled through every cell. It had been so long since I'd been kissed like that. Kissed by a man without apology, who took my mouth like he wanted to conquer it.

"Roman," I moaned, feeling the bulge in his pants as I rubbed myself against him. It was as if something inside of me had snapped, unleashing a craziness I didn't think existed.

And while I knew we were in a parking lot, in full view of the public, I wanted more than what he was giving me.

"Fuck," he groaned against my mouth, one of his hands moving from my ass and palming my breast. "This wasn't what—" The rest of his sentence getting lost in the kiss. "We shouldn't be doing this."

He was right. We shouldn't have been doing any of it, but neither of us was able to stop our hands and mouths as they continued their journey, with or without our consent.

His hand threaded through my hair as his lips owned mine, my body rubbing against his as we barely came up for air. I was too afraid to speak, wanting more than just his kiss, the feeling of his weight against me making me slowly lose my mind.

"Do you live close by?" I heard the words come out of my mouth without being conscious of saying them.

What the hell was I suggesting? I couldn't just sleep with him. Hell, I'd barely even kissed him and we weren't dating, so jumping into bed with him was so bad an idea I had to wonder whether my earlier suggestion of being drugged wasn't accurate.

His mouth stopped, his eyes darkening as he looked at me. "You want to come back to my place?"

"Yes." Again my mouth functioned on autopilot as I tried to work out who the hell I was right now.

His chest expanded as he took a long, deep breath, a guttural "fuck" passing through his lips.

I had no idea what was going through his mind, but his body was more than on board. That sizeable erection wasn't something I'd imagined, and he wasn't squeezing my ass in a way that could be misunderstood as just being friendly.

We shouldn't, I knew that. And for so many more reasons than we worked together. But as my lips pressed against his neck, those reasons didn't seem to make sense.

"I need you to get in the car, Harper." He moved his hands to where mine were and stopped them from moving on his body. "And then I need you to drive yourself home. Can you do that for me?"

Shit.

It was a light blub moment as the magnitude of the mistake I was about to make became evident. And even as disappointment flooded me—I was positive he would have been amazing in bed—I was glad at least one of us was thinking straight. Clearly, it hadn't been me.

He was right. I needed to go home.

"Yes, of course." I tried to smile, trying to pretend I hadn't just propositioned him in the parking lot. "Like I said, I'm not even close to being drunk."

"Good." He nodded, his hands moving either side of my arms. "And you're going to go right home, correct?" he asked again, like he needed reassurance I wasn't going to head to the next bar and possibly try my luck with someone else.

"I promise, I'm going right home."

Positive I'd reached my limit for irresponsibility for one night, home was exactly where I was heading. Besides, we still had work in the morning, and the Cane case—whichever way she went—was going to be huge. We both needed to bring our A game.

"Text me when you're back at your apartment." It wasn't a request. He pulled away from me and watched me straighten.

"Okay." I unlocked my door, my cheeks pinking as I got into my car.

He waited by the driver's side, standing there as I hit the ignition and rolled down my window. "I mean it, the minute you get home I need you to pick up your phone."

"O-kay," I said again, wondering where the sudden concern had come from. But it seemed to be the night for strange happenings so I didn't ask why it was so important that I message.

Maybe one of the planets was in retrograde, leaving a trail of havoc in its wake. It would explain my temporary loss of sanity and Roman's personality flip.

"I'll see you tomorrow, Harper." His hands sunk into his pockets, waiting for me to leave. His usual smile was missing, his body tightly coiled as he stood beside the car.

I gave him a wave, my lips still tingling from the kiss as I turned one last time. "Bye, Roman."

My heart was still pounding as I drove away.

Shit.

OH. MY. GOD.

I am an idiot.

Roman Pierce was the enemy. He was *nothing* like a man I'd ever date even if he was gorgeous. Having a nice face and a sexy body didn't cancel out how cocky, arrogant and—even by his own admission—how much of an asshole he was. In fact, most times he was abrasive and rude.

So, what happened? The first time he showed me a kinder more human side—just enough to prove there was a heart underneath that impressive chest—I threw myself at him, mouth first.

Gah! I was so angry at myself. I hated that I had always thought I was smarter than that. No wonder he walked around like he was God's gift to vaginas, hard not to when you could basically charm your way into anyone's pants. And I'd thought I was immune. Turned out, I was just as dumb as the rest of them.

Thank God—or whoever else was in control—he had the common sense to stop it. I didn't even care why, I was just glad the man used the gray matter between his ears and not the very hard cock between his legs, because we both know I would have gone there.

My body was still vibrating and all we'd done was kiss, my fingers touched my mouth remembering the sensation. I liked it. I liked it a lot which was a problem because even though I knew how bad an idea it was I still wasn't disgusted. Which I should have been. Embarrassed too. And yet, I wasn't.

Instead, I was still feeling giddy which just made me even more confused.

By the time I'd arrived home, Morgan was already asleep. There was the second bullet I'd dodged for the night. While I would have *loved* to tell her how dumb I'd been—kissing a man I'd repeatedly told her I couldn't stand—I was saved from the twenty-four hour psych hold she would have definitely placed me under. Sometimes having a sister in the medical profession was *not* a good thing.

So quietly, after texting him like I'd promised to do and let him know I was home safe, I scrubbed the remnants of Roman's sexiness from my mind and my body. I'll be honest, I was probably in the shower longer than I had to be but hey, you got to do what you got to do when you are exorcising a demon. And when I crawled into bed, I had a plan.

It hadn't been all bad. And before common sense and intelligence started bleeding out my ears, it had actually been really nice. He'd been decent, kind and someone I would enjoy working with. *That* was what we needed to focus on. We could do away with all the previous nonsense and find some kind of middle ground and be friends. Support each other, and drive each other to succeed from a place of mutual respect and appreciation.

All of it would be fine.

There was no need to panic or think the worst, and in the morning we'd talk about it like adults. Then move on like the professionals we were.

Perfect.

I had no idea why I had been so worried, and we would both probably laugh about it months from now. If anything, we should be thankful it happened, giving us the opportunity to have the conversation and move past the silly competitiveness.

Yes, it had been a good thing.

A *brilliant* thing.

That kiss had been pretty brilliant too.

No, I couldn't focus on that. The kiss wasn't the positive in this scenario, it was the outcome that I needed to concentrate on. There would be no more kissing.

No. More. Kissing.

I could live with that.

So, as I closed my eyes—still thinking about the kiss even though I was pretending I wasn't—I felt a sense of calmness wash over me.

Tomorrow was a new day, a great day, and the start of something exciting and wonderful between us. And I couldn't wait.

CHAPTER #8

BY THE TIME I reached the firm, I was feeling even more positive than I had last night. I'd slept like a log, forgoing the regular tossing and turning I usually suffered.

It could have been courtesy of the orgasm I'd given myself in the shower—save the judgment; I was exorcising demons—or it was possible that things were destined to be better.

"Someone looks bright and cheery this morning." Stephanie, Daniel's secretary greeted me as I strolled past her desk.

"I got the first good night's sleep in forever." I took a sip from my morning coffee, unable to hide my smile. "Amazing what a difference a night can make to perspective."

Of course, I wasn't just talking about the sleep, but Stephanie didn't need to know that. The less people who knew about mine and Roman's tiny indiscretion, the better. Besides, nothing *really* happened anyway.

"Well, I'm glad." She handed me a file. "You're going to need that *good* perspective today. Daniel and Roman are waiting in board-room one, Jana Cane has made her decision on her case."

Panic flooded me. "Daniel and Roman are waiting? Was there a memo I missed?" I checked the clock on the wall behind her and it wasn't even eight thirty yet; we hadn't scheduled to meet until nine.

"They're preparing the papers for filing." She gave me a sympathetic smile. "I thought you knew."

"Yes, of course I know," I lied, barely able to contain the 1997 Britney Spears crazy that was bubbling at the surface. "I should get back there." My smile tightened as I powerwalked to the boardroom, dumping my coffee in the trash on the way.

"Lauren." Daniel stood up, gesturing to an empty seat. "I'm glad you're early, although it looks like you might have missed your window to convince Ms. Cane. What a shame too, I had high hopes."

He didn't look disappointed, more bored while Roman sat beside him silent. The smile, the warmth from his eyes that I had seen yesterday was gone and now he was the same as he'd always been. Cold. Distant. Aloof.

"What are you talking about, weren't we scheduled to meet with her this morning?" I was confused, wondering if during my epic sleep I hadn't missed a day. And what could have possibly transpired in the few hours that turned it all around.

"That was the original plan." Daniel sat, giving up on waiting for me to do the same as I kept standing. "But it seemed that Roman delivered some additional information. You were both emailed last night to see if you had anything else to add, and when you didn't respond she decided to go with Roman."

There had been no email. Well, none before I'd left the office. Granted, I didn't check after I went home, but I assumed that anything important would have waited until the morning. Besides, I'd had other things on my mind after dinner.

Shit.

He wouldn't have . . .

No.

He wasn't that evil, *was he?*

"What additional information?" I tried to remain calm even though the evidence didn't look good.

Roman didn't flinch, his voice cool and unemotional as he opened a file and pushed it toward me. "Price Waters knows about the patent and the product. They're looking at launching their own version. So, if she doesn't file soon it's going to be an all-out corporate war."

"And you found this out when?" I locked eyes with Roman, wondering when the hell he had time to prepare a brief when he had been with me the entire time.

"I had my investigator dig around." There was no hesitation in his voice, no apology either as he continued, business as usual. "And when he couriered over his findings to Ms. Cane, he did so with my advice that we needed to move now. Whatever she's going to lose in the divorce, she is going to lose thirty times that if Price Waters beat her to market."

"Are you insane?" Anger, hurt, disbelief, all jostled for position as I tried not to raise my voice. "There's no way Price Waters could have had access to that technology, it would have taken months if not years to develop. They're bluffing."

"They aren't bluffing, Lauren," Daniel interrupted, nodding to the file in front of me I had yet to read. "I saw the raw data myself."

"Then they stole the intellectual property." I couldn't believe Daniel was taking Roman's side, fury currently winning out over hurt. "Either way we can fight this in court."

"That wasn't what the client wanted." Roman's voice was tight but controlled. "You had your chance to convince her—she went with me. We're preparing the terms of her divorce."

"Lauren, I have to agree with Roman on this," Daniel weighed in. "You had the opportunity last night to give one last rebuttal, you didn't take it. And from the looks of things, this will be quicker and cleaner anyway. Now, if you'll excuse me." He stood, buttoning his jacket. "I'm going to work on her patent application while the two of you wrap this up."

For the first time ever in my professional career, I was speechless. I wanted to scream, to hurl myself at Roman and claw his eyes out with my bare hands. But I didn't. Instead, I stood there seething as Daniel walked past me and to the door. "He was just better this time, Lauren. Don't take it too hard."

I barely heard the words as I waited for the door to close.

"You lying piece of shit." I couldn't hold back any longer, keeping my hands to myself as the words flew out of my mouth. "There was no email."

"I may be a piece of shit, Harper," he stayed seated, watching me as I moved closer, "but I didn't lie. Check your inbox."

My handbag dropped on the table as I dug around for my phone.

He watched me, keeping his eyes on me as I opened my emails and saw there was a message unopened. Sent thirty minutes after we'd left the office.

"You played me."

It was obvious that whatever I had thought happened yesterday was an illusion. Roman hadn't miraculously found decency it turned out. And worse than all of that, he was more evil than I had ever anticipated.

"I didn't *play* you." He stood, walking over to where I was frozen. "We went to dinner, *you* missed the message. Did I at any point of the evening tell you not to check your emails? Take your phone and hold it hostage?"

"That's fucking semantics, Roman, and you know it."

I felt sick, nausea bubbling up my throat as I thought back to last night. The invitation. The dinner. How different he'd been as we spent hours, *hours* talking. Only it had just been smoke and mirrors. And then I remembered what he'd said before we'd left the office, *when I'm trying to distract a woman, she won't know it.*

Oh. My. God.

"You're a monster. Was any of it true? All that shit you said about yourself, your brothers? Anything? Did you sit there and lie the entire time?"

And how much further was he willing to go? Should I be thanking him for not sleeping with me? Nice to know he stopped short of being a complete whore.

"Everything I told you last night was the truth." His words razor sharp as he maintained his composure, his usual smile missing in action. "I told you, I didn't lie."

"You can go around and around as much as you want, Roman, but you sure as hell weren't honest." That was the lawyer in him, the argument prepared ready to prove that while he'd been a sorry excuse for a man, he hadn't lied.

Wow, how proud he must be of himself.

"I did what needed to be done."

"No, you stacked the deck." My palm itched to slap his stupid, beautiful face as my throat constricted. "You *kissed* me."

I wanted to cry, to scream, to rage, but I refused to give him the satisfaction. It was bad enough he'd played on my emotions and used me. I wouldn't allow him to enjoy the show as well.

He probably thought the whole thing was hilarious, laughed about it on his way home about how easy I'd been.

I had been a fool to trust him.

"You kissed me back," he reminded me, making me hate him even more. "And you liked it."

That was my limit, feeling my arms that had been idle by my side reach up and physically push him away. It wasn't anywhere close to being satisfying, my need for violence at an unparalleled level as I grabbed my handbag and phone and headed to the door.

"Prepare your own damn motion," I called out over my

shoulder, "and then you can go to hell."

I didn't care that I was running away, or that Daniel had expected me to help Roman. Getting out of that room and away from him was the only thing I could think about.

Striding with purpose down the hall, I put distance between us, and for once he did the smart thing and didn't follow me. I didn't stop walking until I got to the ladies room, pushing open the door to the stall and threw up into the toilet bowl.

The entire evening played over and over in my head, every single word now needing to be dissected. For once I had let my guard down, and he didn't only use it against me professionally but took advantage of me too.

I was going to be sick again.

Unable to stop it, I heaved again into the toilet, tears stinging my eyes as my gut twisted.

It wasn't my finest moment, but I had managed to just get the door closed behind me before I vomited. At least I was able to save myself from further embarrassment; it's not like the day needed to get any worse than it already was.

"Hello?"

Great.

I'd spoken too soon.

"Hey," I called to the mysterious voice beyond the stall. I hoped whoever it was just needed a tampon or something so they could leave me to my misery.

"I'm sorry, I heard you. Are you sick too?" There was a rustling of paper and then a flush. "I haven't stopped all morning, pretty sure it's the stomach flu."

"Yeah, must be going around." I winced, wondering what the etiquette was for bathroom chitchat. "You should probably go home."

"I think—" She didn't get to finish, the rest of the sentence getting lost in some serious retching.

It sounded like a horror movie in there; she definitely needed to go home.

I finished up in my stall, flushing before heading out to the basin to wash my hands, waiting for her to stop. "Are you okay?" I tentatively asked, unsure if I was making it worse by being there.

Still, leaving her wouldn't be right either and unlike *some* people—i.e. the spawn of Satan I'd left in the boardroom—I had a heart.

"Ugh," she groaned from behind the door. "I think I'm dying."

If what I had witnessed had been going on the whole morning, she sounded like she was too.

Well, if nothing else, the woman puking out her eyeballs had stopped me from worrying about myself for a few minutes. There was a positive. "What's your name?"

"Charlotte. I'm one of the new paralegals."

"Okay Charlotte, you think you can make it back to your desk and get your things? I'm going to help get you home."

As much as I hated to admit it, my motives weren't purely altruistic. And I would deal with whatever bad karma I attracted because of that. But if the universe had seemed fit to give me an excuse to get out of work today and not deal with a man I wanted to disembowel, then I was going to take it.

"I can't leave," she groaned, her voice hiccupping. "I'm supposed to be helping Roman Pierce with a case today."

Cue my lack of surprise that *he* was the common denominator to both the women in the bathroom puking.

"There are other paralegals who can help Roman." I was almost positive there was a line of them willing to volunteer. "Why don't you go get your things and we'll go talk to Roman together. Then we'll get you home."

The door opened, a frail-looking redhead whose skin was the color of ash peered back at me. "You would do that for me?"

"Of course." And maybe if we got lucky she would throw up in his lap and ruin is fancy suit. There was no harm in hoping. "I'm Lauren, by the way."

"I know." Her eyes dipped down, tugging at her skirt. "We spoke on the phone two days ago, and I recognized your voice. Oh, wait." Her hand shot to her mouth. "That sounded creepy, I probably shouldn't have said that."

"It's fine." I dismissed her with a wave. "I'm work with Roman Pierce, I'm used to creepy."

She laughed, clutching her stomach as she moved to the basin to clean herself up. Her black eyeliner had smudged, enhancing the Day of the Dead makeover she had going on, but with the help of some wadded up paper towel she was able to make herself look presentable.

"Are you sure this is okay?" She hesitated at the door. "I don't want you to get into any trouble."

"I'm not going to get into any trouble. Besides, I think I have a mild case of it too, so it's probably for the best we both go home."

Plus, one day of working remotely wasn't going to be a problem. Anything Daniel needed done I could manage on my laptop connected to the Wi-Fi at home. Not to mention the class A felony it would help avoid, me being away from Roman seemed like the smartest idea.

Her eyes brightened, taking comfort in my reassurance as she nodded. "Yes, mine started slow and then it got really bad."

Having agreed we were both suffering the stomach flu and needed to go home, I left her to go get her things before meeting her back in the hall. She wasn't looking too hot, with the prospect of her vomiting again looking more likely by the minute. I tried to remind myself that would be a bad thing.

"Harper." I heard his voice from behind me. *Oh, what do you know, it's Mr. Evil Incarnate himself.* God, I hated him.

"Roman." I turned, straightening my shoulders as I shelved the embarrassment and hurt and concentrated on the anger. "It seems Charlotte and I have been struck down with the stomach flu. I need to take a sick day."

He looked at us both with suspicion, his blue eyes flicking to Charlotte and then back to me. "You seemed fine a few minutes ago."

"It came on suddenly." As hard as it was, I met his eyes. "I must have caught some nasty bug. I hear there's a hideous strain going around."

His eyebrow rose and his lips thinned. "Is that so?"

"It's true, Mr. Pierce." Charlotte nodded beside me. "At first I felt a little tired and hot, but it got a whole lot worse very quickly."

She was pale, her hand flying to her mouth as her eyes filled with fear. "Oh no."

Oh no was right.

She dashed into the closest office, grabbing a waste paper basket and giving Roman visual evidence of *our* sudden and horrendous condition. If she'd been just three seconds slower, the display would have been more personal than he probably would have liked.

Such a shame.

"What the hell is going on out here?" Daniel Moss stormed from his office, meeting us in the hall.

"Stomach flu." I grabbed at my gut, doing my best to make myself look ill. Not that it was hard when Roman was in the room. "Both of us."

"Well for God's sake, get out of the office before we have an epidemic." He took a step back, his hand covering his mouth like a mask. "We'll call you if we need you. Charlotte, I'll let your supervisor know. Do you need me to call a cab?"

"It's fine, I have my car," I volunteered. "I can take Charlotte home too."

"Good." He nodded, Charlotte puking again into the waste paper basket.

"We should go." I pushed her toward the elevator, our newly acquired office accessory coming with us. "I'll email from home."

Daniel kept his hand up at his mouth while Roman's eyes narrowed. I didn't care if he believed me or not, he'd have to find someone else to screw over today. I needed distance, time away from him and the situation, to work out what I did next.

The metal doors of the elevator closed behind us as Charlotte clutched the waste paper basket like a life preserver. She might have momentarily settled as we descended to the undercover garage, but I wasn't sure how long our reprieve was going to be.

"I'm not far." I pointed to my silver Mazda parked two rows away. "You want me to take you to an emergency room?"

"No, just home please." Her voice reedy as she followed me to my car.

We both hopped in, and after Charlotte had given me her address—thankfully not too far away—she fell asleep in the passenger seat. It meant there was no more puking but unfortunately left me alone with my thoughts.

How could he?

The single question swirled in my mind as I pulled up to Charlotte's house. She still lived with her folks, so at least I wouldn't have to worry about her dying in her sleep. The duty of care handed over to her mom who met us at the door.

And with my good deed done for the day, I drove to my apartment where I needed to regroup and reevaluate. I might not have been as physically ill as poor Charlotte, but psychologically I wasn't doing too hot.

At work, I expected him to do his worst. Not outright undermine me, but we'd always pushed each other to the limits. In a sick twisted way I think it made us better attorneys.

But what he'd done had crossed the line. He'd made it personal. And I was never going to forgive him.

Feeling drained and confused, I pulled off my work clothes and changed into my sleep shorts and an old T-shirt. I brushed my teeth, cleaned off my makeup and collapsed onto my couch.

I needed revenge.

While it wouldn't change what he'd done, it would make me feel better. Show him he couldn't treat people like disposable commodities and there were consequences. It was too much to hope he'd turn into a decent person, but I wanted him to feel the way he made me feel.

Stupid.

Embarrassed.

Used.

One way or another, he was going down and I was just the woman to do it.

CHAPTER #9

IT SEEMED PLANS of revenge made you sleepy.

Either that, or it was the pint of chocolate chip cookie dough ice cream I ate to drown my sorrows.

We were out of wine, so I had to improvise.

So, when I woke up in the dark with strange hands touching me, I wasn't exactly sure if it was calorie-induced hallucinations or I was being assaulted.

Given my track record for shitty things happening, I wasn't taking a chance either way.

"What the hell." My sister deflected my flying fist of fury, grabbing my hands and restraining me. "It's me, Morgan."

"Shit, I'm sorry." My eyes slowly adjusted to the light. "What time is it?"

Morgan reached across to the lamp on the end table and turned it on. "Just after nine, I had to work a double." She was still in her scrubs. "I saw you passed out on the couched and got worried. There's a stomach flu going around, we were hammered in the E.R."

Hmm. Funny that she'd mentioned that. "Yeah, I came home from work early today, but I'm not sick." *That was questionable.* "I mean, my body isn't sick. Other parts of me . . . well . . . Let's just say I need to scrub the search history on my laptop in case it's ever seized."

She folded her arms across her chest, taking a seat beside me on the couch. "You want to tell me what's going on?"

"I don't want to make you an accessory."

"Lo, come on." She tugged on my arm. "Firstly, if you're going to kill someone and make it look like natural causes, you don't need Google, that's what I'm here for. I'm your sister and that blood oath we took when you were six and I was nine pretty much guarantees I can be counted on to help you dispose of a body or two."

I laughed, shifting into a sitting position. "I'm not sure what the statute is on blood oaths in California, I'm going to have to look that up."

"Secondly," she ignored me, continuing, "if this has to do with that guy you work with and hate, you need to talk to the partners."

"Ugh." I let my head fall on the back of the couch. "I was so, so stupid."

While I hated reliving it all again, I couldn't lie to my sister either. So, I started to recount the whole, diabolical story even if hearing out loud made me feel even more stupid.

"He did what?" Her eyes got huge as her mouth dropped open. "He kissed you so you wouldn't read your emails? Lo, last time I checked that was classified as sexual harassment. You need to call your boss now." She grabbed my cell from the coffee table and waved it in front of me. "He won't get away with this."

"Well . . ." Goddamn it, as much as I hated to admit it, it hadn't been sexual harassment.

Inappropriate, sure.

Unethical, possibly.

Dodgy as hell, very much so.

But as terrible as it sounded, I had *wanted* that kiss. At least I did when I didn't know he was being a fraud. And it had been . . . ugh, amazing.

"I kissed him back. I grabbed him and kissed him and asked to go back to his place." I buried my head in my hands. "Like a desperate moron. *He* was the one who turned me down."

"*You* kissed *him*?" She looked at me as if I was insane. "A man who you swore you wouldn't pee on if he was on fire, that's the guy you kissed?"

I understood the confusion. Because if yesterday morning you had told me that by the end of the day I would have been lip-locked with Roman Pierce and propositioning him in a parking lot, I'd have had your ass committed. But things changed. *He* changed. Except he didn't.

"To be fair, he is probably into some weird peeing fantasy. So even though I have kissed him, I still definitely would not pee on him. Even if he was on fire. And did you miss the part where I told you he charmed me? I should have brought some of the food home for you to take to the lab for a sample. He probably laced it with something."

That would explain a lot actually.

"So," she shifted in her seat, "he charmed you. You guys kissed. And then he blindsided you. And because of this, he convinced the client to go his way."

"Yes," I nodded, her grasp on the situation commendable considering I'd had to be sketchy with details regarding the case. Client, attorney privilege and all that.

Slowly, the smile spread across her face. "Do we know where the loser lives?"

"Nope, but if I did, I would show up on his doorstep and . . ." I tried to think of something horrible. Kicking him in the balls was the front-runner, if not, slightly predictably. "Morgan, are there any kind of drugs I can get over the counter which cause erectile dysfunction?"

Nothing like a case of limp dick to knock him down a peg or two. Of course, I knew what I was suggesting was highly illegal. But it made me feel better to fantasize. And right now, it was all about making me feel better.

"Let's not drug anyone right now," she laughed. "But just know if it comes to it, I have a list as long as my arm that would do the job nicely."

"Excellent." My first real smile of the day made its appearance. "Why don't you get a shower and get out of your scrubs, and I'll order us some late-night dinner."

"That sounds like heaven." Morgan sighed as she lifted herself off the couch. "Get Italian. I'm craving carbs."

As Morgan headed to the bathroom, I grabbed the phone and ordered pasta from *Gino's*. I may have over ordered, risking sending us both into a carb coma but that was the chance I was going to take.

While I waited for the food to arrive, I scanned my bursting-at-the-seems inbox and voice mail, both of which I had ignored since I left the office.

Roman—AKA public enemy number one—had called, texted and emailed, covering all forms of communication just short of sending a raven.

Too bad none of them would be getting a response.

Instead, I checked on Charlotte—she was better but out of action for a few more days, Daniel—he assured me everything was under control and not to come back until I was no longer contagious, and Jana Cane—who I felt needed an apology for my previous lack of response.

Morgan had just gotten out of the shower when the delivery guy from *Gino's* knocked at the door, my stomach rumbling at the thought of the impeding feast.

"What. The. Hell." My eyes bulged as I opened the door. Roman—the asshole—Pierce standing on my threshold. And worse than his unwelcomed presence, he was not holding any bags of food from *Gino's*.

"Are you stalking me now?" My hands planted themselves on my hips, my sleep shorts and old T-shirt not doing me any favors as I tried to be intimidating.

"Yes, I'm stalking you," he deadpanned. "Because I have nothing better to do when I'm swamped on a case than to lurk on someone's doorstep. I delivered the Lieberman files two months ago, I know where you live."

Oh, now with the sarcasm. He really did have his head up his ass.

"Then what are you doing here?" I kept my body braced in the doorway, there was no way he was coming inside, not when he hadn't told me what he was doing here and what his intentions were.

He rolled his eyes, looking bored. "I offered to check in on you. See how you're doing since the sudden onset of this mysterious stomach flu."

"Lo?" Morgan came up beside me, her hair still damp from her shower.

"It's fine, Morgan," I answered her, keeping my eyes on him. I didn't trust him for a second, and I knew exactly what he was capable of when I was distracted. I wouldn't be making that mistake a second time.

"Hey, I have an order here for Lauren." The *Gino's* delivery guy appeared behind Roman. "One of you Lauren?" He looked around to the posse of people assembled at the front door.

"That's me." I raised my hand, taking a step outside the safety of my apartment to grab the food.

Shit.

And double shit.

I'd left the money for the food inside on the coffee table. So, I either called out to Morgan to get the cash while I guarded the door like a Doberman. *Or* I backed myself slowly into the apartment while keeping my eyes on him like he was a leprechaun trying to steal my *Lucky Charms*.

Both of those options had me looking like I belonged in a straightjacket.

"Here." Roman took out a money clip from the inside pocket of his suit jacket and handed the *Gino's* guy a fifty. "That cover it?"

"I can pay for my own dinner." I stopped short of stomping my foot as I called out over my shoulder, "Morgan, grab the cash from the coffee table."

Standing guard at the door like a Doberman it was.

"Just take the money," he said to the bewildered delivery guy, grabbing the food from him before Morgan had a chance to return. He turned to me and smiled. "She gets cranky when she hasn't eaten."

Oh, I was going to kill him.

"You." I lunged forward, Roman using the arm that wasn't holding the food to grab me around the waist. "I hate you so much." I breathed into his face.

Meanwhile, the delivery guy had grabbed the money Roman had given him and was already down the other end of the hall. The unmistakable, "I don't get paid enough for this shit," heard before he disappeared.

"Just calm down." Roman laughed as he wrestled me in his arms. "You're going to hurt yourself."

"Then let me go, asshole." I wriggled, trying to find purchase as my feet dangled in the air. "You're not welcome here."

"What the hell is going on out there?" Morgan's voice boomed from the doorway. "Both of you need to calm down. And Roman, put my sister down."

She didn't need a formal introduction. I'd fed her enough

information to deduce that the good-looking jerk at the door was the *same* good-looking jerk I worked with and hated.

"Are you going to be civil?" He didn't let go, clinching me closer to his body.

"Are you going to stop acting like a dick?" I fired back, unconcerned that I was wearing next to nothing, pressed up against the firm and toned body of Roman Pierce. Ironically, that included his dick.

In another time or place, it *might* have been enjoyable, not so much now.

"Okay, both of you, stop." Morgan grabbed the food from Roman's hand, the one that wasn't currently wrapped around me. "Someone is going to end up calling the cops, most likely, me."

"I'm going to let you go, slowly," he whispered in my ear. "Then we're going to talk."

"Fine."

He may have thought I was agreeing, but I was doing anything but submitting. No, I was just pacifying him, luring him into a false sense of complaisance because wriggling out of his bear hug had proven too difficult. I was out-muscled by his weight and his size in a physical confrontation, but mentally, I was still boss.

The tension around my body started to ease with my feet finally feeling the floor under them. He seemed hesitant but when he saw I didn't lash out, he unwrapped his arms. "Can we do this inside?"

The last thing I wanted was Roman polluting the sanctity of my home. I was going to have to hit whatever room he entered with a heavy dose of *Febreze* and *Lysol*. Even then I would probably have to sage the place and get a blessing from the Pope just to be sure.

But my options were limited and the sooner we got this over with the sooner I could self medicate with pasta and garlic bread.

"Fine." I stepped aside, giving him room to enter my apartment.

His huge body strode in with confidence, and if he was worried about me staking him through the heart—I'll admit, it crossed my mind—he didn't seem concerned.

"Hi, we haven't properly met." He grinned, sticking out his hand trying to bewitch my sister. "I'm Roman."

She smiled back—traitor—accepting his hand while juggling our food. "I'm Morgan."

"Morgan, I need you to give me a minute alone with Roman." I closed the door behind me, wanting to expedite the process.

"Thank you, I appreciate that." He had the nerve to smile at me.

"Don't thank me, asshole," I snapped, wanting to smack the smug right out of him as I narrowed my eyes. "She's a nurse, so legally bound to save your sorry jerk ass if I try to kill you. Trust me, I'm not doing you a favor."

He looked mildly amused, his lips twitching at the edges but had the sense not to laugh. "I'll take my chances then."

"I'm going into the kitchen." Morgan side-eyed Roman before turning to me. "Lo, don't mess up the rug, I just had it steam cleaned." She gave me a chin tip before disappearing.

I didn't waste time, facing him head on. "What is it that you want?"

"Why did you leave today?" He ignored my question, remaining standing considering I hadn't invited him to sit. "And don't tell me it was the stomach flu, I know you're not sick."

"You made me sick, you and your *lies*."

"I told you, I never lied to you." He kept his voice controlled. "Look, I get you're pissed. Fine, be *pissed*." He moved closer. "But you can't tell me that with the new evidence that my way wasn't the right way to go. Take your ego out of it. You know the best thing for our client was to settle the divorce."

The nerve of him.

Suggesting I was only arguing with him to be right? Ha! He must be confusing me with himself.

"Take *your* ego out of it." My finger pointed with accusation. "If you were so convinced that it was the best way, why didn't you just tell me outright? Or give me a chance to argue my point?"

You know, handle it like partners, I didn't add. He could say whatever he wanted, but he wouldn't convince me that his intentions hadn't been deceitful.

His brow lifted, taunting me. "What did I tell you last night?"

"I'm sorry, when?" I leaned in, waving my arms around. "When you were bullshitting about your thirty-five brothers? Or when you pretended to be a person with feelings? I'm not sure what part of the conversation you want me to focus on."

"At the car, Harper." His eyes connected with mine.

He had to remind me that last night hadn't *just* been talking, didn't he? Like it wasn't bad enough I couldn't eradicate the thoughts from my mind using self-hypnosis, I needed to get a refresher from the only other person who had been there

I hated him.

Really, *really* hated him.

"You listen to me." My skin heated as I jabbed a finger into his stupid firm chest. "I allowed myself to believe that the person I was having dinner with was a true representation of himself, and because of that, I reciprocated, behaving in a manner I usually wouldn't, with you. This is not a character flaw, it's called *humanity*, and I will not allow you or anyone else to make me feel bad about that."

Fire burned through my veins as I spewed out exactly what I was thinking.

The corner of his mouth twitched, broadening into a smile. "You want to regret it, but you can't, can you?"

Oh. No. He. Did. Not.

"Did you hear anything I said, you big moronic jerk?"

"I told you to go home and text me, *Lauren*." It was the first time he'd *ever* said my first name, stunning me into silence. "I made you promise to pick up your goddamn phone, and send me a message."

"So you want a Nobel Peace Prize because you cared about me getting home safe?" My voice was quieter than it had been, but no less venomous. "Just an FYI, the big knife in my back kind of negates the kind gesture."

"No." He breathed, his shoulders squaring off as his body completely dominated the space, overwhelming me. "I assumed you'd check your fucking emails like you *always* do. Yes, I went behind your back. And yes, I didn't tell you about it because I knew you would fight me for the sake of fucking fighting. Because you get off on it, the same as I do. But we needed to settle, it is a good deal for the client, and if Daniel had brought this to the table you would have agreed."

I couldn't speak, the words getting lost in my throat as he stalked closer.

"But I told you to message me because I assumed you would see the email." He didn't shout. Didn't need to. Each word cracked like a whip, demanding my full attention. "And then you would call me and we'd fight about it. But ultimately you would decide I was right."

I shook my head, not willing to admit he might be right. "You don't know that."

"Yes, I do. Like I know I'm right about this."

His mouth was on mine before I had a chance to work out what was happening, his tongue parting my lips as hands found their way onto my ass.

His hands.

On *my* ass.

While he was kissing me.

And I wasn't stopping him.

A moan escaped my lips as he pressed against me and it felt so, so good. Last night had been no fluke as my skin felt like it was lit on fire, losing myself in the kiss, in his scent, in . . .

Oh. My. God. I needed to stop him.

"What the hell are you doing?" Common sense decided to show up and I pushed him away. "Have you lost your damn mind?"

"No. I'm thinking very clearly." His hands were still on my ass, and I hadn't asked him to move them.

I should probably do that.

Now, Lauren! Tell him to move his hands.

"You said . . . Last night . . . You." *What the hell was I trying to say?* Crap, his hands. That's right. "And take your hands off my ass."

Oh, thank you, God.

His hands lifted, bringing them where I could see them as he held them up but didn't move. "Tell me I'm wrong. Tell me I'm wrong about the case and tell me I'm wrong about this." He dared me, his mouth hovering dangerously close to mine.

Conflict flared in me as my body and mind warred with itself. Our lips were so close; all I had to do was reach up and kiss him like I was dying to do. But I also wanted to grab a kitchen knife and find out for real if the large intestine was five feet long. He was tall, so maybe his would be longer.

Although, Morgan had said not to mess up the rug.

Shit, none of this was helping.

"Get out of my apartment." I took a step back, moving out of the way of temptation and hopefully back to sanity. "You need to go."

"I'll go if that's what you want, Harper." He was back to using my last name as he smirked. "Enjoy your dinner, we'll discuss *this* tomorrow."

I narrowed my eyes as I leered at him. "We're not discussing shit. And here," I added, grabbing the money from the coffee table, "I don't want you paying for my dinner."

He looked down at my hand but made no move to accept it. "Tell me, Harper. Is it the paying for dinner or the kiss that you have the problem with? Because you didn't seem to have an issue with either last night." The jerk had the nerve to smile.

"Get out." The words morphed into growl as I pointed to the door. "Get out of my apartment."

"See you in the morning." He laughed, straightening his tie. "Say goodbye to your sister for me. And by the way," his eyes dropped down to my breasts. "That T-shirt leaves little to the imagination. Not that I'm complaining, they are even more spectacular than I imagined."

My hands fisted at my sides and my fingernails dug into my palms. He wanted me to argue, to yell, to fight. So I didn't. I was too worked up to be embarrassed, not caring about what he could and couldn't see through the thin fabric of my T-shirt. Instead, I summoned all my will to keep my mouth shut, subliminally promising him that while he might be able to see my boobs, he'd never touch them again. Mentally, I had killed him three times by the time he'd reached the door.

He looked over his shoulder, giving me one last look at his smug, ever-present grin. Then he left, closing the door with a forceful pull.

"Well." Morgan walked back in, forking her spaghetti and meatballs out of the foil takeaway container. "Here I was thinking I would eat dinner and maybe watch some cable. Who knew I'd be walking into my very own Telenovela at home."

I rolled my eyes, my body still jangling with irritation even though he'd left. "Oh, stop. He is just infuriating and I hate him."

"Yeah, it was hard to tell from the kitchen." She took another mouthful of dinner, chewing thoroughly before adding, "I think kissing him back was probably *not* the way to go. A slap would have been more authentic. Maybe a knee to the groin?"

My head shook, breathing out a slow regretful breath. "I don't know what's wrong with me. I can't stand him, I can see literally no redeeming features and yet when he kisses me, I can't seem to stop."

I wanted to be disgusted. To tell Morgan—and myself—that I'd hated the kiss and the way he'd touched me, but I couldn't.

There was something wrong with me.

"I must have contracted some horrible infection that is eating away at the rational part of my brain." There had to be a logical explanation, because letting my libido be in control was too stupid for words.

"Or you're just attracted to him," she tried to reason, lowering the foil takeaway container to the coffee table and forgetting about her dinner. "He's extremely good looking. Very tall, blond and hot. And he's not intimidated by you." She waved her fork around, continuing her diagnosis. "Isn't that the reason why you claim it's hard to find a date?"

I scoffed, wondering if my sister hadn't contracted the brain-eating disease as well. "I know you aren't suggesting I date him. Because there isn't a chance in hell."

"Who said anything about dating him?" She laughed. "You said it yourself, you're not interested in dates and having a boyfriend. *You'd have to spend too much time with them.*" She mimicked my previous relationship discussion. "I'm just saying I get the attraction. And I think him pushing your buttons is part of the appeal."

"Well, I still think I'm sick." I held onto the last shred of denial I could. The alternative was too horrible to even contemplate.

"Yes, you could be sick." She gave me a sympathetic nod. "We can get some blood drawn if it makes you feel better. *Or* you can admit that he is the first guy in a long time that has challenged you, and you find it sexy. And *he* is sexy. So of course you want to have sex with him."

Those were not words I wanted to hear, especially not from my smart and rational sister.

"Maybe. I don't know." I shrugged, feeling exposed. And it had nothing to do with my lack of clothing. "He's just so horrible."

"Yeah." She agreed, grabbing my hand. "But at least you know what you're getting."

"Ugh." I groaned, closing my eyes even more confused than ever. "Let's go eat dinner. I need to go over the case."

"So you're going back tomorrow?"

"Yes, I might be swinging wildly, alternating between hating him and being attracted to him." I still couldn't believe I was saying it out loud. "But he's not going to stop me from doing my job. Besides, leaving him unchecked is dangerous. I have an obligation to my boss and the firm."

"Good for you." Morgan gave me a gentle punch in the arm. "Now, let's go eat our free dinner."

CHAPTER #10

I HAD STUMBLED on the definition of a true paradox.

I hated Roman Pierce.

I wanted to destroy Roman Pierce.

But unfortunately, I wanted to sleep with him as well.

It could only be explained because maybe desire and hostility were so closely related emotions that the mind got confused. I mean, I didn't study psychology, but I was almost positive they resided in the same part of the brain. Or at least that is what I told myself, and it made me feel better.

So, while there was no feeling of affection, love and romance—the opposite being more accurate. There *was* an undeniable attraction and lust that crawled through my body like a virus.

See, I knew I was sick.

And as much as I hated to admit it, Roman was right.

Not about kissing me.

Although . . . ugh.

About the Jana Cane case, and settling was *probably*—and I said that word begrudgingly—the best way to go.

Oh, I still thought we had a fighting chance in court against both her soon-to-be ex-husband and Price Waters, who had very obviously gotten their hands on some insider information. But, I also knew that she didn't want her new patent and product launch marred by legal red tape, which would drain her resources. Not to mention Daniel had already filed a *cease and desist* against Price Waters, giving them a chance to politely bow out before he buried them in subpoenas. And after the patent was filed, anything they did with their ill-gotten information would mean serious fines and jail time. They were greedy, but not outright stupid.

My previous day's "stomach flu" had seemed to miraculously disappear the next morning. As much as seeing Roman and dealing with the confusing and volatile emotions did *not* seem like a good time, I needed to get back to work. Besides, the son of a bitch didn't get the satisfaction of running me out of town. Or the office, as the case was.

Ironically, I wasn't exactly sure what his intentions were when I hadn't seen him most of the day.

I hadn't been intentionally avoiding him, walking into to the firm with my chin held high, ready to do battle. But after assuring Daniel I wasn't Typhoid Mary and whatever nastiness that had struck me down yesterday was gone—easy to promise when you hadn't been sick in the first place—I hadn't seen Roman at all.

And after a sleepless and sexually frustrated night readying myself for the showdown, I was actually disappointed.

Instead of striding in with his devastatingly sexy smile, ego the size of Mount Rushmore and taunting me with further seduction, he was hidden away in his tiny, windowless office next door.

No rolling of his eyes, quip of his lips or calling me *Harper*. Nothing.

And when I asked Daniel what had Roman so busy—casually, like I couldn't have been more bored if I tried—I'd been informed he was putting the finishing touches on the reconfigured timeline to send to opposing counsel. Which made sense of course, but it *could* and *should* have been something we'd done together.

What the hell was wrong with me?

I should have been grateful, ecstatic that I didn't have to deal with his ridiculous arrogance for a while. But there were no feelings of gratitude as I rested my hand on the wall that separated our almost identical offices.

Tension crackled through the Sheetrock, the lingering memory of his kiss and touch gnawed at me like a sewer rat, no matter how much I didn't want it to. The gutter—with said sewer rat—was exactly where my mind was as I imagined clawing through the wall and throwing him across his desk.

And I reverted to my previous statement.

What. The. Hell. Was. Wrong. With. Me?

Trying to ignore what was obviously a serious case of psychosis, I returned to my desk and *tried* to do some work.

I didn't like my chances.

Excitement shot through my spine when a few moments later there was a knock at my door, and I knew it was *him* before he'd even walked in.

My heart pounded as I lifted my head to look at him with fake disinterest. "What do you want?"

"Hmm, what do I want?" His eyebrow rose, locking the door behind him and taking the air from the tiny space with him. "Pushing you up against the wall and kissing you would be a good start. I haven't been able to get your amazing tits off my mind." His eyes dropped to my breasts.

My choice in outfit today *might* have been intentional. The white, sheer fabric of my blouse clung to my body like a second skin and was completely inappropriate for work when I wasn't wearing a jacket.

Which I wasn't currently while alone in my office.

Except, I was no longer alone.

"You're delusional and disgusting." I glared at him, pretending that heat hadn't spread across my skin the minute he'd walked in.

"Am I?" He moved closer, not looking convinced. "Did you think about it last night, Harper? Think about the way I touched you and the way I *could* touch you?"

His long legs had efficiently taken him from the door to where I was sitting in just a few steps. I pretended not to notice how strong his thighs looked stretching the fabric of his pants as he perched himself on the edge of my desk.

"Didn't give it or you a second thought." I dismissed him with a wave. "I know you like to think you're a big deal, but you really aren't that amazing. I feel sorry for you."

"Really?" He laughed, the light hitting his perfect blue eyes as he grinned. "And was it sympathy that made you moan in my mouth? Or rub up against my cock?" He leaned forward edging his mouth right near my ear. "Do you think if I stuck my hand up your skirt right now that it would be *sympathy* I felt, or would it be something else?"

My throat tightened as I squeezed my legs together.

It wasn't just his hand I wanted him to stick up my skirt. And if he touched me—even just an innocent graze across my arm—I would probably explode.

He was a demon, an incarnation of evil in a designer suit who could obliterate my hormones with a single sexy smile.

"I have work to do." I coughed, too obvious that he was getting to me.

"Yes, you do." He lowered his head, teasing my mouth with his hot breath. "Fuck, you drive me insane."

I could no longer be held accountable as our mouths met in a thrilling frenzied crash. We had already established that psychologically I was compromised by the weird evil phenomenon and was powerless to fight it.

And then there was that mouth of his which was a problem all on its own. Seducing me with kisses that could stroke my G-spot solely with his lips. I had either not had sex in such a long time I'd forgotten how it worked, or the man had sold his soul to the Devil. Pretty sure at this point I didn't care which of those theories proved to be correct as long as he kept kissing me.

Or was I kissing him?

Oh my God, I didn't care which as long as it didn't stop.

My body rose out of the seat as my fingers threaded through his slick blond hair, and like a magnet finding north, I couldn't stop the contact.

He palmed my ass, pushing me back against the wall—like he promised in the first place—and let his mouth do the Devil's work.

He was hard, his firm length straining against his pants as he bunched up the hem of my skirt and hooked my leg on his hip.

I rocked against him, his erection stroking me through his pants and my underwear as his hands and lips explored me.

It was the third time I'd been kissed by Roman. The third time, and I wasn't sure how it could get any better. It was like having sex fully clothed with the most banal parts of my body becoming highly sensitive erogenous zones. He could kiss my freaking finger and I'd probably come.

"Are you wet, Harper?" He moved his mouth and sucked the exposed skin of my throat.

"No, not at all," I lied, unable to stop my hands from grabbing his shirt and pulling him closer. "You do nothing for me."

"You're such a filthy liar." His fingers traveled up my leg and edged at my panties. "I bet I could touch you right now and you'd be soaked."

Breaths were sucked in and out in ragged pants, blistering need consuming me. "If I am, it's because I'm thinking about someone else."

My lie made him grin, teasing me further as he pushed my panties to the side. "Is he doing this to you?" A finger plunged into me without warning, filling me while his thumb circled my clit. "Mmmmm. Harper."

I bucked against his hand, getting lost in the friction.

He brought his lips to my ear and groaned, "Whose hand are you fucking right now?"

A moan escaped my lips as I closed my eyes.

"Not yours, anyone but yours."

So much deceit and in a twisted way it just made it more exciting.

"I could make you come like this, Harper," he teased. "I thought about it all night, all fucking morning too. Walking in here and making you come exactly like this."

"You can try, but I doubt you can."

Lies.

Every single word so far from the truth, but I couldn't stop.

I didn't want to stop.

He grinned at every denial, my feigned indifference exciting him even more as he pushed in another finger, pumping me while his thumb continued to circle.

"Feel my fingers inside of you?" He brought his mouth closer, biting my bottom lip with a taunt. "Feel how good that feels? That's not even close to how amazing it would feel with my cock."

"It's not—" I'd lost the ability to lie. Wanting to tell him some bullshit about barely feeling a thing or being more aroused at the DMV, but as I tried to form words, nothing came out.

"You're so close." His mouth pressed against mine and with a few more strokes he had me unraveling. "Yes. God. Yes."

They had been his words because I'd lost the ability to say my own. My fingers dug into his biceps as my hips bucked, every part of me shaking as waves and waves of euphoria washed over me.

"I expected you to be more vocal." He laughed, his mouth against my skin while I reined in my breathing. "You're rarely at a loss for words."

"Maybe if you actually made me come, I'd be a little more excited." Our eyes locked, my fingers slithering down my body where his hand was still between my legs. "Better luck next time."

"Oh, you think I didn't feel that?" He pumped inside of me one last time before pulling out his fingers. "Tell yourself whatever you want, but I made you come, and you liked it."

"I can understand your confusion." I yanked down my skirt, steadying myself on my feet. "Jerking yourself off is a lot different than doing it to a woman. You might want to work on your technique though."

He laughed, pulling out a tissue from the box of Kleenex I kept on my desk and wiped his hand. "If you want me to do it again, Harper, all you have to do is ask. But I have work to do, so it's going to have to wait until later."

"Don't you get tired of embarrassing yourself?" I scoffed, the tingles still echoing through my body. "I'm not that desperate."

And I didn't know why, but I wanted to kiss him again.

To put my hand against his pants and feel him hard, stroke him slow and tease him just like he teased me. But I kept my hands to myself, folding my arms across my chest as he followed my eyes down to his crotch.

Shit.

He'd seen me looking.

"Maybe if you're good, I'll let you play with it later." He shot me a wink. "Some of us have work to do first."

I shook my head, glaring at the door. "You can leave anytime, Roman. This is my office."

He casually tossed the tissue that had been in his hand into the waste paper basket. "Oh, I know that. I was going into tell you about your new assignment, but then we got sidetracked."

That was one hell of a sidetrack.

I'd walked into a room before and been absentminded, sometimes even forgetting why I'd gone in there in the first place. But I'd never been so distracted I'd stuck my hands down some man's pants and jerked him off without the intention of doing so.

Not sure if that said more about him or me.

"What new assignment?" I asked, refusing to acknowledge the other part of his statement.

His lips twisted as he sunk his hands into his pockets. "ITP. Fiber Optics acquisition. You lost the bet."

"Are you serious, right now?" I struggled to wrap my head around the disbelief.

"Of course I am, you didn't think I was going to let it go, did you?" He fought his grin. "You might want to get on it soon though, it will take forever to go through the prospective candidates. ITP insists you do the vetting for them, and they've been looking for a while."

"You are such a bastard." I tossed out the insult wondering how only a few minutes ago I had let him touch me.

Wanted it.

Enjoyed it.

He shrugged nonchalantly. "I've been called worse. I'll let you get to work. I have a ton of paperwork I need to get through myself."

Ignoring his still very visible erection and my irritation, he turned, unlocked the door and left.

Walked out of my office without another word.

I fell back into my chair, my limbs still shaky. I wasn't sure if it was from the amazing orgasm or how much I seemed to like and hate him both at the same time.

Even more troubling was that I was angrier at him for seeming

to be unaffected by it all rather than at myself for my lack of judgment. I mean, obviously he had a hard-on and he'd been aroused.
But he'd walked in, walked out, and seemed more amused by it
than anything else.

I wanted to march into his office and do the same to him. Put
my hands on him, tease him to the brink of madness and then tell
him to go alphabetize the Roberson files. There were six genera-
tions of Robersons. It would take him a while.

Instead, I shook my head, looking at the door he'd closed and
wondering what else I could do to bug the hell out him.

And if that was how good I felt when he touched me, imagine
how amazing the sex would be.

Ugh.

Torment him, sleep with him—maybe they wouldn't have to
be mutually exclusive?

There was only one way to find out.

OTHER THAN OUR brief interlude, we remained on our mutual
respective sides of the wall.

My new assignment—the ITP account—was boring as hell.

They were just another tech company in Palo Alto looking
for greater dominance and more muscle in an already saturated
market. But the skinny-jean-black-frame-wearing-thirty-something
CEO was a multimillionaire who was still making money when so
many other companies had iDied. So, of course when they said,
"jump", we said, "Would that be a vertical or horizontal leap?"

Bored.

Bored and agitated, and the day crawled along painfully slow.

So, when the time display on my phone buzzed at five o'clock,
I grabbed my handbag and jumped out of my desk chair like my
office was on fire.

I hesitated at his door just for a moment, bringing my ear discreetly to the wood and not entirely sure on what I was hoping to accomplish. The low rumble of his voice echoed through the room. He sounded like he was on the phone, but I could only make out every second word. My skin goosebumped as I heard footsteps come closer, pausing as he returned to his call.

"I'm going to have to skip dinner tonight, I have no idea when I'll get out of here." His voice was clear like he was standing right there opposite me with only the door between us.

I held my breath, my heart pounding as I waited to see if he'd continue.

"Look, I know you're pissed, but I completely understand where she is coming from. My advice is sign the fucking thing, shove it in a drawer and move on."

Huh? Sounded like business but his language was more familiar than he normal would be with a client. And what about the dinner invitation he had to decline?

My feet stood frozen in place, curious to hear more while still conscious about being discovered eavesdropping.

At any moment he could open the door, finding me stalking him like a pathetic loser. Or someone we worked with might see, attracting their own set of questions. But instead of cutting my losses and leaving before either of those things happened, I decided the risk was worth it and stayed.

"Eric." He said a name, which happened to belong to the eldest of the Pierce hoard. The mystery of the caller had been solved; he was talking to his brother. "If she hadn't come to me, it would have been someone else. You know that while I don't always show it, I care about her, and I will make sure she does not get fucked over."

Her?

What *her?*

I assumed Roman had a steady stream of willing women. I'd

often joked about his "roster" and he'd eluded the same himself. He didn't date those women though, he *fucked* them. Then he left, as he so elegantly put it.

And in the year that we had been working together, he didn't seem to have been in *any* kind of relationship, let alone a serious one. But whoever he was talking about with Eric obviously wasn't one of these fuck toys.

A feeling I didn't understand swirled in my lower gut.

Jealousy?

Anger?

Did I have any right to care?

But as irrational as any of it felt, I stayed, wanting more information.

"As your fucking attorney, I'm telling you not to fight this." His voice rose in agitation. "Do I need to remind you about the millions of dollars in assets?"

What the hell?

His brother was a *millionaire?*

Who the hell was the man who hours ago had his hands in my pants, teasing me to insanity? I knew nothing about him. Literally nothing.

"Fine. We can argue about this later." Footsteps started again. "I'll stop by on the weekend before you fly out . . ." The rest of the conversation reduced to an inaudible garble.

While I had initially been more concerned with my unresolved sexual frustration, my detective work raised more important questions.

And before I kissed him again—or anything else—I was going to find out exactly who he was.

CHAPTER #11

HE WAS AGONIZINGLY close.

All afternoon we had spent inches away from each other finalizing the details for the Cane divorce. After spending the day and a half in purgatory vetting companies for ITP, I was given a reprieve when Daniel asked me to help Roman wrap it up.

The double entendre wasn't even funny.

Neither of us spoke about what happened yesterday in my office. I hadn't waltzed in and given him a blowjob like I had fantasized about. Nor had he bent me over my desk and had sex with me—I had more than one fantasy.

In fact, there hadn't been any inappropriate touching at all.

Neither of us had been miraculously cured either. I watched as he raked his hand through his hair in frustration when I bent in front of him, the undone button of my shirt showing just enough cleavage.

And I battled the distraction whenever he'd reach across the table, his big, strong body, a finger touch just out of reach.

Neither one of us caved.

It was like the ultimate game of sexual chicken, just waiting to see which one of us was the first to flinch.

But it wasn't just my inability to resist him that I had to deal with. No, I had a more important issue to resolve. Information, namely who he was, and what he was involved with.

And I had still yet to find out who the woman was that he apparently "cared about."

I'd been up all night, tossing and turning, building my version of the truth. And my constructed reality wasn't pretty.

Eric, the older brother, was some kind of underworld drug lord.

I'd come to the hypothesis after an extensive online search. There were no investment bankers, property developers or any other kind of businessmen named Eric Pierce that I could find.

It would also explain the whole Heart and Vine connection too. It would make sense that someone with ties to illegal activity would need some legitimate businesses to launder their money. And obviously Roman was the middleman who made that all happen.

Having a lawyer as part of the syndicate made perfect sense, and one that was related to you by blood was even better.

The other brothers were probably involved too, their roles in the intricate crime web not yet ascertained.

And the woman?

She was Roman's secret wife.

Probably of South American origin with unmatched beauty, she had been married off young when her father hadn't been able to pay a debt. She despised him—didn't we all?—spending her days locked in a villa where she daydreamed about his murder. And while he hadn't wanted any part of the sham marriage—I assumed since he seemed to be such a commitment-phobe—he was honor-bound to do his part for his family.

He felt sorry for her, knowing that she was trapped in an impossible situation, and over time had learned to "care for her"—that was where that part came in.

And to cope with a loveless marriage to a woman who systematically plotted his death—I could probably help her with that—he whored himself around, using sex as a panacea.

Shit, or maybe I needed to take some freaking Ambien or something. Surely it was the lack of sleep making me sound like a crazy person. That, *or* it could be that a drug lord and his secret South American wife had recently been prosecuted. One of my friends was an assistant to the DA and had mentioned it over drinks. She made shitty money, but her stories were always great. Criminals were all the same, and why should Roman's family be any different.

"Harper?"

My head snapped to attention as the sexy whore bastard said my name.

"Sorry, what was that?" I tried to smile sweetly, remembering to stick with the plan.

Do not call any attention to yourself.

He watched me as he spoke. "I said, can you email me the deposition from Tuesday?"

"Sure thing." My lips thinned into a tight smile. "I'll do it right now."

I hated that I still found him attractive.

That even though I knew—okay, assumed—he was involved in bad shit, his face and his body did things to mine that I did not understand.

I was a terrible person.

But there was a silver lining.

If I could somehow find a way to get justice for those—me included—that he and his brothers had wronged, then surely it would be worth it. I just needed more information. And in order to do that I needed him to trust me and believe it was business as usual.

Which is why I was still flirting with him.

It killed me—fine, it wasn't completely terrible, shelve your judgment—to pretend, but I did it. And I would continue to do it until I knew everything.

Hell, I could be the key to a major crime investigation; I almost had no choice in seeing this all the way through.

My fingers tapped on my laptop, the sentence having been written three times and still didn't make sense before I stopped typing. "What are you doing tonight?"

"Not this." He didn't lift his head continuing with his own document hell. "I swear they should hand out a prenup with the diamond ring. Why anyone would get married is a mystery, but getting hitched without the paperwork is just plain stupid."

I fought the urge to roll my eyes, lacking complete surprise at his romantic deficiency. He'd probably been soured by his own experience.

"I'm almost positive that most people don't get married believing they are going to get divorced."

Unless you were Roman Pierce. And then he probably made you so crazy that divorce was all you thought about. Divorce or death, it was a fifty-fifty split.

"Yeah, well most people are idiots," he deadpanned, blowing out a frustrated breath.

"Speaking of idiots." I couldn't help myself, smiling sweetly as I pushed my laptop to the side. "What are your plans tonight?"

His fingers paused midstroke, looking at me with suspicion. "Why?"

Shit, I had been too eager. I should have insulted him more.

"I need to buy you dinner," I said casually, like it was the most natural thing in the world. "You know, to pay you back for buying mine. So if you don't have plans, we'll do that."

As far as lame excuses, it was the lamest. So ridiculously stupid it was almost an insult to my intelligence. But, I needed a reason to get him alone to talk and as far as workable ones, it would do.

Twice he'd paid for my dinner, and it was common knowledge I didn't like being indebted to people. Even more so when it was him. So, in fitting with my personality, it would make sense I would want to even the score.

He looked amused, ignoring his computer entirely as he turned to face me. "I'm sorry, did I miss a question somewhere?"

"I asked you what your plans are, *that* was the question." I rolled my eyes, wondering why he had to make everything so difficult. "So, are you free or not?"

"I can probably clear my evening for you, Harper." His eyes caught mine. "If you say, please."

"Don't do me any favors, Roman." I was already regretting my decision, wondering if I wasn't getting in over my head. "This is a yes or no proposition and the offer has an expiration time as well."

"Yes, Harper. We'll have dinner." He waved his hand, decreeing it so as he gave me a smirk. "I'll pick you up at eight."

Whoa, what just happened?

How did we get from me extending an invitation to him controlling the tone? And picking me up at eight? That *wasn't* happening.

"I have a car and can drive myself. We can meet there," I was quick to add, knowing that being alone with him was dangerous.

It's when I made stupid decisions, like allowing him to kiss me. And other things.

I couldn't trust myself, and I especially couldn't trust him.

"*Or* I can pick you up at eight, like I just said I was going to." He eyed me hard, leaving no room for debate. "You can pick where we go. That's my final offer."

It never ceased to amaze me how much he could twist things around to suit himself. That was why I needed to keep my wits around him. "You know bullying people isn't a compromise."

"I'm not bullying you. You want to go to dinner. I want to

drive," he reasoned, making it seem like I was the one being irrational. "No one is forcing you to do anything."

I wasn't even going to try to argue with his jaded logic, the thought process making my head hurt.

Just agree to whatever, have dinner, find out information, and seek vengeance.

"Fine, whatever. Eight," I conceded, shaking my head.

He was barely able to contain his grin. "Wear something sexy."

His secret wife wasn't going to have to worry about killing him; I was going to do that for her.

I narrowed my eyes as I clenched my teeth. "This is *not* a date, Roman."

"Who said it was?" His brow scrunched in confusion. "I just think if you're going to be shoving your tits in my face all night, I might as well get a better look. That is what you've been doing." He pointed to my chest, his lips twitching into a smile. "Not that I'm complaining."

"Maybe this is a bad idea after all."

It wasn't just a bad idea, it was dangerous.

I had no idea what I was getting into and I'd made extremely poor choices when it came to him.

I had kissed him three times, the last time going a lot further than just kissing.

What's more, I liked it. I wanted to regret it and yet, there was something in me that held onto the memory like it had been a good thing. The recall heated my body quicker than any man should and I wasn't sure if presented the opportunity another time that I wouldn't do it again.

Even now, knowing he was probably married and was involved in an evil crime racket. I was on the fast track to being one of those women who wrote love letters to prisoners and dreamed of the day they'd finally make parole.

Shit.

Shit.

Shit.

My eyes snapped to his, his pupils expanding as he bit on his lower lip. "It's too late to change your mind. Now email me those depositions, the sooner we get out of here the better."

Shit.

The potential for this to end badly was huge.

"SO, YOU'RE DATING him?" Morgan had been switched to night shift and was just about to leave when I got home. She stood at the door with a dinner-filled Tupperware container in her hand, her brow furrowing in concern.

"It's not a date," I assured her, dumping my handbag on the kitchen table. "I told you, we're just going to talk."

My theory on Roman and his family hadn't been shared yet. Firstly, because I knew Morgan would worry, and she had enough on her plate saving people on a daily basis in the ER. And secondly, because all I had right now was suspicion. I needed solid evidence, and the less people who knew, the better.

"This has trouble all over it, but I guess I should be grateful you are willing to do something other than work. Baby steps. We may even get you into the regular habit of having fun." She looked at her watch, grabbing her keys and her phone. "I need to go or I'm going to be late. Just remember to be careful, and if you sleep with him use protection. I stuffed condoms in your top drawer last week."

"I don't need help with fun. I have a lot of *fun*." I screwed up my face in horror. *I did, didn't I?*

Sure, I worked hard, but so did she, and I could definitely relax when needed. Her eagerness for me to "date" someone who

I'd been vocally averse to was probably a hint it had been a while. Maybe she was right, and I was a little uptight? Ugh, too much to process right now, especially when I had no idea where the night was going to lead and whether or not any fun would be had.

"And I'm not going to sleep with him," I scoffed, hoping the rest of me was as certain as my mouth was. "I told you, dinner and talking, that is all."

"Whatever you say, Lo." Morgan waved goodbye, looking unconvinced. "I've got to run but know it's okay to let your hair down a little. Given half a chance, I might attempt it myself."

As the door slammed shut, the clock started to tick, and I was both nervous and excited for what the night would bring.

One way or another I wanted some answers, and I'd probably have better luck with that if I eased off the *bitch* and added a little more *charm*. It worked for him, didn't it?

So, giving myself a mental pep talk, I quickly stripped down, showered and redressed in "something sexy." Not because he'd told me to or because it was a date. But because dressing that way made me feel more confident, and I figured I had a better chance at learning the truth if he was distracted by my boobs. Yes, I was going to use a little cleavage as well as my brain, there were just some problems that needed the whole toolbox.

The red dress I picked plunged dangerously low in the front. I'd only worn it one other time on a date and that night ended with a drunken homeless person tossing garbage at me and calling me a whore. I was hoping that this time around I'd get a better outcome.

My less than average breast size meant I didn't need a bra, with the rest of the dress molding to my skin all the way to just below mid thigh. It didn't leave a lot to the imagination, and unlike the night where I'd been accosted by the homeless person, this time around it had been intentional.

In an effort to tame my long heavy brown hair, I blew it out, with my tresses eventually submitted into large, loose curls. I was just putting on the finishing touches of my makeup when I heard the buzzer at my door.

It was only seven thirty; he was early.

"Hey." I opened the door, still missing my shoes and the matching handbag. "Come in, I'm almost done."

His eyes flared as they rolled down my body, his lips thinning into a tight line. "Have you decided where we're going?"

"Um yeah, Niko's." I nodded for him to follow me into the living room before slipping into my shoes. "It's this cute little place off Hollywood." My back was turned to him as I adjusted in my heels and continued talking. "Their menu is a fusion of sort of everything but apparently it works. And I heard the food is—" The breath eased of my lungs as I turned back to face him finding him closer than I anticipated. I slammed into his chest, his body unyielding.

He smelled amazing, the fresh manly scent of his cologne wafting up my nose as my face hovered inches from his chest. He wasn't wearing his usual suit either, dressing down in a pair of charcoal tailored pants and a black button down shirt. No tie. No jacket. And no idea how to convince myself that I didn't want to maul him within an inch of his life even though he was probably a married, dirty lawyer with a family in organized crime.

"Where's your sister?" He didn't move, his firm body flush against mine.

"Working." I took a step back, giving us some distance, deliberately not giving him any more information than I already had.

It was one thing to be alone with him in my apartment just before we left for dinner, it was another for him to know that no one would be home when we got back either.

I had meant what I said when I told Morgan I wasn't going to sleep with him. But I wasn't about to give a diabetic person a piece of cake and see what would happen either. And as far as irresponsibility went, me being alone with Roman, and giving the diabetic the cake were one and the same.

"We should probably go, traffic." I grabbed my handbag, the international female sign for let's get out of here, and walked back over to the front door.

He waited a minute, being creepy a little longer as he stared before he decided he was going to join me. The sooner we got out of there, the better.

"My car is parked out front." He opened the door, moving to the side to give me room to step outside and lock up behind us.

I felt his eyes on me the entire time, the icy blue weight of his stare dissecting every single one of my movements as he followed me down the hall.

Never had I been so glad we only lived on the second floor. It was easier to walk down a couple flight of stairs than step into the confined space of an elevator. I needed to remember that at the end of the night and say goodbye to him in the car.

"So . . ." I attempted breaking the awkward silence as I opened the external security door and stepped out. "I'm meeting with Chase Anderson next week." It wasn't great conversation but it would have to do. At least I didn't sound moronic or flick my hair. And I hadn't fallen face first into his lap either so it was winning all around.

"Why?" His response was clipped, sounding annoyed as he joined me on the sidewalk.

"Because I've narrowed down a few options for the acquisition." I assumed a meeting with the CEO of ITP would be self-explanatory, especially since losing the stupid bet against him had been responsible. "When we spoke yesterday, he made it clear that he wanted to deal with me directly."

"I'd heard rumors he was very *hands on*." His eyes dipped

down to my breasts, only this time, he wasn't smiling. "I should probably go with you."

"Thanks, but I think I can handle it by myself." And I didn't need his help with something I could have handled as a first year associate.

He eyed me cautiously, his smile yet to return. "I didn't say you couldn't handle it, I said I should go."

"Then let me rephrase it." I stopped, nailing him with a look guaranteed to shut down the conversation. "I am going by myself."

"Suit yourself." He wisely didn't continue to argue as he waited for me to continue walking. "Let's go."

It was a perfect spring night outside. Warm enough that I didn't need a jacket, with a slight breeze cooling the air before it hit skin. It seemed that even the weather was conspiring against me, the mood feeling a lot more date-like than I would have liked as we walked to the curb where he was parked.

I had never seen Roman's car. Trivial information about stuff like that had previously been decided to be a waste of my time. Who cared? Besides, it was probably something black and sleek that complimented his preference for dark suits. A sedan, possibly with a personalized number plate, because that wasn't douchey at all. Eye roll.

So, unless we were planning on stealing a car before we headed out to dinner, I was confused when we stopped beside an older model cherry red convertible.

"You drive a 1980's Porsche?" My eyes bulged. The rounded curves looked like they had just been polished to shiny perfection.

Tonight was just full of surprises, the car, the first no doubt of many.

He laughed, amused by my reaction as he pulled the keys out of his pocket. "Nice try, but it's a '72 Ferrari."

"You drive a *Ferrari?*" I didn't bother trying to hide the shock.

"How much are you getting paid?"

Even though we hadn't known each other before coming to work at Moss, Byrne and Carter, we'd been hired at the same time. Brought in as a powerhouse duo or some other bullshit recruitment line, and as far as I knew our offers had been identical.

But if he could afford a freaking *Ferrari*, then one of us was getting severely underpaid. Probably the one who didn't drive an Italian sports car if I had to take a guess.

"Feeling a little worried I'm making more than you?" He opened the passenger side door, waiting for me to get in. He rolled his eyes as I stayed in my spot, my wide eyes darting between him and the shiny car. "Relax, it was a gift from my brother."

He gave me a tight smile as I slid into the soft leather tan seat. The interior even smelled expensive as I watched him walk around to the driver's side and climb in.

"Eric?" I buckled my seatbelt, probably not needing positive confirmation on exactly who had played Oprah with the fancy cars.

"Yes, Eric," he clipped, inserting the key in the ignition and starting the engine.

He was definitely a drug lord.

"Well, that was nice of him." My fingers ran over the leather interior as we pulled out into traffic. "I love my sister but she's never given me a car. What does he do again?" I casually threw out, hoping that in the midst of regular conversation something would slip.

"Business," he volleyed back with a one-word answer that gave me absolutely nothing.

I took a deep breath, trying to look casual as I gazed out of the windshield. "That's a pretty wide area, want to narrow it down a little?"

"So, I tell you he bought me a Ferrari, and you're suddenly interested in him. Subtle, Harper. Very subtle." He speared me with some serious side eye and laughed.

"Please, Roman." I couldn't believe he'd think I'd be that shallow. "I was trying to make conversation. But for the record, it would take a lot more than a car for me to be interested in *your* brother."

Oh, I was interested, just not for the reasons he thought. While he assumed my questions about Eric were in hopes of snagging me a rich guy who might dazzle me with presents, I wanted the deeper, darker story that he seemed intent on not telling me. He might not know it yet, but all of that was changing.

If he wasn't going to give me the lowdown on Eric, maybe I could get a read on the other two. He'd already told me the youngest was in college. I figured they had tried to keep him insulated, hoping he'd go legit. That hadn't worked out so well for Michael Corleone in the Godfather, let's hope young Alex Pierce didn't end up being the worst of the bunch.

"So, what about your other brothers then? Dave and Nick, right?"

"You paid attention." He nodded as he shifted gears. "They're in the same line of work as Eric."

I knew it.

"Like a family business?"

"You could say that."

"Not you though."

"No, not me. Are you done with the inquisition?"

No.

"Yes."

It was clear that when it came to his family he was tight-lipped and evasive. Which would make sense, considering the nature of the family *business*.

Deciding I should probably try to ply him with a little wine before I attempted to cross-examine, I eased back into my seat and listened to the purr of the engine.

We turned onto a side street and found parking not far from Niko's, the noise from the restaurant spilling out onto the street.

"This is Niko's?" Roman's brow knitted as he craned his neck to see. "This crowded, noisy shithole is where you want to eat?"

"You said I could choose." I unhooked my seatbelt. "So, let's go before we lose our table."

I'd intentionally chosen somewhere crowded. I figured if it was noisy and impersonal, the sexual tension might be kicked down a notch too. Hopefully he'd relax a little, like he did at our first dinner at Heart and Vine.

"You're afraid to be alone with me." He smirked as if reading my thoughts.

I rolled my eyes, blowing out an exaggerated sigh. "Could your ego be any bigger? The food is good here, it's relaxed—the venue has nothing to do with you."

He unhooked his seatbelt, tipping his chin to the entrance. "So we're here because of the food?"

"Why else?"

My answer had seemed to satisfy him as he popped open his door and climbed out of the car. I joined him on the sidewalk, adjusting my dress as he locked the doors.

He had an intrigued look on his face as we walked to the host station in silence. I had no idea what was going through his mind, but I had a feeling he was up to something.

"Hi, do you have a reservation?" The hostess who greeted us looked like she'd had better nights.

"Yes, I have a table for two booked—"

"Excuse me, do you have a takeout menu?" Roman interrupted before I could give my name.

"Yes, we do." The hostess gave Roman an appreciative smile. "You guys want to order to go?"

"No."

"Yes." Roman drowned out my rebuttal, taking the menu he'd been handed and pulled me to the side.

"What are you doing?" I hissed, too annoyed he was changing my plans to notice he'd put his hand around my waist.

"You said you liked this place because of the food." He looked around the room like he was disgusted. "So we're getting the food and then we're getting out of here. Your place or mine, I don't have a preference."

My jaw tightened, as did my hand around his forearm. "I'm not going home with you."

"Fine, your place it is." He decided with a sweep of his hand. "Now hurry up and order, I'm hungry."

I was just about to argue when his phone buzzed, the soft beeping coming from his pants pocket. He slid it out, looking at the screen before silencing it and sliding it back in.

"Girlfriend?" I asked curiously, my hands anchoring on my hips.

"I told you I'm not dating anyone," he answered, looking at the menu he'd been handed as the phone once again beeped.

"You can take the call, you know," I offered, curious to know if he was avoiding the call because of the caller or because of me. "Whoever it is, they are obviously trying to get ahold of you."

"I'll get to it later." He dismissed it without even looking up. "What's not going to get us food poisoning in this place?"

He was infuriating, I wanted to take that menu he was so intent on reading and shove it right down his throat.

"I think food poisoning might improve your disposition." I glanced at the menu, having already decided I was ordering the braised chicken with a baked potato. "You should try the steak, I hear it comes with a side of joy."

He laughed, his hand moving lower on my hip. "Steak it is then."

We placed our order to go against my better judgment. And

after a heated hushed argument at the counter, I paid, collecting our food so we could return to the car. In less than thirty minutes, I was going to be faced with the reality of being alone with Roman in my apartment.

He's an asshole, I reminded myself.

And you hate him.

My body unconvinced that either of those two reasons were good enough not to sleep with him.

"I'm not sleeping with you," I said the minute I was sitting in the car. "We're eating, talking and then you're leaving."

"Whatever you want, Harper." He grinned as he pulled out into traffic. "Anything we do will be your decision."

CHAPTER #12

I HAD TALKED a good game.

Kept the conversation innocent enough on the entire drive and even managed to wrangle out that his parents were divorced. His father had remarried but his mother hadn't, and it would be a cold day in hell before he'd ever take the walk down the aisle himself.

I assumed this was because of his forced marriage to his South American mafia princess but there was a reasonable possibility I'd been wrong about that.

Firstly, if they were going to force her to marry someone, they would have chosen a better candidate.

Roman was too visible, his career too exposed to be able to harbor a secret, possibly illegal, immigrant wife. They needed him for important things like beating a RICO charge or helping legitimize the millions in drug money. The wife would be wasted on him.

It was more likely that I had an overactive imagination and was overly suspicious. That, and sleep deprivation, chased with copious amounts of caffeine didn't exactly set me up to make the most rational of choices. Maybe I was trying to rationalize insanity to explain away my attraction to Roman. Because the more I thought about it, the more ridiculous it sounded. Just the marriage part, everything else was still plausible until proven otherwise.

And I pretended it didn't thrill me that the threat of his ficti-tious forced marriage was over, and I didn't have to wear the stain of his infidelity on my soul.

Not that we'd slept together—it was a fine line, and I knew I was dancing on it—but it still made my skin crawl that I might be party to someone else's deceit. Fictional forced marriage or otherwise.

And even though I reminded myself of the dinner-talk-no-sex plan, I had barely gotten into my apartment when he slammed the door shut behind us and pushed me up against the wall. The paper bag that housed our dinner tumbled to the floor as he pressed his mouth against mine. His hand moved to the back of my neck and pulled me closer.

"We're not supposed to be—" I stalled out, the rest of my sentence getting lost when I felt him hard. "We were supposed to be having dinner."

"Then tell me to stop." He rubbed against me. "Because there is only one thing I want to be eating right now, and they didn't serve it at Niko's."

It was wrong.

So wrong.

Oh God, then why did it feel so good?

"Roman." My back arched, feeling more of him as my body made contact. I wanted to tell him to stop, but I couldn't make my mouth say the words.

"God, I want you." He sucked against my skin. "More than I've ever wanted any woman." There was a gentle bite against my collarbone. "And all I keep thinking about is peeling this sexy fucking dress off and being inside of you."

"That isn't a good idea," I said for my benefit as much as his. "I don't even like you." My attempt to rationalize not making much sense as I continued to kiss him.

"Then hate me and fuck me," he whispered against my mouth, his teeth pulling against my bottom lip. "I promise I'll make you come harder than you did on my hand."

I yanked at the waist of his tailored pants, desperate to touch him. My fingers fumbled for the zipper, pulling it down roughly as my hand wrapped around him.

"Fuck," he growled through his tight jaw, breathing heavily through his nose as I stroked. "That feels so good."

"Bedroom." I kicked off my shoes, the dinner forgotten as my fist locked around his shirt and pulled him to my room. "And the first time you made me come wasn't that great, I'm expecting you to make good on that promise to be better."

"You going to continue to be a lying bitch?" He grabbed my ass, hauling me onto his body as he carried me to my bed.

"Stop talking and kiss me."

My fingers busied themselves at the buttons of his black shirt, each one revealing a little more toned, tanned skin underneath. It was even better than I remembered it, the hard lines rippling under my fingertips.

He tossed me against my mattress, pulling his shirt off and throwing it to the floor. He turned on the lamp on my nightstand, his beautiful muscular skin catching the light as he flexed. "When I get you naked, we're going to have sex, so think carefully about what you want."

"If your mouth is going to continue to move, Roman, please find a better use for it." I stretched out on the bed, pulling him down on top of me.

He pushed aside the front of my dress exposing my puckered nipple, his head bending as his tongue swirled around it. "Like this?"

"Yes." My back arched, loving the feeling of his hot breath on my skin. Whatever my reasons were for not sleeping with him, they no longer mattered.

I knew there wasn't a deep emotional connection.

I knew there would be no long lasting relationship,

But if all either of us wanted was sex, maybe we could push all of that other stuff aside and just enjoy each other for a while.

And I would take the repercussions and serve my penance as long as he continued to make me feel good.

Oh, how he made me feel *good*.

"If you are fond of this dress, then I recommend you take it off now." His impatient hands yanked at the back trying to find a way out of it.

"Don't bust the zipper, give me a minute." I awkwardly reached around and got it started, his hands taking over and pulling it down the rest of the way.

"Get it off." He fisted the fabric, pulling it over my head before tossing it to the floor. His hungry eyes devoured my mostly naked skin as he stripped off his shoes, socks and pants. The hard ridge of his cock strained against the front of his boxer briefs.

"You wear this for me?" His finger flicked at the edge of my lacy black thong. "Hoping I'd see it?"

His hands grabbed me around the waist, flipping me over before he rubbed his erection along the seam of my ass. "I hate to disappoint you but I'm not interested in lingerie. I'm after what's underneath."

"It wasn't for you," I lied, my hands fisting the sheets either side of me as he slid down the thong. The limited coverage the fabric had been providing gone, exposing me—completely naked.

"You are such a liar." He smacked my bare cheek, the heat of his open palm replaced by his lips. "And I don't think I've ever been harder in my life."

I wasn't sure if he meant that, or if they were words he said to every woman, but I was too turned on to care. I allowed myself the fantasy, that he meant those words just for me.

With his hands on my hips, he lifted my ass, forcing me onto all fours. I didn't have time to ask him what he was doing, his tongue lapping my heat as he thrust in a finger.

"Fuck, you taste so good." His tongue ran the length of my pussy, getting me wetter with each pass. "I could eat you all night."

"More," I begged, my face pressed against the mattress as I bucked against his mouth. Not being able to see what he was doing heightening every sensation.

He didn't stop, using his mouth and his tongue to bring me closer; every cell in my body feeling like it was going to simultaneously explode.

"Condom," he barked out, his fingers still inside of me as he moved further up the bed. At some point he'd stripped off his boxer briefs, his naked skin blanketing me from behind. "I need to be inside of you now."

"Top drawer." I thanked Morgan and her safety-first mentality, pointing to my nightstand where I hoped she'd put more than one.

With a quick hand he dove into the drawer and pulled out the box, grabbing me around the waist when I tried to flip over with a very firm, "No."

"I want you like this." He held me still as I heard the packet tear. "Exactly like this."

With one steady thrust he filled me, his hips grinding against my ass as his fingers dug into my waist. I couldn't move, the sensation overwhelming me.

"Harper?" He stopped, his breathing heavy. "You okay?"

"Yes," I moaned, slowly circling my hips. "Don't stop."

He growled as he started to move again, picking up speed. "You feel amazing. Every single inch of you is fucking amazing."

I wanted it to go longer, for the tingles in my body to last all night. But it felt too good, whatever control I had was lost as an orgasm exploded inside of me.

"Yes," I screamed into the mattress, my body bucking against him. "Oh my God, yes." I said it over and over, unable to stop.

"Lauren." He said my name, my *real* name, as he pumped harder and faster, the heat inside of me continuing to rise. "You feel too good."

He came with a shout, both of us shaking as we collapsed on the bed. Our arms and legs were tangled as I felt him slide out, our matching breaths panting as we lay together in a mess of limbs.

I rolled over to face him, my skin covered in a thin sheen of sweat. "I wasn't supposed to sleep with you, jerk."

"Then I won't spend the night. I'll fuck you a few more times, and you can sleep alone." He pulled me closer as his mouth went to mine. "But go ahead and tell me you didn't enjoy it. I'll be ready in a few minutes for round two, and you bitchy gets me hard."

"You are a sick individual." I pushed roughly against his chest. "And that is never happening again."

I wish I knew I meant it. Wish I had the sort of willpower to know I would chalk it up to a bad decision and we'd go back to spewing obscenities against boardroom table. But no man had ever made me feel that good, and I wasn't sure I wanted it to stop. Even if it was the biggest mistake of my life, oh God, did I want to do it again.

"Tell yourself whatever you need to, Harper." He shifted on the bed. "But we both know that it's not going to stop."

As I went to argue, he placed his fingers on my mouth. "Save it." His thumb pressed against my lips. "And the next time, I'm going to watch you while you come."

He replaced his hand with his lips, kissing me before lifting himself off the bed. "I need the bathroom, I'll be back in a minute."

"It's the first door on the right." I rolled onto my back so I could watch his perfect ass walk out of my bedroom.

I hadn't had a chance to appreciate his body before. I had tried to twist around and see, but mostly I gave up, pressing my face against the bed as he took me from behind.

But I felt him.

Felt his big, toned body dominating mine, and what I saw in the few seconds before he'd walked out the door was unbelievably outstanding.

I waited, anchoring my hands behind my neck as my eyes stayed glued to my doorway, waiting to see him waltz back in his flawless naked perfection.

"You want something?" His mouth twisted at the side, taking his time as he strolled back to my bed.

My mouth opened and then closed, my eyes dropping down to his hips.

Wow.

He was huge.

It wasn't just his cock, which was impressive in its own right, but the rest of his body was like a testimony to genetic excellence.

"Yeah, I thought so." He threw back his head and laughed. "Tell me again how you don't want to *sleep* with me."

Every single inch of immaculate muscle flexed like a well-timed symphony, my eyes feasting on all that skin as he bent to kiss me. He was without a doubt the most beautiful man I had ever seen.

Too bad it probably wouldn't work out between us.

"We work together. It would be bad." I fished for the most obvious reason, forgetting the thirty thousand other ones I'd had before I'd seen him without his clothes on.

"You already hate me." He laughed. "You've got to come up with a better excuse than that."

"So, we're going to have sex?" *Was I actually agreeing to this?* "But somehow keep things professional at work?"

"Yes, we can be adults." His gorgeous body lowered onto the

bed. "Working alongside you pushes me to be better. I like having you breathing down my neck." His lips twisted into a grin. "Doesn't mean I can't be sucking yours at the same time."

"I'm not one of those women who are going to get all swoony and start being soft," I warned. There was no way I'd throw away my career or ambition for a man no matter how good he was in bed. "I will go toe to toe with you every single time regardless of how many times you make me come."

His finger trailed up my leg, gripping my thigh tight. "Good, because you're not going to get a free pass from me either. If anything," he pushed my legs apart, "I'm going to be *harder* on you."

A sick thrill ran through my body. I knew I was playing with fire, but I had the box of matches in my hands and I wasn't about to toss them away.

I didn't want a *boyfriend*; I didn't have time for it. But if my biggest adversary ended up being the best sex I'd ever had, then who said I couldn't do both.

"There has to be rules." My hand moved to his, stopping it from moving further up my thigh. "The two areas stay separated, always. Throw whatever you want at me, Roman, but it doesn't get personal."

"Agreed." He nodded, his eyes focusing on my mouth. "I'll play fair. Now, you're done talking? I want to lay you out and watch you scream my name while I bury myself in you."

My skin heated as a wicked grin spread across my lips. "Don't be offended if I scream out someone else's name instead. I figured it's nicer than calling out asshole or cocksucker."

"No one else's name," he warned as his eyes darkened. "I prefer asshole or cocksucker."

He was just about to kiss me when his phone buzzed, the repetitive trill coming from the pile of clothes on the floor at the end of my bed. His chest heaved with a frustrated breath, his jaw tightening. "I have to get that."

"Sure." I watched him move off the bed, curious if it was the same caller who had been ignored earlier.

While I had agreed to a sex-only relationship with him, I still knew very little about his life. And whether he wanted to give me that information or not, I was going to find out.

His head shook, raking fingers through his hair as he bent down to the pants that had been discarded on the floor and pulled out his phone.

If he'd been surprised by the caller, he didn't show it. His face impassive as he looked at the screen, hit the button and answered. "Roman."

My heart thumped as I waited for him to excuse himself or signal to me that he was walking into the living room to take it, but he didn't. His eyes stayed on me as he listened to whoever was on the other end of the line.

"Are you sure you want to do that?" He paused, shaking his head. "Yes, I know someone, but I would rather handle this in house." Another pause, his grip around the phone tightening. "Fine. I'll see you later."

He ended the call, tossing the phone onto the floor in frustration. Whatever had been said was obviously not what he'd wanted to hear; tension spreading across his forehead as he reached down and pulled on his boxer briefs. "Round two is going to have to wait."

"Is everything okay?" I watched as he pulled on his pants, continuing to get dressed. Round two wasn't only on hold, he was *leaving*.

"It will be." He reached into his back pocket and pulled out his wallet.

What the hell?

My eyes widened as he peeled off a hundred dollar bill and held it out toward me. "Here, you need to take this."

"Are you fucking *insane?*" I slapped his hand and the money away. "Do you think I'm a fucking prostitute?"

Rage filled me as I searched my immediate space for a weapon. While we weren't exactly in a place of love and devotion when we fell into bed together, I assumed he didn't think I was a whore either.

I was going to *kill* him.

Screw Morgan and her just-steam-cleaned rug.

"No, I think you're a fucking *lawyer.*" He pushed the money closer, ignoring my death stare. "Take it as an advance on your retainer."

What. The. Hell.

"What?" My eyes moved from his hand to his face with none of it making sense. If this was some kind of joke, then he was giving one hell of a performance. I was Alice, tumbling down the rabbit hole with no sense of who or what would be on the other side.

"You need to come with me tonight and I need you in the capacity to represent someone." He put the money on the bed and pulled on his shirt, his deft fingers moving steadily up the buttons. "What happens at the meeting will fall under privilege, you understand?"

"What?" I said again because all those words had just made me more confused. He was hiring *me* as a *lawyer?* I had been wrong, it wasn't a rabbit hole I'd fallen into; I'd stumbled headfirst into a John Grisham novel.

"My brother is being a pain in my ass." Next came his socks and shoes. "He wants a second legal opinion, but it's a sensitive matter." The bed compressed under his weight as he took a seat and picked up the hundred again. "Take the money, Lauren, we need to go."

If I'd had even an ounce of common sense, I'd have told him to shove his money, his crazy-ass family, and whatever insanity he was inviting me into.

Forget that I'd just slept with a man I openly disliked—and considered doing it again for reasons beyond my comprehension—and walk out the door. And once I was outside of that door hustle to the closest police station—and possibly psychiatrist—and file a report. I wasn't sure if it was him or me who deserved to be locked up, but one of us needed to be for sure.

Clearly common sense was in short supply.

"We need to go *now*?" I heard myself say, suddenly becoming conscious I had picked up the money. I couldn't believe I wasn't only considering it, but some warped and twisted part of me was excited.

I needed to take up a freaking hobby or something.

Maybe I could start insider trading, or overbill my clients. Obviously I had a death wish and wanted to ruin my career so why stop at legal representation to a bunch of mobsters.

And if by some miracle, I didn't end up being disbarred or dismembered, Morgan was going to kill me herself if she ever found out I'd put myself in jeopardy. I don't think this was the *fun* she had in mind.

"Yes, now." He handed me my dress. "Please."

"Okay, give me a few minutes." My voice sounded weird as I grabbed my clothes and hopped off the bed. This was by far the most reckless thing I'd ever done and all I could think about was whether or not I had time to put on makeup as I raced to the bathroom, redressing and cleaning myself up. My pulse hammered under my skin as I looked in the mirror.

The dress was far from appropriate.

Did I even bother with a jacket to cover up with to give the illusion of professionalism? Was anyone really going to care?

I seriously needed to get out more.

The idea that I was willingly going to meet a man I suspected was a criminal, sign up to help him, and be *excited* about it spoke volumes of my epic fall from grace. My attire was the least of my problems.

And yet as I freshened up and adjusted my dress, my skin tingled with a buzz that I'd never felt before.

It was totally going to suck if this ended badly. And here I thought the worst thing that was going to happen tonight was my questionable sexual decisions. Ha, if only.

"Harper, you ready to go?" Roman knocked on the bathroom door while I gave myself one last look in the mirror.

I was sure nobody was going to care about my personal appearance, but if I ended up going down tonight, I wanted to make it easier on the coroner.

"Yes, ready." I opened the door, slipping on my shoes as I grabbed my handbag and phone. "You going to tell me where we're going and what the hell we're going to do when we get there?"

He took a deep breath, his eyes locking on me. "After tonight, you're going to know things about me. Things that most people don't."

This was so bad.

And yet there was I, going anyway.

"Roman, I took the money." *Did those words really just come out of my mouth?* "I am not going to tell anyone anything. But I'm warning you, if you or your brother drag me into some shady shit, this will not end well for either of you."

He barked out a laugh, his hands settling on my hips. "You keep talking like that and you're going to get me hard. Relax." His head lowered, planting a kiss on my lips. "This is perfectly legal, but you're going to have to trust me. And I will tell you everything *after* you meet him."

"Okay." *Was it?* A little late now to be having second thoughts. "Let's go."

THERE WERE A million questions running around in my head, and at least half of those should have been asked before I hopped back into Roman's Ferrari and drove with him into the hills.

Beverly Hills.

If Eric Pierce's millionaire status was ever in doubt, it was solidly put to rest as we drove past lines of high fences and thick hedges. Not that I expected anything less, I'd heard Bugsy Siegel used to have a house around here too.

And of those questions—thought and needing to be asked—none of them had left my lips, keeping my mouth shut and my eyes open as we pulled up to a large, black, iron gate.

"Two grand." I watched as the gate slowly slid open. "That hundred you gave me back at the apartment isn't close to cutting it."

As the words left my mouth, two thoughts went through my head.

One, who the hell was I right now?

And two, I probably should have asked for more.

Two K was nothing to a man who lived in a house like that, but even though I had strong fears for my sanity, I wasn't going to totally go Wolf of Wall Street. Somewhere in all this craziness,

I had to hang onto my humanity. Or at least that was what I told myself I was doing.

"You're shaking me down?" He laughed, putting the car into gear as we moved down the driveway. "I'll make sure you get the rest of your money."

The property was stunning, beautiful manicured lawns with security lighting illuminating the mansion we stopped in front of.

I think *millionaire* had been underselling it. I took a deep breath as Roman killed the ignition.

"Ready?" Roman's hand stalled on the handle, looking over at me before opening his door.

"I am." I opened my side before I had a chance to change my mind.

Roman waited for me to join him, both of us climbing the stairs to the impressive front door. My pulse raced as he rang the buzzer, waiting for it open.

A tall, handsome, dark-haired man I assumed was Eric answered the door. They didn't look related, but who was I to judge. "You take the scenic route? His Lordship is wearing out the carpet in the living room."

"I was busy." Roman looked impatient, tipping his head to the man who'd answered the door. "This is Ryan. He's my brother's manservant."

"You're a dick." Ryan flipped him off before turning to me. "Yes, I work for Eric, but I'm also a friend. Ryan." His hand extended, waiting for me to shake it.

He must be the *consigliere*. Got it.

I accepted his handshake as I introduced myself. "Lauren Harper. Pleased to meet you."

I wasn't sure if I was, but I wasn't unpleased either.

Ryan had kind eyes, and anyone who called Roman a dick to his face was okay in my book. I also had to wonder if it was a

prerequisite to be good looking and hot to join the Pierce Crew.
The two members I'd met so far could have easily been featured in
Vogue. Maybe the mobster edition. There was an editorial gold mine.

"Pleasure's mine." Ryan grinned. "I'd love to keep being social, but you guys need to deal with him. This is waaaaay above
my pay grade."

He outstretched his arm inviting us in, Roman placing his
hand on my lower back as we walked inside.

My pulse raced as we walked through the lavish hall, my eyes
trying to not be expanded to full capacity as I took it all in.

Ryan led the way, his confident strides coming to a stop beside
an open door. "Here you go." His head tipped to the direction of
the room. "Tia is with Lila over at my place, let me know when
it's safe to come back."

I wasn't sure if those names were supposed to make sense,
but I nodded as I stepped into the room. A tall blond man with an
amazing ass—ah, it was a family trait I see—had his back toward
us, his head down as his hand gripped the mantel.

Roman stood beside me, taking a breath. "Eric, we're here."

Eric rolled his shoulders as he straightened, shaking his head
before he turned around. He was taller than Roman, but just as
toned. His powerhouse body wrapped in a pair of designer jeans
and T-shirt as opposed to the suits his brother favored. His blond
hair was slightly longer, looking mussed from excessive finger
raking and his face—

"Holy shit." The words slipped out of my mouth as the breath
got stuck in my throat. My chest felt tight, my lungs struggling
to expand.

Oh. My. God.

"Breathe." Roman squeezed my arm. "This is my brother,
Eric."

"Eric Larsson is your *brother*?" I managed to wheeze out. "Your brother is freaking *Eric Larsson?*" The question repeated in case it had been missed the first time.

I wasn't sure if it was more shocking that I was standing in front of a movie star in his own house, or that I had been working alongside his brother for over a year and not known. In my head it didn't make sense, like there was a piece of the equation missing. I was prepared to meet a drug lord, not one of Hollywood's A-list. And how insane was it that in my head, an evening with a criminal made more sense.

How could it be? The question rolled around in my head as the family resemblance became unmistakable.

Roman *Pierce* was actually Roman *Larsson.*

"You didn't tell her?" Eric narrowed his eyes at his brother. "Typical."

"Oh, give me a break, like you were so forthcoming with Tia." Roman rolled his eyes. "Do you want our help or not?"

I punched him as hard as I could in the arm, my mind still in free fall. "What the hell, Roman?"

"Jesus, Harper." He rubbed his arm, his grin making an appearance. "I never took you as the violent type. Looks like we're both learning something new."

Eric came closer, putting out his hand. "You'll have to excuse my brother. I'm Eric."

"I'm Lauren." I tried to find some professionalism, the question of how it was all possible left unanswered. "I work with your soon-to-be-deceased brother. I hope you weren't too close."

"I like her." He nodded to his brother. "She's obviously smart."

The entire backstory I'd built for Roman and his family fell apart at the seams. And the reason I hadn't been able to find information on Eric, Nick, Dave or even Alex *Pierce* online was because they didn't exist. The family was not entrenched in the deep underworld like I first thought. Instead, their oldest sibling was super famous, the others probably in some other form of *show* business, and Roman was . . . well, there weren't enough words for what he was right now.

"Can someone please fill me in on why I am standing in Eric Larsson's living room?" I looked between the two brothers, hoping one of them would give me something that sounded like the truth. I assumed it would be Eric who came through; Roman had proven he couldn't be trusted. "Why the hell do you have different last names?"

"I use Pierce for professional reasons," Roman spoke, surprising me. "In both our lines of work we have the ability to attract crazies. I figured this was the best way to reduce the need for damage control. I can practice law without worrying about some guilty asshole coming after my family, and I can separate myself from the insanity that comes with the Larsson last name. I'm not ashamed of my family, Harper, I've just chosen to not let it define me."

Wow.

That was more honest than I'd expected, and in a weird kind of way it made sense. Not that I wasn't still mad as hell at him for blindsiding me. Oh no, he wasn't getting off that easy. But if Morgan wasn't an ER nurse and instead had a massive multimillion-dollar recording career, I might have done the same thing.

Maybe.

The jury was still out.

"Pierce is our mother's maiden name," Eric added, giving me a sympathetic smile. "Roman changed it before he graduated from Yale."

Trying to work out if that meant he *hadn't* been lying was making my head hurt. Getting into the particulars would have to wait for later, for now, my reason for being there hadn't been addressed. Unless it was to freak me the hell out, and then it had been mission accomplished.

"Why am I here, Eric?"

A look passed between Roman and Eric, Roman finally speaking. "She's good, she won't say anything."

"My soon-to-be-wife, Tia, is insisting I sign a prenuptial agreement." His hands balled into fists at his side while his jaw tightened. "I think planning for the end of a marriage before it's even begun is bullshit and a bad idea. She went to Roman behind my back and had it drawn up." A murderous look was fired at his brother, and suddenly the mysterious phone calls made sense.

"I told you, it's *not* about planning for the end," Roman snapped, frustration apparent on both sides. "She is just trying to protect you because she loves you. And I can respect that."

"And I told you, I don't need protecting," he fired back, the *nice guy* he seemed to be a few moments ago disappearing as he started pacing like a caged lion.

"I love her." He stopped, looking directly at his brother as he continued. "I am *always* going to love her, and nothing that ever happens is going to change that. So if it ends between us for some reason, she can have it all. I don't give a shit. You think I'm going to care about how much money I have in the bank?"

It was clear that in front of me was not the Eric Larsson I'd seen in the movies. That guy was good looking, talented, hot beyond comprehension with more money than he could spend in one lifetime. But *that* Eric Larsson wasn't in this room.

Instead, there was a man who was very much in love with a woman. And he didn't want to enter into a lifelong commitment with an exit strategy.

The romantic in me wanted to weep, curl myself at his feet and ask if any of his brothers were as sweet and amazing as he was. Not Roman obviously, because we'd already established he was a jerk. But there were a few others, so I was still in there with a chance.

The lawyer in me, however, was horrified. Marriages broke

up all the time, and while it was all fantastic when you were in love and happy, it could turn ugly on a dime. Which was all he'd probably end up with if he got divorced without a prenup.

"Eric, I can understand why you aren't thrilled that your fiancée went to Roman." I'd have preferred my loved one cozying up next to a cobra, but that was another story. "But I have to agree with him, you need to sign it."

"She isn't marrying me for my money." His voice rose, deep lines of tension edging at his face. "We do not need this."

"And no one is calling her a gold digger," Roman added, continuing to be unhelpful. "This isn't about that. If you love her as much as you say you do, you will sign it. She has already said she won't marry you without it."

Wow. Those were fighting words, and no wonder it looked like the war of *Asgard* was about to take place in Eric's living room. Loki—Roman was definitely the evil brother—had seriously pissed off Thor, and it was probably wrong of me to be enjoying it.

"I'm not signing *anything* until someone other than Roman looks over it." Eric's eyes fell to me, the *someone* in question obviously being yours truly.

"She gets anything she wants. *Anything.*" Eric glared at his brother. "And the New York house is hers outright. Fuck, she can have this one too. And you will be the one to talk to her, not him." He pointed at Roman, the anger still apparent before he turned back to me. "You are not my lawyer, you are *hers*, you got it? This is not about protecting me."

I nodded, confident it was not going to be a problem. After all, I had no loyalties to either of them. "Yes, I can do that."

"I mean it, Lauren." Eric nailed me with a hard look. "Whatever she wants written in that thing is hers."

"I am looking over it before you sign it." Roman's shoulders squared out, his tension obvious. "I'm still *your* fucking attorney."

A silent dialogue passed between them, words I'm sure had already been said or would be later. And if *Thor* was about to rain down a shitstorm of pain and fury, *Loki* didn't look scared.

"I'm not sure how friendly you and Roman are." Eric gave up glaring at his brother to address me. "But in this, you are on opposites sides of the table. You have a problem with that?"

"Please," I scoffed, unable to stifle the chuckle. "I don't even *like* your brother, being friendly with him isn't in my repertoire."

"She's right." Roman shrugged. "She is more a pain in my ass than anything else."

I smiled sweetly at Roman. "That would be because you're a dick."

"Excellent, you're going to love Tia." Eric clapped. "I'll be back in a minute."

Eric disappeared, leaving me alone with Roman. The urge to punch him right in the junk was strong, but so was the desire to kiss him. I couldn't decide which would give me greater satisfaction.

"Were you ever going to tell me?" I stared at him, the accusation thick in the air. "We've been working together for over a year and I didn't even know your *real* last name."

"Does it matter what my last name is? I'm still the same person." He shrugged. "You know my reasons, and I stand behind them. And I'll remind you that as Tia's attorney you can't break privilege, that includes who I am to her."

I laughed, shaking my head that he'd assume I'd use the information against him. "I've never broken privilege and I'm not about to start now, asshole. But get ready, Roman *Larsson*, as you so helpfully pointed out, I am *Tia's* attorney."

He moved closer, his eyes filled with heat. For some sick reason fighting with each other was an aphrodisiac, and he was just as in to it as I was.

"Bring it, Harper."

We stared each other down, the air crackling between us. And had I not been in his brother's living room, minutes away from meeting a new client, I would have torn his clothes off and shown him exactly what I was *bringing*.

After this was over, we were definitely going back to my apartment.

CHAPTER #14

TIA WAS A firecracker.

Slightly crazy with moderate success in her own right as a columnist, she was very clear about what she wanted.

"So, you work with Roman?" she asked, her eyes narrowed in suspicion. I had a hunch not a lot got past her.

"Yes, but don't hold that against me." I smiled as I continued to scribble on the notepad she'd provided. "Now, let's get the terms straight so I can draw up a new agreement."

We sat in a formal living area toward the front of the palatial home. Roman and Eric were at the other end of the house, hopefully putting on hold their Norse God war while I consulted with my new client.

The original prenuptial agreement had been compiled by Roman. And while it had been sensible—giving Tia a generous settlement should the marriage be dissolved—it gave her zero property entitlements and no claim to any of Eric's future earnings regardless of how long they ended up being married.

I could see why Eric had been infuriated; the deal was reasonable, but not necessarily *fair*.

It was true that Tia was coming into the marriage with virtually no assets and little financial contributions, but she added value in other ways. She had taken over the running of the household, helped coordinate his schedule, and gave immeasurable moral and emotional support. All of those things meant she had less time to expand her own career and personal wealth development.

And while she insisted that she was happy, and that she had no aspirations to accept any of the book deals she'd been offered, she could have parlayed her modest column into a multimillion-dollar deal of her own.

There had even been interest to turn her unconventional love story—the ordinary girl who met her famous number one crush and they fell madly in love—into a movie. Again, something she'd declined. Not to mention she'd given up her life in New York and followed Eric to Los Angeles.

All those reasons combined deserved *more* than just money.

"So, under the new agreement, the house in Brooklyn is yours regardless of how long the marriage lasts." As I spoke I made amendments to Roman's agreement, the new one to be drawn up later. "And then there is a sliding scale on your settlement. That increases the longer you are together and if any children are produced from the marriage. At a minimum you will walk away with ten percent, at most twenty-five."

"It sounds so clinical." She shook her head. "But I'm not entitled to the house. He bought it before we were even engaged. And twenty-five percent is not what I asked Roman for; we agreed that a lump sum would be fair, with alimony if we had kids. I get to keep any gifts, but I'm not doing this for money."

"Okay." I stopped writing, lowering my pen. "Roman is Eric's attorney, which means his version of fair is incredibly slanted. And I know you aren't after his money, that's obvious considering you're the one asking for this. But legally, this is what you are entitled to, and more importantly, if you want Eric to agree then we're going to have to go in with a decent offer. He was willing to give you *everything*; he's not going to sign something that doesn't even give you a place to live."

"He was so angry." She looked at the papers in front of us. "I thought he was going to kill Roman."

From what I could see of Roman's family, they were . . . well *normal* for want of a better word. While he was a movie star, Eric didn't come with the air of superiority that usually accompanied high-end clients. His relationship with Roman seemed similar to the one I shared with Morgan, affectionate with a healthy dose of sibling mischief underneath. No doubt their teenage years had been fun. And Tia . . . five minutes alone with her and you could tell she'd never do a thing to hurt Eric. I knew Roman would have seen that too. Loyalty and trust were things he valued more than anything, considering I had only *just* had a glimpse into his world now after knowing him for over a year.

"Roman evokes that reaction in a lot of people. Feelings of wanting to murder him, I mean." I laughed, my own earlier thoughts of strangling him not far from my mind. "So don't be too hard on your man, he's just thinking like the rest of us. It's good to see fame or family doesn't make you immune." I chuckled, wondering if we should start a support group and chant Kumbaya or some shit until murder impulses subsided.

"So, what happens now?" Tia folded her hands in her lap. "We've been arguing about this for three days straight, but I meant what I said about not getting married until this is signed."

It had been the first thing she had told me when we sat down. That despite her looming wedding date, she wouldn't say "I do" until he'd signed on the dotted line. I could usually sniff out a bluff, and this wasn't one.

"Ordinarily I'd go higher than what we agreed, let opposing counsel argue and then settle on what we've laid out. But since your wedding is so soon, I'm going to give Roman our final offer and get it filed as soon as possible."

I pushed the papers aside, the impersonality of it all so startling. And while I saw the necessity of it, it didn't mean I didn't have a heart.

"I know this seems really hardcore. The best-case scenario, the day you both sign is the last time either of you will see it again. But Roman and I are currently dealing with a high-profile divorce as we speak, and it can get ugly. It's insurance, just like any other kind. You don't drive a car intending to crash but you still have a policy, right?"

She laughed, her lips spreading into a genuine smile. "Yeah, I can see that." She nodded, tucking a lock of hair behind her ear. "Hey, I know this is a weird request, but can you include in the alimony a clause where he has to supply me with one lipstick a month? When we first met I bought some insane amount of red lipstick and it became an inside joke. Hopefully, he'll see the funny side of it, and maybe it will make him laugh."

I picked up my pen, announcing it out loud as I added, "One lipstick a month." I paused, thinking on what was best for my client. "We should probably add in a color preference too because men are hideously bad at a color wheel. It would suck if you ended up with something like coral, it just wouldn't work with your skin tone."

More laughing, this time from both of us as I made the final amendment.

There was a knock at the door, Eric and Roman entering after Tia had called out they could come in. It seemed in the great battle of *Asgard*, both had survived.

"You guys done?" Eric was the first to speak, the tension on his face still visible.

"We sure are." I rose from the couch and gathered my papers. "I'll finalize it and then give it to Roman for you to sign. I should have it back to you by tomorrow afternoon."

"Thank you." Eric held out his hand. "And sorry you had to get dragged into this."

"Hey, don't thank me." I returned his handshake, giving him a playful grin. "You haven't seen it yet. There's a lipstick clause, and it isn't favorable for you."

He laughed—his smile almost identical to his brother's—dropping his hand as he sidled up to Tia. "Sounds like interesting reading. Now if you guys don't mind, I'd like to put this behind us and concentrate on making up with my fiancée."

"We're leaving." Roman placed his hand on my lower back. "We'll be sending our respective bills in the morning."

After a quick goodbye, Tia and Eric walked us back out to Roman's car. It was startling how much had changed since we first arrived.

I bit my lip, sliding into the passenger seat as he joined me in the car.

"I understand why you didn't tell me about your family. It can't have been easy living in Eric's shadow, especially considering how good-looking he is." I fanned myself. "Are your other brothers hot as well?"

His lips fought the grin, spearing me with a look as he started the ignition. "Wow, that's original. You can tell me how much better looking my brother is after I take you home and fuck you."

"Who says that's what we're going to do?" I pretended to look horrified. "Besides, I'm starving, some loser took me out to dinner and then didn't let me eat it."

"I didn't hear you complaining when I was eating you." He laughed giving me a wicked grin.

"Just shut up," I pushed playfully against his arm, "and we're going to need to hit drive thru on the way back."

He did as instructed for a change, passing a drive thru on the way back to my apartment. I was so hungry I ate in the car. He did the same, balancing his burger on his lap as he drove.

There was unspoken agreement when he'd parked the car.

I hadn't invited him to come up with me, but I hadn't asked him to leave either. And even though there was a part of me that simmered uncomfortably, wishing I knew more about him, it wasn't that part that was currently in control.

It didn't seem important, at least not for right now.

Funnily enough it didn't get any more important as the night wore on either, any further talk about him and his family disregarded in favor of other things.

He was really good at *other* things.

Really, *really* good.

"IT'S MORNING." HE kissed my lips, his hand sliding down my hip. "I should go home."

"Yeah, you should." I yawned, my body as well as my mind feeling exhausted. "Or not, I really don't care either way."

He laughed, his mouth pressed against my shoulder. "Your indifference is sexy as hell, but I've got a family breakfast with my mother later this morning. Something about her eldest son getting married has made her sentimental, and my presence is required."

"Yeah, I can understand how that would be a foreign concept for you, being around people who are kind and love you." I rolled over to face him. "Don't let it go to your head, they probably tolerate you at best."

He shook his head, biting back the grin. "Thanks for keeping my ego in check. I'll be sure to call you if at anytime I start feeling too good about myself."

My arms wrapped around his neck and I kissed him again. He didn't flinch, kissing me back like it was the most normal thing in the world. And even though I didn't want to admit it, him spending the night hadn't been terrible. I wondered if he felt the same, and if that had been the reason he'd stayed.

I watched as he moved off the bed and grabbed his clothes, redressing for the second time in my room. Only this time he would be leaving, and I might not get to see him until Monday.

"I'll email you the revised prenup in a few hours, give you a chance to go over it." My eyes stayed on him while he pulled on his pants.

"It's Saturday morning, why don't you go back to sleep and then get it to me later this afternoon." He finished buttoning his shirt. "I'll email you if there are any problems."

Ordinarily I wasn't a huge fan of sleeping in. But as I stretched out in my bed, the side he'd just left still warm, it sounded like a fantastic idea.

I pulled up the covers and sighed. "Okay."

"No argument?" His eyebrow rose, looking genuinely surprised.

"Just leave already," I groaned, tossing a pillow at him. "I was in a good mood, why do you have to ruin everything?"

He caught the pillow, tossing it back so that it landed on the bed. "I'm not used to you being agreeable, I'm not sure I like it."

"Momentary lapse in judgment." I rolled my eyes. "Rest assured, it won't happen again."

He laughed, strolling over to my side of the bed, and kissed me one last time. "Enjoy your weekend. Stay out of trouble."

"Back at you." I finger waved before turning on my side, listening as he showed himself out and pulled the door closed behind him.

The room felt larger without him in it, the air noticeably cooler. I chalked it up to fatigue—or insanity—because no man could influence space and temperature with his sheer presence.

Ugh, I needed to go back to sleep.

As my eyes closed, I heard the creak of the front door open. Obviously, the lock hadn't engaged properly on his way out—convenient, and not unlike him. It made me grin like an idiot, my heartbeat increasing just at the thought that he was coming back.

He hadn't been able to leave after all.

Jerk.

"Couldn't help yourself, huh?" I called out, my smile pressed against the pillow. "I knew you'd end up crawling back."

"Are you talking to me?" My sister appeared in my doorway. She was still in her scrubs, her keys dangling from her fingers.

I sat up, grabbing the sheet to cover myself, trying to look casual. "I thought you were someone else."

"Oh really? Someone else has keys to our apartment?" Her hip leaned against the doorjamb, her amused smile telling me she hadn't been fooled.

There was no point trying to hide it; she was probably going to find out later anyway. Besides, it's not like I hadn't had men stay over before.

"Roman just left," I said, trying to not to sound as pleased as I did.

Her grin stayed in place as she swung the keys around her finger. "I know. I saw him."

"You just couldn't tell me, huh?" I shook my head, my nakedness meaning I couldn't get out bed and kick her ass. "You had to make me say it."

She laughed, enjoying making me squirm. "It's so much more fun to watch you admit you were wrong. Must have been one hell of a dinner and talk." Her finger pointed accusingly at the condom wrapper on the floor. "Last time I checked, a *chat* didn't require protection."

"You can never be too careful these days." I shrugged, my

innocence oozing from every pore as I batted my lashes. "It was a *serious* conversation."

Morgan laughed, not buying my declarations of purity for a second. "Ones that involve penises generally are. You want to talk about it or can I go fall into a heap and sleep a few hours?"

"Go sleep." I waved her off, intending to do some of that myself. "It can wait a few hours."

"Awesome, I'm going to crash." She yawned, the weariness of her shift catching up with her. "Don't wake me unless the apartment's on fire. I have night shift again."

She punctuated her parting instructions with another yawn as she turned and walked out of my room.

And once again I was alone.

With a stupid grin on my face.

Sleep wasn't going to be as easy to come by as I first thought.

I HAD GIVEN Morgan a basic rundown of the previous night's events.

It had been heavily edited. Names and places redacted so I didn't violate anything, which meant that she was unaware of the Larsson/Pierce connection.

And for now, that information was staying locked down, even if she was my sister.

"How's the firm feel about two of its associates dating?" she asked over a bowl of Cap'n Crunch.

It was closer to lunch than breakfast, but neither of us was in the mood to cook. So instead we sat around our kitchen table eating cereal and talking about my love life. It had been more fun when she had been the subject of the interrogation. I was positive this was payback for the shit I gave her when she was dating the paramedic.

"Well . . ." I pushed the spoon around in my bowl. "We're not exactly dating. Neither of us have time for a relationship, so we're just kind of doing *this*."

It was delusional to assume I was suddenly going to stop having sex with Roman. *Are you kidding?* And toss away the best orgasms ever given to me by a man *or* myself? Yeah, I wasn't stupid, and if he wanted to continue to be my life-size sex toy, I would happily be his.

"You mean where you go out for dinner and sleep with each other? The *thing* that sounds exactly like dating?" The sarcasm dripped from her still smirking lips.

"Whatever," I laughed.

Enough coffee hadn't been consumed in order to explain all the reasons why regular dating wouldn't work with us. And I was more than happy with the way things were, even if Morgan wanted to read more into it.

After breakfast and a shower, I sat down and went through my notes from my meeting with Tia. Even though Roman wasn't expecting the paperwork until the afternoon, it was a good way to occupy my mind. Other than wondering whether or not I was going to see him again over the weekend.

I didn't.

See him again that is.

We spoke briefly on the phone Saturday night after he'd checked his email and told me that Eric was signing the papers. It sounded like he was at a bar or out somewhere for dinner, the background noise making it obvious he wasn't sitting home alone like I was.

I didn't ask him where he was, or if he was with someone, and he didn't offer to tell me. Instead, the conversation was kept on point so that after I hung up I could obsess about it for the rest of the night like a moron.

Not that I expected him to . . . well, I wasn't sure what I was expecting him to do. Hell, I didn't even know what I was expecting of myself.

It was clear no boundaries had been set, and I wasn't sure if I'd just been worked into the rotation like Carla. An extra player added to his growing board of chess pieces. I wasn't even sure I was mad, the lack of definition partially my fault. No one forced me to sleep with him, and I hadn't offered him exclusivity either.

I hated that even though I didn't really have a right to, the thought of him with someone else made me jealous, uncomfortable in the reality that he'd not felt the same way about me.

One thing was for sure, I was almost positive none of the previous women who'd shared his bed knew about Eric. I held tight that he'd trusted me enough to let me in, even if it was just a little. Surely that meant I was more than just a *piece of ass*.

It was definitely too confusing to think about it. So, I took the weekend to forget about work, Roman, and everything else, and just be a little self-indulgent for a while.

With Morgan working all weekend, I went and booked myself into a spa. The previously unexplored secret society of fluffy white bathrobes and mysterious skin practices hadn't been something I'd ever been interested in. Because paying a woman in a fake doctor's coat to touch me seemed stupid.

But boy had I been wrong.

My face, body and hair were treated to such pampering it almost felt illicit, leaving every part of me feeling like a million bucks. I didn't even care that I had handed over more cash than I did for my first car; the full-package they'd talked me into was worth every cent. I suspected that those aromatherapy diffusers pumped out more than just essential oils, and by the time I was done, I was too blissed out to care.

And as Saturday slipped into Sunday, I hardly thought about

Roman at all. Images of his perfect body and beautiful face were completely banished from my mind.

Mostly.

Maybe I thought about him a little.

CHAPTER #15

"RUNNING LATE, HARPER?" Roman was sitting behind my desk in my chair when I walked in. He looked amazing as usual, his shirt perfectly pressed underneath his perfectly tailored suit.

I wondered what time he got up in the morning in order to look that good, and if he had an army of sweatshop tailors held hostage in his closet so he could satisfy his fetish for expensive designer threads.

My smile was automatic, spreading across my lips as I walked over to my desk and dumped my handbag. His eyes flared as they moved up my bare legs. My figure-hugging dress was shorter than I usually wore to work, but I was inspired after my time at the spa, my skin so silky soft.

"Actually, I've been working for hours already, I had a morning meeting." My finger pointed from him to the ceiling, a subtle hint he needed to get up.

He stood slowly, his eyes moving up and down my body. "What meeting?" He reached out, his fingers curling around my hair. "This is different too."

"Thank you for noticing." I flicked my hair back over my shoulder, secretly thrilled he'd noticed. I'd had it trimmed and styled while at the spa and loved how it now framed my face. "And my meeting was with ITP. They had business in L.A, so I met them at the Beverly Wilshire for breakfast." I lowered myself into my vacated seat, taking care to cross my legs for maximum impact.

It was childish, and probably a little ridiculous, but I liked watching him squirm. And I felt somewhat justified, he'd taken up space in my head during the weekend so I was going to commandeer a little of his now.

"You went to see Chase Anderson, looking like that?" His hand waved in my direction and I assumed it was my dress that concerned him. Unless he was talking about my new hair, the stylist had said I was going to stop traffic.

I stared down at my outfit with an adequate amount of fake shock. "What's wrong with the way I look?"

What he didn't know was that I hadn't met with Chase Anderson. Chase rarely got out of bed before ten a.m., so I instead had my initial meeting with his COO, Anita Anderson, who was also his sister. And unsurprisingly enough, Anita hadn't cared about my hair or my outfit. She was more concerned with the results of my vetting so when her brother did wander in sometime midmorning she could give him the short list.

I probably could have mentioned that, but I didn't.

"Are you trying to be cute?" His hand moved to my knee, his fingers gripping my leg tightly.

"Cute?" I shoved his hand aside, "No, I wasn't trying to be *cute*. So, if all you came in here for was to critique my wardrobe choices, you should probably go. I have work to do."

The muscles in his jaw tensed as he lowered himself down, his butt resting on the edge of the desk in front of me. "And what if I'm not done here?" A finger trailed up my leg. "Actually, I'm fairly sure I'm *not* done."

I leaned forward, bringing my mouth closer. "And what do you suggest, Roman? You want to pull up my dress and have a quickie in my office?" I was only half joking, with no intention of turning him down if he did exactly that.

His eyes darkened as he focused on my shiny red lips. "Daniel is expecting us in his office."

My fingers tiptoed up his leg, moving to the front of his pants where I found him hard. He didn't stop me, watching as my palm flattened against the fly and rubbed against it.

"Too bad." I peered at him under my thick dark lashes. "I took what you said about not being interested in lingerie to heart, so I'm not wearing any." His length thickened under my hand as I held it still. "You should probably do something about this though. I'm not sure walking around with a hard-on is very professional."

I grabbed him hard, a hiss passing through his lips as I stood, keeping my grip around him. "And if you ever call me cute again, it won't be your cock I grab, it will be your balls. I promise that won't be as much fun."

His fingers wrapped around my wrist, holding my hand hostage. "I'll take my chances." He used my hold to continue to stroke him. "We'll talk about you, this dress, your lack of underwear, and Chase Anderson after I fuck you. You should message Daniel and let him know we're both going to be late."

It gave me a sick thrill to make him crazy. To watch a man who notoriously had it all together, crack a little at the edges just like the rest of us. I wondered if there'd been signs of it earlier and I hadn't noticed or if this was brand new.

He planted his hands on my hips, opening his legs and pulling me into the gap in between. His mouth was on mine, swallowing my gasp as he pulled up the hem of my dress.

I was conscious the door wasn't locked, that at any time someone could walk in and see what we were doing. The thought we might get caught just made it hotter as my hands gripped his shirt.

Our mouths tangled, hot breaths exchanged as his hand landed on my ass.

"Jesus." He grabbed my bare skin, squeezing it. "Send the goddamn message we're going to be late and get up on the desk."

I didn't argue, grabbing my phone from my bag as he lifted me onto the desk, his hand bunching up my dress as I fumbled with the letters.

It was crazy, my eyes moving from my cell screen and then looking over my shoulder to the door as I heard the sound of his zipper.

"Never thought I'd need to carry condoms at work." He pulled one out of his back pocket and tore it open. "But I'm glad I am."

He pushed down his pants and boxer briefs so they hung on his hips, giving himself a firm couple of pumps as he rolled on the condom before his attention turned to me. "You send the message?" He kissed me before I had a chance to answer, one of his fingers plunging into me.

"Yes," I moaned, arching into him as my body heated under his touch.

He added another finger, pressing his mouth against my lips. "Shhhh."

It was hard to stay quiet as his eyes locked onto mine, feeling his hand pump into me.

"Do it." I gripped his shoulders, my pretty painted fingernails digging into his precious expensive suit.

He pulled out his fingers and filled me with his cock in a hard, fast thrust. The slight sting making my eyes water from my body not being fully ready.

"You okay?" he asked, holding himself still as I adjusted to him.

The sweet ache throbbed between my legs as I nodded, tilting my hips so he could get deeper. "Don't stop."

We moved in a frenzy, our bodies crashing against each other as office supplies tumbled off my desk.

It had never been like this. Excitement peaked inside of me so fast that I came in a rush, a scream escaping from my mouth as he clamped a hand around it. "Not so loud." He breathed at my neck as he rocked against me. "Lauren." He moaned my name as his powerful body came undone.

He pressed his forehead to mine as we sucked in matching ragged breaths. "I'm still not done," he whispered as he kissed my lips. "We'll pick this up a little later when I have more time. You go first, and I'll meet you in Daniel's office in a few minutes."

My arms and legs felt like jelly as I nodded, grabbing a couple of tissues from the box that had been tossed on the floor, and cleaned myself up as quickly as I could.

Maybe jealousy ran on both sides? The idea that perhaps he felt the way I had been feeling over the weekend gave me a secret thrill. Even if I wasn't entirely correct, there was an underlying lack of control that we both seemed to share. He wasn't made of stone like I'd first thought, and I very much liked the glimpse of chaos that poked through underneath.

Sitting through the meeting with our boss was going to be a challenge, even more so since I wasn't wearing underwear. I left Roman in my office after a quick look in my compact mirror confirmed I didn't look like I'd just screwed a man on my desk. That was the one benefit of it being fast, the potential havoc on my hair and makeup had been greatly reduced. Not that I complained, the smile fixed on my face as I adjusted my dress and strolled out.

"I don't like waiting, Lauren." Daniel was on his laptop when I walked in, his fingers continuing to type as I took a seat. "Where the hell is Roman?"

"Performing a human sacrifice." I smiled as my knees pressed together, making sure I didn't inadvertently flash my boss. "It's the only way to stop from changing into his true reptilian form."

The edges of Daniel's mouth twitched, shaking his head but not looking up. "You know, if you both weren't so goddamn good at your jobs, I'd have fired one of you. Less aggravation that way."

He was lying through his teeth and he knew it. The reason he'd hired us in the first place was *because* we were so good together. "It would be Roman, right?" I laughed, knowing we were both safe.

"What would be Roman?"

Speak of the Devil; the man himself strode in, not even a hair out of place.

"I was just telling Lauren how there are days I want to fire you both." Daniel gave up on his computer, watching as the man I'd been having sex with moments ago took a seat beside me like nothing had happened.

Roman straightened his tie, flashing Daniel his trademark cocky grin. "Don't be ridiculous. Who would take our place?" He screwed his face up in disgust. "Lewis? Preston? They're so far up Carter's ass, he opens his mouth and they gargle for him. And pretty sure neither of them can spell *conviction*, let alone get one."

"You done?" Daniel folded his arms looking amused. "Believe it or not, there was a reason I called you in here."

"You want to parade us through the office like conquering generals." He winked, before tipping his head to me. "Don't worry, Harper, I'll share the adulation with you this one time."

"Do you have any humility?" I shook my head trying to not look amused. In truth, his egomaniac routine was kind of hot. "Like *any* at all?"

"Nope."

"You know," Daniel leaned back in his chair, studying us both. "At some point, I'd like you to at least pretend you've seen my name is one of the ones out there on the wall. Give me the illusion that you listen to me." He held his hand up, stopping whatever comeback Roman had brewing. "It was good work on the Cane divorce.

I know it's not finalized just yet, but I was glad you were able to put your differences aside to get the job done. We're signing Jana as a major client and part of that is a restructure of her company. I want to make sure she isn't susceptible to sharks—either in husband form or otherwise—moving forward."

Roman's brow furrowed as he shifted forward in his chair. "So you want us to go through and make sure there's no leaks in the boat?"

"No." I kept my eyes locked on Daniel, this time knowing exactly what he meant. "He wants us to take her out of the boat entirely."

"I always knew you were the smarter one." Daniel gave me an appreciative grin. "I want her business rock solid, and if her innovations stay on target, she could well be our biggest client."

"I'll tie up the divorce and after Harper dumps the ITP acquisition, we can get started." Roman stood, wrongly assuming the meeting had finished and everything had been decided.

"I'm not dumping anything." I joined him on my feet, tipping my chin to look him in the eyes. "I've vetted all the companies. When Chase Anderson makes his decision, I will be the one who finishes that deal." Anger spiked inside of me.

"Let someone else handle it." He dismissed me with a casual wave of his hand. "Anything else?" He turned to Daniel, ignoring me.

"Not from me, but I'm sure Lauren might have a few words for you." He grinned pointing to the door. "Why don't you head out of my office and let her yell at you in private."

"Thank you." I gave Daniel a quick nod before turning to Roman. "Let's go."

I didn't wait for him to agree, heading to the door and walking out. Roman was only a couple of steps behind me when he grabbed my arm. "Your office or mine?"

"Yours." I shook off his arm, wanting the opportunity to storm off. It wasn't easy, his longer legs keeping up easily with me as the eyes of our colleagues followed us down the hall.

They were well versed in our process; the one that usually involved heated discussion behind closed doors. I guess they assumed everyone else was safe as long as we were yelling at each other.

Roman got to his office first, overtaking me and flinging open the door. I stepped in, helping him out by slamming it behind us.

"What makes you think you can tell me which cases I need to drop?" I glared at him, my skin prickling with annoyance.

"You didn't even want the case." He glared back, seeming confused about why I was upset. "You had to take it because you lost the bet. You should be thanking me for getting you off the hook."

"Thanking you?" I wasn't sure whether I wanted to laugh or choke him. "Yes, I didn't want it, but I have it now and I don't just dump clients halfway through a deal. What kind of message does that send?"

Going through the ITP paperwork and their fiber optics acquisition was like reading the Yellow Pages. Long, boring, and time-consuming that yielded limited reward and even less thanks. Chase Anderson might be happy to have an associate vet for him, but when it came time to sign, he'd want a partner. For no other reason than men like him and their egos wanted to feel important. But while I suffered through the brain-numbing hoop jumping, I also wasn't in the habit of leaving a job unfinished. Especially not when I'd already put in so much work.

"He will be dealt with by someone else." He moved forward, forcing me to stand my ground. "Besides, he's been dragging his feet for months, he's not even close to making a decision."

"Well, he sounded pretty close to it when I spoke to him." I sneered back, the lie passing easily through my lips. We'd barely spoken and he hadn't been close to deciding shit, but I wasn't going to admit it.

Roman's jaw tightened, his eyes dipping down to my body. "And did he tell you that while he was staring at your tits or you ass?"

My hand lifted without thinking, ready to slap him when he caught it. I was so angry, I didn't even care that I'd gone from thinking about hitting him to actually following through.

"You asshole." I tried to rip my hand from his grip to no avail. "I have never used my body to work a client, and it's offensive that you'd even think that."

"I know that." He didn't let go, his fingers staying locked around my wrist. "But Chase Anderson is a prick and him seeing you in this dress is making me fucking crazy."

I stopped struggling, burning hot and cold by his admission. I still wasn't sure how I felt about it; both thrilled and appalled that anything involving me made him crazy.

"Then why did you give me the freaking case in the first place?" It was his doing I was even dealing with Chase.

"Because he usually only deals with partners." His eyes heated as he captured my chin with his hand. "He's never met with an associate before, and I had no idea he'd meet with you."

I should have put him out of his misery and told him that my meeting hadn't been with Chase, but I didn't. I wasn't sure if it was jealousy or he just didn't like someone else playing with his toys, but I liked it. Maybe more than I should.

"I'm not dropping the case," I said, the defiance in my voice making his pupils dilate.

His mouth lowered, brushing against my lips. "Because you want to piss me off, or for another reason?"

My chin tilted higher, closing what little distance there was between us, and I kissed him. Full, deep on the mouth, as my fingers threaded in his hair. "Because no one tells me what to do." I moaned between kisses. "That it pisses you off is just a bonus."

His hands moved down my body, kissing down my neck. "Fine, we'll discuss it later."

"Or we won't." I laughed, not willing to concede anything despite the very compelling argument his body was making.

"I have to say, I like our new way of settling arguments." He squeezed my ass, nibbling at my collarbone.

I laughed, anger taking a backseat to other emotions. "Nothing was settled, Roman, you're just thinking with your penis so you're no longer worried about what is going through your mind."

"Harper." He stopped kissing me, a smirk spreading across his lips. "If you think I wasn't thinking with my *penis* every single time we argued, then you are delusional."

"You're a sick man, Roman Pierce." I half-heartedly pushed him away.

"Yeah, but *you're* sleeping with me." He kept his arms locked around me, my poor attempt of a shove doing nothing to move him. "So, what's that say about you? You want to throw more stones at the glass house, go right ahead."

"Hmm, maybe I've decided to stop all that nonsense." Not likely, considering what we had done on my desk this morning and would probably happen on his desk if I didn't put a stop to it.

"Your sister home tonight?" He ignored my last statement, and either he didn't believe me or—like always when he didn't like the topic of conversation—he pretended he didn't hear it.

"Yes, she just came off three nights in a row." We'd had the changing of the guard at the front door when I left and she'd just gotten home. "She has the next two days off."

"You want to have dinner with her before you come back to my place?"

It never ceased to amaze me just how cocky he was, that he had zero fear of rejection. It was like he was made of bulletproof body armor, it went beyond confidence and into a whole other realm.

"You know, Roman, you should probably ask me first before you just assume." I'm not sure why I bothered, there wasn't a chance I was spending my night alone.

"Really? You *aren't* going to come to my place so I can fuck you properly?" He laughed, an amused look of his face. "We can go back to yours if you want, but we both know you struggle to be quiet, and you just said your sister is going to be home."

I pushed against his chest, this time a little more forcefully. "I'm leaving, you jerk. But yes, fine, whatever, we'll go to your place."

"Glad you saw it my way." He slowly eased his hold, enabling me to untangle myself from his body. "Let me know if you have a preference for dinner. I'll make a reservation."

His invitation made me stop; my feet no longer interested in walking out the door. "You want to have dinner with me?"

"Didn't we already establish that?" He raised an eyebrow. "I know I just didn't have a conversation with myself."

I knew dinner had been mentioned, but I assumed I'd just go see him later. For sex, which was what I assumed we were doing. Dinner felt like it might be more, and something I wasn't expecting.

"Why?" I heard myself ask, wondering why he'd do that when I had already agreed to sleep with him.

"Have dinner with you?" He cocked his head to the side like it was me who was the puzzle. "Because I want to and I like it. I enjoy our dinner conversations. It's . . ." He searched for the word. "I just like it." He shook his head, giving no further explanation and I was almost positive he knew what he'd wanted to say but didn't. "So while I'm sure you'd probably prefer the company of your sister, I'd rather you eat with me. I'll let you choose where and what time of course, as long as it's not Niko's." The edges of his lips curled into a grin.

"Wow." I didn't bother trying to hide my surprise, both at his honesty *and* that he wanted to spend time with me outside the bedroom. I wasn't sure I was expecting either.

"This is my version of a compromise." He shot me a wink, seeming to be proud of himself. "You should try it by dropping Anderson as a client."

"That wouldn't be a compromise," I pointed out. "That is getting your way."

A wicked grin spread across his lips. "I see no problem with that, I *like* getting my way."

He was a menace and if I didn't leave soon, it would dissolve into trouble for sure. We'd already tempted fate once this morning, having sex in my office with an unlocked door, I wasn't confident we'd be as lucky the second time around.

Not to say I wasn't tempted, we could lock the door this time around.

No.

I should go.

"See you later, Roman." I turned, giving him a finger wave as I made my way to the door. "I'm going to have dinner with my sister tonight and then I'll come see you after."

His eyes darkened as he watched my hand open the door. "I thought we agreed you were having dinner with me."

I tossed over my shoulder as I walked out, "We agreed nothing."

CHAPTER #16

MORGAN MADE CHICKEN potpie, it was flaky and delicious, and I savored every mouthful.

"You are never allowed to get married." I took another forkful, loading it with culinary goodness. "Or if you do, you aren't allowed to move out. I will die if I have to fend for myself."

Morgan laughed, finishing off the rest of her dinner. "The drama. You could learn you know. If you can read, you can cook, you just need to follow the recipe."

"And deprive you of this." I waved my fork at what was left of the pie. "No, I wouldn't be so cruel."

She grabbed her plate, rinsing it off before loading it into the dishwasher. "So." She paused, raising an eyebrow. "Are we going to talk about the elephant in the room?"

"If this is your way of telling me I'm putting on weight, you can save it." I spoke around the last forkful. "I don't care, your cooking is worth it."

"You aren't putting on weight." She leaned her hip against the kitchen counter as she gave me a pointed look. "Roman. You. Sleeping together."

Morgan had worked nights all weekend, which meant she had

slept during the day. It was the excuse I gave her for my spa time, not wanting to wake her by being noisy in the apartment. Of course she saw right through my transparent and lame attempt to forget about Roman, but was kind enough not to push. But now, all bets were off with the news that after dinner I was going to spend the night at his apartment.

"It's no big deal." I joined her by the sink, shrugging as I rinsed off my dinner plate to illustrate that it was indeed no big deal. "I don't know if it's going to be a nightly thing, we're just keeping it casual for right now."

"Lo, you work together." Her hand reached across and clasped mine. "Please promise me you are going to be really careful. You love your job. I don't want that to change if things go south with Roman."

"It won't," I promised, my fingers squeezed hers back. "It's just fun for now and when it stops being fun, we'll go back to not sleeping with each other. We're going to argue regardless, so that part won't be different."

She sighed seeming to be unconvinced. "Okay. Well, you know what you're doing."

I didn't think she was confident that I did know, but at least she was being supportive.

"He invited me to dinner," I admitted, Roman's offer to have dinner unmentioned when I came home.

Morgan looked surprised, the shift in the conversation hopefully taking away some of her concern. "And?"

"And it was sort of weird. Like he was going to say something and then he didn't." I paraphrased trying to remember exactly what he'd said. "By his own admission, he doesn't date a lot and his only reasoning was that he *liked* it."

"Liked dinner?" Morgan screwed up her face in confusion.

"Dinner with me, wiseass." I rolled my eyes. "Maybe I should send you instead so you can try and work him out. I can't say that part of me isn't curious and slightly confused."

I was only half joking. Tempted to find a way to send my sister in my place or have her observe us, purely for experimental purposes. To sit in as an independent observer and dissect his behavior and throw some light on his possible motives. Her training as a nurse made her brilliant at gauging people, and working in the ER made her excellent at problem solving even if the situation was unpredictable. She was a double threat, and I respected and valued her opinion.

"So, why did you say no?" She asked the same question I had asked myself.

And that was when I lied through my teeth.

"Because I wanted to see you. I mean, he isn't my whole life or anything," I clarified, realizing how ridiculous it sounded that I'd rather spend a night eating pie with my sister rather than the hot man I was sleeping with. "Maybe I just want to keep him guessing." Only thing was, it was me who was guessing, and I wasn't sure what the hell I was doing. "But I'm going to see him tonight."

She nodded not suspecting my reason was bogus because for the most part, it sounded convincing. It was rational and even normal to not rush into a—what exactly were we doing?—"relationship." And sure, that was partly true.

But the real reason why I had said no to dinner was because I was worried about his reasons, which as far as I was concerned were unclear. He liked it. Did he mean he liked me, or that he wasn't eating alone? Was I good company, or did he like me in particular? I hated how even the questions in my own head made me feel vulnerable and how much I wanted it to be personal.

That he wanted me across that table, and no one else.

Because suddenly I was needy and would rather live in ignorance than the truth where I was replaceable.

He'd respected me before. We'd had our differences sure, but he'd never treated me like I was less because I was a woman. I didn't want things to change, and I didn't want to stop sleeping with him either.

So instead I buried my head in the sand, claiming ignorance for a little while longer. Because what I didn't know couldn't hurt me.

I wasn't sure when exactly I'd turned idiot, but my transition seemed to be complete. And it was a downward spiral I didn't care to stop.

THE MINUTE I'D walked through the door of Roman's apartment, he had his hands on me.

Then his mouth.

Then everything else.

He blanketed me, consumed me, drank me in whole, as we forgot about the argument at work, my refusal to have dinner with him, and everything else that didn't involve the present moment.

I was in his bedroom before I'd gotten a chance to check out his décor, naked before I'd said hello, and had him inside of me before my back hit the mattress. It was fast and hard, which was exactly how I wanted it, and how I'd wanted him.

The second time was slower, but no less intense, and by the third my mind had become a wasteland, complete dominion given to my body as he worshiped me.

And I never wanted it to stop.

"You staying or going?" His lips kissed my shoulder while his arms held me captive. I liked the way it felt, and how I felt inside of them.

"Going."

He kissed me again.

"Staying."

I'd changed my mind.

He smiled against my skin, and I assumed this was once again his version of a compromise, AKA him getting his way.

"Good. I'll think of a creative way to wake you in the morning."

I didn't want to fight him, loving the idea of staying curled up beside him and even more excited that he liked that too. Maybe he did like me—as in *me*, personally—to be around? The idea that he wanted me to stay with him delighted me more than just spending the night. I snuggled in closer, feeling his arms around me.

"What if I decide to wake you?" I grinned in the darkness.

He chuckled, his hand moving to my breast. "Blowjob."

I sighed, pretending that was not exactly what I had been thinking. "So predictable, and in no way creative."

"Fine, hand job *followed* by a blowjob." He pulled me in tighter. "Extra points for creativity if you can perform both while sliding my cock between these beautiful tits." His hands closed around the "tits" of which he spoke.

"Or me, my mouth, hands and tits can stay asleep and see what you come up with." I didn't turn around, but I knew he was grinning. "Yeah, that sounds like a better plan." I snuggled up close pretending to go to sleep.

It didn't take long and I was no longer pretending, my eyes staying shut as my breathing evened out. My body and mind drifted into complete darkness as I fell asleep in his arms.

Morning had indeed been creative, opening my eyes to my naked body covered in pancakes. The flat fluffy disks had been strategically placed on my breasts as I woke to warm syrup being poured over me.

"What the hell are you doing?" I tried to sit up as syrup leaked onto the sheets. It was a gooey mess that was going to ruin his bed linen but he didn't seem to care, pushing me back down as his finger trailed up my ribs.

"I made myself breakfast." He lowered his mouth to the pancake that had slipped from my breast and took a nibble, his tongue gathering syrup until it reached my firm peak. I moaned as he closed his mouth, sucking me hard as I laid back down.

"No breakfast for me?" I asked as he feasted on my body, occasionally taking a bite from a pancake as well.

He flattened his tongue against my belly, running it down to the top of my pussy and stopped. "What do you want, Lauren?"

It was like he rationed out saying my name, saving it for those times when it would have maximum impact. Every single time I was surprised when he didn't call me *Harper*, making my skin tingle as a word I had heard a million times before sounded different coming from his mouth.

I craved it, like a drug.

"Kiss me, Roman."

And in a hot sticky mess of pancakes and syrup he did just that, lifting me off the bed and carrying me to the shower where we had sex. We never did get to finish breakfast.

I left him with his ruined sheets and went back to my apartment. There I showered again, changed, getting a knowing look from my sister before I went to work.

He was already in his office when I arrived, wearing his fancy suit and sipping on coffee as he went through files on his desk.

"No coffee for me?" I stood in his open doorway, my hip leaning against the jamb.

"I tried to give you breakfast in bed but you didn't seem interested in it." He hid his smile behind the paper cup. "So now you'll have to get your own coffee."

"I'd like to take that coffee and pour it in your lap." I rolled my eyes, making sure I kept my voice low so no one else could hear.

It was risky, while we weren't doing *anything* other than talking, it wasn't exactly office appropriate conversation. His door was open and I hadn't even stepped inside, the idea we were rolling the dice made it just that little bit more exciting.

He took another sip, licking the remnants of coffee from his lips. "If you want to give me a blowjob, Harper, you just need to ask. No need to ruin a perfectly good suit."

"You're pretty obsessed with yourself, you know that?" I yawned, pretending to look bored. "Does narcissism come naturally or is it a concentrated effort?"

"Hey, is it safe to come in?" Stephanie smiled at us both, strolling past me to Roman's desk. "Hoping there's a cease fire long enough so I can go through these reports with Roman."

We hadn't even noticed the arrival of Daniel's secretary, completely oblivious as to what was going on around us. God knows how long she'd been standing there, and what she'd heard.

"Ah, yeah, I was just leaving." My words came out slightly fumbled and not at all smooth. We'd been stupid and that had been too close. "I'll talk to you later, Pierce."

"I'd say it was my pleasure, Harper." He gave me a cocky grin. "But we both know it was all yours."

It was lucky that Stephanie was busy getting herself seated so she completely missed my eyes bulging and my mouth dropping open.

He couldn't help himself, pushing the envelope a little more because he could.

I flipped him off discreetly, not waiting for a response as I closed the door and went into the next office. Mine, the shared wall separating us yet again.

It was both new and weird as I sat down at my desk, wondering how the dynamic was going to work. But it did.

During business hours, it was exactly that—business.

Roman was still argumentative with a tendency to be a jerk and our conversations were constantly heated. And in the boardroom, we often found ourselves in fierce disagreement like we always had been. But they now involved kissing and touching whenever we'd get a private moment alone, the risk of getting caught increasing every time.

Dating—even in the loosest possible terms—was discouraged among employees. While it was not an outright violation of our contracts, Moss, Byrne and Carter didn't want to have to deal with the mess if there was a Charlie Sheen/Denise Richards style breakup.

So technically we weren't breaking any rules, but it would have been frowned upon. And there was no way I would do anything to risk the partners' respect, especially not Daniel, who went to bat for me every time.

So we walked the knife's edge, alternating between fighting and flirting, both giving me just as much of a thrill.

And when the day ended, we left separately, reuniting later at either his place or mine. We alternated to make it fair, but I warned him that if he ever tried that syrup shit at my apartment he'd be losing testicles. While his breakfast in bed routine was hot as hell, there was no way I was messing up my obscene thread count Egyptian cotton sheets.

I loved our angry, high-powered days *and* our wild, crazy nights. Thankful for right now, I didn't have to make a choice.

"PLANS TONIGHT, HARPER?" He waltzed in like he always did, not bothering to knock. It used to drive me insane, now I didn't mind it as much.

"You taking a survey, Pierce?" I didn't bother looking up from my screen, knowing he hated when he wasn't acknowledged with eye contact. It gave me a stupid thrill to push his buttons.

He casually strode to my desk, his hand reaching across and shutting off my monitor. "I said, what are your plans tonight, Lauren?"

There was always something about it when he called me Lauren. Nothing I could pinpoint, but no matter what was going on, how much I was trying to play the game, that one word—my name—unarmed me in the most curious way.

"I'm having sex with you." I smiled sweetly, turning to give him the attention he wanted.

God, he was sexy. So powerful, yet so contained, wrapped in an amazingly cut suit. I doubted there was ever a time where he didn't look good, or that he wasn't in control, but the possibility I might see him unraveled excited me more than it should.

"I like these plans." His finger skated across my jaw. "But *before* sex, I want to do something else."

There was an almost childlike glow to his perfect blue eyes while his mouth curled into a mischievous grin.

"Dinner?" I teased, desperate to know what he had in mind but pretending I didn't care. "Dinner would be good actually, I'm pretty hungry and it's been a long week."

"I'll feed you after." He smirked, reaching across and brushing a kiss against my lips. "What I need for you to do is go home and get changed. And as much as I like these amazing legs of yours, wear jeans and bring a jacket. I'll pick you up in about an hour." He didn't kiss me again, pulling back as he took a step toward the door.

"You're not going to tell me what we're doing?" I stood up, wondering why the mystery. "It better not be something lame like hiking or sports related. I hate that stuff in the daylight; I'm interested in doing it in the dark."

He laughed, hesitating with his hand on the doorknob. "I promise you'll like it. It's something I like to do from time to time, and it's been a while."

God, I hope he wasn't talking about some weird sex club where he was hoping to have a threesome. Why the jeans though? Gah, I had no freaking idea.

"Roman." Nerves spiked inside of me, mostly excited but a little worried.

He winked, cracking open the door. "Trust me, I won't hurt you." And then he walked out.

He wouldn't hurt me.

I wasn't sure what those words meant. Sexually? Emotionally? Physically? Too many possibilities I couldn't even begin to process. But as dangerous as it sounded, I wanted to find out.

Whatever work I'd hoped to finish was ignored as I logged off my computer, grabbed my bag and left the office. I didn't even bother saying goodbye to anyone, making a beeline for my car and drove straight home.

"Hey!" Morgan met me at the front door of our apartment. It was one of the few times we were getting home at the same time. "Why the rush, you need to pee or something?"

I didn't even bother trying to hide my smile. "I'm going on an adventure with Roman. He's going to be here soon and I need to change." I pushed open the door, undressing on my way through the house.

"Bring condoms," she shouted after me. "I have a feeling you're going to be needing them."

My feet barely touched the floor as I quickly dressed in jeans and T-shirt, and freshened up my makeup. My pulse thumped wildly as I debated if I looked okay, the knock at the door almost making my heart stop.

"She'll be out in a minute." I heard Morgan's voice with Roman responding. I wasn't able to hear what he said, giving myself one final look in the mirror before I stepped out of my room.

Oh. My. God.

Wow.

My eyelids peeled back as any words I was hoping to speak got lost on their way out of my mouth. I wasn't even sure I was still able to breathe, my body paralyzed as I stood unable to move.

His grin widened, looking extremely pleased with himself. "You're going to need a jacket or a sweater."

Roman Pierce, a man who I was almost positive had been born in a suit, was wearing a pair of jeans. Not just any old jeans either, these looked like they'd been custom made to showcase the perfect curve of his thighs and ass, like an advertisement for the good time that was promised inside of them. He topped the look off with a fitted black T-shirt—the cotton stretching across his chest like body paint, a leather jacket that he'd left open so I could admire the body-paint-T-shirt thing happening underneath, and a pair of heavy black boots.

And if not for the cocky smile hiding under the slight shadow of stubble, there was no way I would have believed it was him.

"Roman?" I finally found my voice, wondering if he hadn't been possessed by an alternate being or spirit on the way over. The man standing in front of me, not the man I knew.

"Sweater or jacket, Harper." He tilted his head to the side. "I want to get on the road."

I nodded, not bothering to ask any more questions because who the hell cared what we were doing when he looked like that. Instead, I ran to my bedroom and grabbed a jacket, hoping I hadn't imagined the whole thing.

"You better bring her back in one piece," my sister warned as I returned; her eyes narrowing as she looked at Roman. "If there is one scratch on her, you are a dead man."

"Noted." He nodded, not at all worried by my sister's curious warning. She obviously knew more than I did, Roman grabbing my hand. "You ready?"

There was no hesitation.

"Yes."

His arm moved around me, leading me out the front door as we waved goodbye to Morgan. He decided to take the elevator, his lips on me the minute the metal doors closed.

"Roman," I moaned into his mouth, my hands clutching at his T-shirt. "You are so freaking hot."

He chuckled, his teeth pulling at my bottom lip. "Really? I'm not an asshole or cocksucker today? Well, that's different."

The elevator doors opened before I could continue to maul him with my mouth, which I guess was a good thing because I wasn't sure I'd be able to stop if I kissed him again.

His hand draped on my hip as he led me outside, the night air still a little warm, especially since we were wearing jackets.

"Where's your car?" I looked around, his cherry red Ferrari not anywhere to be seen.

"We're not taking my car." We stopped at the curb, his eyes gleaming with the same childlike excitement he'd shown earlier in the office. "We're taking my bike."

I hadn't been paying attention, too distracted by the sexed-up version of Roman who had shown up to take me out to notice we'd stopped in front of a motorbike.

Not just any old motorbike either. It was black and sleek, accented with florescent green, and looked like its only purpose was to go fast.

"That isn't a bike," I pointed out, my hand reaching out and touching the gas tank. "It is a reckless menace."

He handed me a helmet, his grin widening. "So you should feel right at home on it. Just make sure you hold on."

I watched as he slid on his own helmet, the dark visor hiding his eyes as he threw a leg over his bike. The action so natural he'd obviously done it a million times before and yet so completely at odds with whom I knew him to be.

"Get on." He shuffled forward, his hands gripping the handlebars as his feet steadied the bike. "She gets impatient if she sits too long." His voice barely audible underneath the helmet.

"Well, that makes two of us," I mumbled under my breath as I pulled on the helmet and settled in behind him. It was probably the hottest non-sexual thing I'd ever done, my arms wrapping around his waist as he fired up the ignition.

The engine rumbled, sending vibrations through my body. And as the bike moved forward, it pushed me closer to Roman, my knees gripping him as well as my arms.

I didn't need to be able to see his face to know he was probably grinning. Which was funny because so was I, a new kind of excitement spiking as we took off on the road.

He commanded the bike the way he did a courtroom, with confidence and authority. There was no hesitation in his movements, no sign of fear as we traveled through traffic leaving Los Angeles as we headed in the direction of Santa Monica.

There had been no discussion on where we were going, and I didn't care, the landscape passing in a rush as we roared down the interstate.

And if I had assumed the beach was our destination, I'd have been wrong as we jumped on the 405 and passed Brentwood and then Bel Air, finally slowing when we reached Mulholland Drive.

He turned his head, his helmet bobbing in a nod as we continued down the road, winding around the mountains between the L.A. Basin and the Valley, the view absolutely breathtaking.

I'd been there once, after graduating high school, with my sister. We'd taken Morgan's beat-up Hyundai and laughed the entire time. But as I rode on the back of the bike with Roman, it felt like I was seeing it for the first time. Everything new and amazing—more beautiful than I'd ever seen before.

We pulled off at a lookout, his boots hitting the gravel as he steadied the bike and pushed down the kickstand. The roar and vibrations stopped as he cut the ignition and pulled off his helmet.

"You doing okay?" His fingers undid my chinstrap before helping me off the bike.

I could barely speak, my feet feeling slight unsteady on solid ground as I shook out my hair and wrapped my arms around him. "That was amazing. It was by far one of the coolest things I've ever done."

And then he kissed me, his lips sweeping across mine with the headlamp of the bike being the only light.

My hand gripped his jacket, pulling him closer as he took my helmet and put it on the seat. Both sets of fingers now free to roam over his chest while his found their way onto my ass.

"I like this, Lauren. Being out here with you." His lips moved to my neck as my nails dug into the leather of his jacket.

"Thank you for bringing me here, I love it." I kissed him back, each movement of my mouth more desperate than the last. I needed to get closer, the contact not enough as I sucked in hard breaths, my body needing more of him.

"You keep doing that," he squeezed my ass, "and the sex is going to happen sooner than I planned."

"Maybe you need to revise your plan," I teased, one hundred percent okay with stripping down and having him take me right there in the dirt.

He shook his head, shooting me wink. "Not yet, but I promise it will be worth the wait."

We made out a little more, dry humping like teenagers until he gently pulled away. I would have been happy to stay out all night, looking at those mountains and kissing him, but apparently he had ideas about dinner or something so we got back on the bike.

My body eased against his with a new calmness as we rode back to his apartment. And there was no doubt there had been a shift. There was something deeper, more intimate between us. It both excited and terrified me at the same time.

Was it too soon? We'd know each other over a year, but all of this was still so new. Was it reckless to try for something more than what we had? I wanted it, wanted him, and I believed he wanted me too. But I couldn't shake the feeling that things were too good to be true and something bad was bound to happen.

I closed my eyes and pressed myself against him, shutting out the thoughts of doom. There would be time to think about all of that after, but for now, I just wanted to enjoy being with a man who was deliciously complicated, but also—while incredibly well hidden—was also very sweet.

We parked the bike and then ordered pizza, my half without

the heart attack processed meat he seemed to love.

And when dinner was over, he made love to me slowly on his leather couch. He took his time, worshipping my body with his mouth and his hands, making me come twice before he'd even entered me.

I wasn't sure if it had been the night air, the bike or something else, but it just felt different and part of that unnerved me.

"You staying?" He kissed my neck, our arms and legs a tangled mess on the sofa.

"I should go." I closed my eyes not wanting to leave but not sure staying was a good idea either.

I didn't want to ruin it, not after everything had been so perfect. Staying felt greedy, like I was somehow tempting fate. I couldn't risk it, not yet until I was one hundred percent sure.

His hands gripped me tighter. "I didn't ask what you *should* do, I asked you what you were *going* to do. Are you staying?"

"No," I said, regretting it the second after I'd said it.

"Okay, let's get dressed and I'll take you back." His arms unwrapped as his weight shifted.

He didn't argue, didn't ask me to reconsider, and I'd be lying if I didn't admit that part of me was disappointed.

I'd never been the type of person who'd wanted to be begged, desperately wanted by a man so badly that he'd never let me go. To me, it symbolized weakness on both our parts.

But as I watched him get dressed, seeming to be unaffected by me leaving, I realized maybe I'd been wrong. It wasn't weak to want someone, or to be wanted in return. It was human nature, something we were designed to do.

I shook off the feeling, ignoring the urge to stay as I gathered up my clothes from the floor. "I'm just going to the bathroom," I called over my shoulder as I slinked off naked. Human nature or not, I'd committed to going home so that's where I was going.

He was already dressed when I reemerged, still wearing those amazing jeans and T-shirt but this time minus the jacket. His hair was still mussed from the helmet and the sex, making him look both adorable and seductive at the same time.

You said no to that, I reminded myself, again questioning my decision as I walked over to him.

"We'll take the car this time." He dropped a soft kiss on my lips. "You ready to go?"

"I sure am."

No, I'm not.

My fingers linked with his as we walked out to his car. He opened the passenger side door and waited for me to get in before going around to the driver's side.

"Thanks for tonight, Roman." My fists knotted awkwardly in my lap. "I had a really good time."

He grinned, starting the ignition and pulling out of his parking garage. "Good, that's what it's all about, Harper."

Music played softly as we drove back to my place, his hand occasionally resting on my knee in between changing gears. It felt so good being beside him that I wished I lived in San Diego, the drive ending way too soon.

He didn't get out of the car when we got to my apartment; he reached across and gave me one last kiss and watched me get out. I felt his eyes on me as I unlocked the security door, waiting in his idling car until I was safely inside.

Then I climbed the stairs to my front door, Morgan waiting up for me as usual.

"You live," she cheered as I walked through the living room. "Good, that means Roman does too. You know I hate motorbikes. I should force him to come sit in on just one trauma accident and see how he feels about those death traps."

"It was fine." I yawned, suddenly feeling more tired than I'd been all night. "He was careful and it was fun."

"Yeah, yeah." She rose to her feet. "Let's agree to disagree, shall we. I'll see you in the morning." She waved as she headed to her bedroom.

"Uh-hmm," I mumbled as I waved back. "I'll be here."

Instead of being tucked up beside Roman, I chose to go to bed alone and conflicted.

So much for being smart.

Dumbass.

HE DIDN'T CALL Saturday.

Or Sunday.

I checked my phone maybe a dozen times to make sure it was on, the battery was charged, and that I had service. And even though all those things had been in my favor, he still didn't call.

And the worst part was, I didn't call either.

It was exactly like last weekend, a weird sort of limbo where I wanted to pick up the phone and tell him to come over, but I didn't.

Because he hadn't called, so I didn't think I should either.

Ugh.

When did I turn into a moron with no backbone? I couldn't decide if the lack of communication made me look like a badass, or if it was just plain stupid.

By Monday morning, the jury was still out.

"On your desk."

The sound of his voice made my head snap to attention, I had come in early and wasn't expecting to see him so soon.

I tried to sound casual, leaning back leisurely in my chair. "Why do I need to be on my desk, Roman?"

He locked the door behind him as he moved closer. "You *know* why."

Just like last week, he pulled me out of my chair and kissed me roughly, only this time it had been without the argumentative foreplay. There wasn't a lot of talk at all to be honest, his mouth dominating mine as he edged me to my desk.

While Friday night he'd been soft and slow, Monday he was hard and fast.

Both of us clawed at each other, him lifting my skirt and pulling down my panties, while I undid his pants and yanked down his boxer briefs.

Almost as if the separation had made us crazed, he couldn't get the condom on quick enough, thrusting inside of me the minute he was covered.

And I had been more than ready.

I'd thought about him all weekend, about doing this, about kissing him, about being with him.

He was giving me what I had wanted Friday night before I left.

Showing me how desperately he wanted me.

And it didn't feel weak at all.

We both came in a panted rush, his mouth finding mine as he kissed me.

"You have a good weekend?" His lips moved down to my neck where he sucked my skin hard.

I grinned, the sensation driving me crazy while he was still inside of me. "You know, I've had better."

"We should work on that then." His tongue traveled up along my throat to my jaw. "Now that we've taken care of that, we should probably get ready for that nine a.m. meeting. Daniel will be pissed if we're late."

He grabbed the tissues off my desk and cleaned up before helping me do the same.

I straightened my skirt, fishing my underwear off the floor and slipping them back on. "If I recall, last week was your fault."

He laughed, standing up to adjust himself in his pants. "Yeah, all *my* fault. I remember how much you complained." He leaned forward and kissed me. "Now, if you're done tossing accusations, we've got a big week."

"There's the door, Pierce." I pointed to said door. "No one is keeping you here."

"I know where the door is, Harper. I'm exercising my right not to use it." He zipped, shooting me a wink before he left. "We'll pick up from where we left off tonight. If your sister is working, we'll go back to your house. Less chance of you running off. I'm not sure I'll be so accommodating in letting you go this time around."

I swallowed hard as he closed the door behind him, my body still tingling from his kisses and his touch.

Morgan was working tonight, but even if she wasn't, it wouldn't have changed anything.

I wanted him.

And he wanted me.

I wasn't running anywhere.

CHAPTER #18

THERE WAS A certain amount of anxiety that came with Friday.

We had spent every night together during the week, but no talk of what was expected for the two days between now and Monday.

Last weekend we had spent it apart, like the one before that.

There had been no discussion and/or plan for it, the abstinence more stupidity than anything else. We just said goodbye after our amazing Friday night date until our hello sex on my desk on Monday.

And while the first time it had been his doing, last weekend it had been all mine. It was stupid really, the thought that I couldn't tell him I wanted to be with him on the weekends too. And while I didn't think he'd spend them with other people, I envied those hours he'd spent alone, wishing he'd spent them with me. My pulse still raced when I thought about it, wondering if he'd thought about me, like I'd thought about him.

But this week had been different, and I wasn't sure I could quit him cold turkey even if it was only for forty-eight hours.

The whole day he didn't say anything. Made no plans for dinner or ask about Morgan's work schedule—anything to hint that he wanted to see me.

Nothing.

And with daylight hours expiring, I was starting to get edgy. I didn't want another weekend without him. The sweet burn of addiction licked at my heels as my mood turned to irritation.

But I wasn't going to be the first one to crack.

It was almost five and I was just about to leave, when he opened the door of my office, came inside and closed it behind him.

"Are you going home?" His eyes snared on the handbag over my shoulder and my phone in my hand. It wasn't a hard deduction to make that I was leaving for the day.

"Yes, all done."

I gave him nothing, *nothing*, as I stood unable to actually leave unless he moved from in front of the door. It might have taken a while, but I was patient. I hadn't come that far to throw in the towel.

He didn't move, his tall strong frame tensed as his eyes moved over my body. "I'm taking you to dinner tonight. Wear something nice. Pick you up at seven."

"I'm sorry, did you ask me something?" My head tilted to the side as I narrowed my eyes. "I heard a bunch of words, sounded like a list of demands or something."

"No, Harper." His eyes darkened, stalking closer. "A demand would have been to tell you to get on your knees and suck my dick. Me taking you to dinner is continuing with the exact thing we have been doing all week. Do you still want me to ask, or can we stop pretending it's not what both of us want?"

"I wasn't sure." It was the first time I'd shown him any vulnerability, nervous about seeming weak. "I didn't want to assume."

"That's the difference between you and me." His fingers ran up my arms, ghosting my skin before they settled on my chin. "I don't waste time thinking about things I don't want."

He pulled my body flush against his as he kissed me, every part of him unapologetic as his hands crawled over me. It was more than just flirting, the kisses getting deeper as I reached down between us and palmed him.

Hard.

So hard for me and the doubt and hesitation I'd felt all through the day eased away in a heady, heated rush.

I heard his zipper, one of his hands disappearing from my body as he undid his pants.

Desk sex had been a Monday thing. Something we had used to knock the edge off after the weekend break, a quick gorge on each other so we could get through the day until we could resume our weekday nocturnal debauchery.

But it was Friday, and if he had plans to take me to dinner and sleep with me, there wasn't going to be a break this time.

We had all night.

Why the sudden urgency?

"What are you doing?" My hand replaced his down at his fly, pulling free his hard length and giving it a stroke.

His fingers reached underneath the hem of my dress, climbing higher toward my underwear. "You would think with the amount of times we've done this, that would be self explanatory."

"But why not wait?" My body wanted him even if my brain didn't understand it, my mouth kissing him even though I'd asked the question.

There was a desperation in his voice that I hadn't heard before, need ringing in each breath as he looked at me. "Because I can't wait."

My handbag dropped to the floor as I reached behind him and locked the door. Mondays seemed safer; everyone too busy or distracted—less chance of them walking in on us when they had deadlines breathing down their necks.

Friday didn't give the same assurances with the odds of someone stopping on their way out the door, huge.

"Roman, we shouldn't do this here." I hated saying no, hated that I was the one being responsible, because I loved being reckless with him.

He blew out a long steady breath, his chest falling on the exhale. "You're right."

I'd never heard him say those words, ever. Not to me, to the partners, or in a courtroom. If anything, he'd actively avoided them. Using creative workarounds to agree without admitting fault or error. It was an art form, and when I wasn't a recipient of his smooth redirection, it was beautiful to watch.

"You think I'm right?" My hands fisted at his shirt, pressing him further against the door.

"One time, Harper, so I hope you enjoyed it," he warned. "You won't get me to say it again."

"I don't need you to." I kissed him again, this time it was me who was the aggressor. His body accepted mine as I rocked against him, needing as much contact as I could get.

"I thought we agreed this wasn't a good idea." He chuckled, letting me set the tempo as he watched with curiosity.

I slid my underwear down my legs, rational thought flying out the window as excitement flooded me.

He had given *me* something he'd never given anyone else. Other women might have had his body, occupied his mind, and even shared his time, but the significance of that admission was not wasted on me. His defenses had been lowered, whether he'd intended to or not, and in that brief moment, he had shown me a part I'd never seen.

Like I had been vulnerable earlier, so had he, and there was something so freaking hot about that, I couldn't wait either.

"We did agree, but I changed my mind. So shut up and we'll both stop pretending this isn't what we want."

His eyes darkened as his own words were thrown back at him

while rough hands shoved down pants. "I need a condom. Now."

My fingers fished into his pocket and I knew I'd find one there. It had become a habit I was fond of, and right now so glad he was always so prepared.

I tore open the package and slid it on him, licking my lips as I rolled it down.

"Bend over." His hands grabbed my hips and spun me away from him, moving me forward toward my desk. With flat palms, I braced myself, looking at him over my shoulder as he lifted my dress to my waist and situated himself behind me. "Did you think I was going to give this up for two whole days?" His hands slid up my legs, moving closer to my center. "Not a chance."

"Stop talking, Roman," I begged, wanting him to touch me. "You're not here for conversation."

He laughed, a single finger edging down the crease of my ass, teasing me. "No, I'm not." He dipped lower, coating himself in my heat. "Conversation is overrated."

One finger, then two, entered me as my hips rocked against him—the sensation feeling so good and all he'd used was his hand.

"That feels—" The words got lost in my throat as he played, alternating between thrusting inside of me and rubbing my clit. The anticipation building as the head of his cock nudged at my entrance.

"Roman, please."

"I don't think you've ever begged me before." He pushed in a little, nowhere near enough as he held me still. "I like it when you beg, Lauren."

"Then I won't." I tried to push back, hoping to get him deeper. "I don't care what you like."

He rocked his hips a little more, giving me another inch. "You are such a liar." Another inch. "God, you feel so good."

A moan echoed throughout the room, and I realized it was

mine, the sound escaping from my lips as he thrust all the way, filling me. "More."

He didn't stop, finding his rhythm as one hand steadied me and the other played with my clit. My knuckles turned white as they tented against the top of the desk, the tips of my fingers gripping the wood as I circled my hips against him.

Alternating between fast and slow, hard and soft, he drove into me.

Madness. Sweet madness, and I couldn't get enough.

"Roman," I bit down on my lip to stop myself from screaming. "Please."

He laughed, possibly amused that my refusal to beg hadn't lasted long but I didn't care. I wanted him, wanted him so much I ached.

"Come for me, Lauren."

He thrust into me and I came apart. My body shook as rivulets of pleasure ran through me, Roman finding his finish soon after. My hand clamped over my mouth as I squeezed my eyes shut trying to be quiet. Our labored breathing sounded louder in the silent room.

"I'm not done." He continued to move, slowly rocking in and out. "I love feeling you come. Feeling you squeeze my cock."

I liked it too, staying still as the tiny pulses continued to radiate through me.

"Driving home is going to be interesting." I twisted to look at him. "My legs feel like jelly."

He slowly pulled out, grabbing the tissues off the desk and cleaned us both up. "Don't forget what I said, dinner at seven."

"Yes, I remember. Dress nice." I lifted off the desk and straightened myself. "Where are you taking me?"

I wondered if the *dress nice* part had been for his benefit or if we were going somewhere that had a dress code. After last Friday's adventure, I didn't care to ask any questions. I knew I was going to love whatever he had planned.

Done with removing the condom, he zipped up, giving me a smile I knew meant trouble. "You'll see when you get there."

"Great." I should have known better than to expect a straight answer. "Can't wait."

CHAPTER #19

SITTING IN HIS Ferrari would never feel ordinary.

It wasn't that it was a flashy Italian sports car, or that it cost an obscene amount of money. It was that I was sitting inside a Ferrari *with* Roman.

A man who, in the past, I could barely stand to be around.

And while my feelings had definitely changed, other things hadn't.

At work, he had remained the same. Unyielding in his sometimes stubborn stance, fierce and with a tendency to be a prick. We battled across the table as much as we'd done before, with Roman pulling no punches despite sleeping in my bed.

He didn't coddle me, treat me different or give me a break. He expected my best, and I thrived because of it. And in turn he was the same brilliant asshole who seemed to have a photographic memory when it came to the law.

There wasn't a doubt in my mind that working alongside of him—even if we were on opposite sides of an issue—made me a better attorney.

And I loved that he wasn't threatened.

I rolled my head to the side, staring out the window as I smiled in silent contentment as we drove. He still hadn't told me where we were going, and other than telling me that I looked amazing—the A-line satin floral skirt and black off the shoulder top meeting his standard of *nice*—he was being cagey.

But the pieces of the puzzle started to fall into place when we arrived in the residential part of Beverly Hills. The *expensive* part, with their big iron gates.

"We're going to your brother's house?" I wasn't sure if I was nervous or excited, my fingers curling around my seatbelt as we got closer to Eric's house.

"Yeah, it's the rehearsal dinner for his and Tia's wedding, and my presence is required even though I'm not in the wedding. I couldn't get out of it," he said casually, like we were heading to a friend's house for barbeque.

"Oh my God," I screamed, my eyelids peeling back to wide-eyed panic. "Stop the car."

He ignored both my animated waving and insistence to stop, shrugging like I had been the crazy one. "Why?"

I almost choked, unsure of how he could not understand how bad an idea it was. It was as if common sense had been left on the curb somewhere and in its place was a bunch of dumb.

"You can not take me on a *date* to your brother's rehearsal dinner." I stated the obvious, because clearly he couldn't get there on his own. "What the hell is wrong with you?" I shoved his arm hoping he might take the hint and pull over.

"What do you mean, what is wrong with me?" He laughed, keeping his eyes on the road and showing no signs of slowing down. "We're going to my brother's house for dinner, it's not a big deal."

I scoffed, the amount of ridiculous in that statement almost too much to bear.

"Even if he *wasn't* a famous actor—which he is—and even if I *hadn't* only met him once—which I did—this kind of event is usually for family and close friends, by invite only. You can't just bring some random date who hasn't even met the rest of your family," I continued, because that wasn't even close to all I had to say on the matter. "Not to mention that I was his fiancée's attorney for the prenuptial agreement he didn't want. I don't think he's going to be thrilled to see me, and I'm almost positive they will not want me there."

It wasn't that I was offended by it either. I was unrelated, known purely in a professional capacity, and that interaction hadn't been the most pleasant, especially for Eric. I knew I was a good person, and *I* didn't want me there.

Roman dismissed me with a wave of his hand. "Who cares what he wants, I want you there. Besides, he's so freaking happy he's getting married, he's not going to give a shit either way. Trust me, I bet he doesn't even notice."

"He *is* going to notice." I coughed back the laugh. "And did you even think to ask?" Again, drawing him a road map to Obvious Town. "First, ask Eric considering you are hijacking his dinner for your own purposes. And then me, to see if I even wanted to go. It's like you literally have no regard for anyone but yourself."

This wasn't some case he could dictate, and I wasn't some witness he could manipulate. He had deliberately not told me, which just made the situation worse. Because if it were *no big deal* like he eluded, he would have mentioned it. He might have tried to slide it by me, but I knew his style.

"You would have said no, my way was better." He wasn't even trying to hide his smile, the whole thing seeming to be amusing.

Dead.

Or at least he would be after I mentally calculated my chances of survival after the crash the impeding throat punch would cause.

Old car, safety features in 1972 weren't the best.

If only we'd been having the conversation in a Volvo, or

something with a roll cage.

"Of course I would have said no." *Anyone with the ability to reason and some compassion would have said no.* "For all the reasons previously listed and more."

"Well, it's too late now." He nodded to the familiar black iron gate. "We're here."

A mix of curse words and promises of grievous bodily harm were mumbled under my breath as he pulled up alongside a metal box, the large gate rolling open after he'd entered the code.

"Just so you know," I warned, my fingernails digging into my palms as the car slowly moved forward. "After this is over, we are *not* spending the night together." It would be just him and his hand tonight; sex was off the table.

He laughed, his smile dripping with smugness as he turned to me. "I kind of guessed that. Why do you think we did what we did in your office before we left?"

"You are such a pig." I shook my head in disbelief. I still wasn't sure if I was feeling manipulated or elated that he wanted me to meet his family. Either way, he was still in the doghouse as panic and anger bubbled to the surface.

"Come on, Harper, it will be fine." His hand reached over to my knee. "My whole family will be there. Tia's too. You said you wanted to meet the rest of my brothers, here's your chance."

He was right. I was more than just mildly curious about his family. And had this been under different circumstances, on neutral territory, I would have loved the opportunity.

But for reasons beyond his comprehension, I wanted to make a good impression with his family, and I needed time to prepare. It was like being thrown into a murder trial having done no prep, needing to make up your defense while standing in front of the jury, naked.

"Don't be surprised if by the end of the night I trade you in for one of your brothers." It was an empty threat, but he didn't know that. "You brought it on yourself."

He didn't seem convinced, twisting his lips into a grin. "I'm irreplaceable, besides they would bore you."

We stopped at the end of the long driveway, pulling up in front of Eric's house. The exterior lights were on with music from the back of the house spilling to the front.

There were already a number of parked cars, with Roman's Ferrari not looking out of place alongside the collection of high-class hood ornaments.

I sat in my seat, needing a minute to collect myself before stepping out. The last time I'd been sitting in front of Eric's house in the car, I was anticipating a scene from Donnie Brasco. Now, I had no idea what to expect.

It was a wedding rehearsal dinner for God's sake; awkward didn't even begin to cover it.

Roman opened the passenger side door, having made his way around while I continued my internal debate. He held out his hand to help me out which I ignored, choosing to straighten my skirt instead.

If he was bothered by it, he didn't show it, waiting until I was done before putting his arm around my waist. His hand pressed against my hip as we walked together.

His hands on me in public was still new, but I loved it. I took every stolen touch when I could, just in case. I hoped it wouldn't stop, but part of me wasn't sure, wanting the contact and the re-assurance that came with it.

I didn't argue about him holding me, even though I was mad. I was too busy worrying about more pressing issues like what his family would think of me, as I let him lead me up the stairs to the front door.

We stopped in front of the large wooden door, Roman's hand

hesitating on the buzzer. "If it makes you feel any better, I told him I was bringing a date."

"No, it doesn't make me feel better," I said honestly. "Because you calling me a *date* means you didn't tell him it was me. It's lying by omission, you jerk." I elbowed him, hating that I still found him attractive even though he infuriated me.

"I disagree, counselor." He finally pressed the buzzer, smiling as he pulled me closer. "I gave him every opportunity to ask me who the date was, he didn't ask. You are in fact, my date, so there are no grounds for the accusation of a lie."

My smile tightened as I heard the door unlock. "There's no jury to glamour, Roman. Save the performance."

"WOW." Wide eyes greeted me, the man on the other side of the door surprised as he took us in. "Am I seeing what I think I'm seeing?"

"Who is it?" Another voice, a second set of masculine wide eyes joined the first at the door. "Holy shit!"

The men were obviously related, with similar features to the man standing beside me, while sporting slightly darker eyes and hair. It was clear they were two of the brothers I hadn't met.

Tall, good-looking and athletic—it was like the Larsson family had been genetically engineered for optimum sexual appeal. The thought of them all in a room together made me uneasy; I wasn't sure that all that testosterone wasn't going to make me spontaneously ovulate. Thank God I was on the pill, one of these Larssons was bound to get someone pregnant.

"When Eric said Roman was bringing a date," Larsson number one extended his hand, his eyes moving between me and the member of his kin whose fingers were wrapped around my waist. "I didn't realize he meant an *actual* person. Hi, I'm Nick."

I accepted his handshake, the warmth of his smile making me return one of my own as I introduced myself. "Lauren."

"And I'm Dave." He pushed Nick out of the way, his fingers wrapping around mine as he leaned forward. "He didn't kidnap you did he?" A cheeky grin spread across his lips. "Blink twice if you're not here of your own free will."

A real laugh bubbled up my throat, the tension in my body slightly easing. Both of them were not only attractive in their own right, but had their own version of adorable charm.

"I can't believe I'm related to a pack of morons." Roman shook his head, popping each of his brothers in the arm. "Don't you have some dog food commercial to shoot or something?" He bit back the smile.

Dave scoffed, puffing up his chest. "That was one time, and I'm still getting call backs over it. Not to mention bitches find me irresistible."

"He means *actual* bitches." Nick slapped his brother across the back. "There isn't a female dog around who isn't attracted to him." He leaned in closer. "Pity he doesn't have the same luck with women of his own kind."

Roman rolled his eyes, leading us through the door into the main foyer as I laughed, Nick and Dave seeming to enjoy my reaction.

"Well, since the idiots have already introduced themselves, there is no need for me to do it." Roman took turns in giving each of them a shoulder hug that bordered on a tackle. "They are smarter than they look, but sadly they don't act like it."

"Is someone talking?" Nick looked around, ignoring his brother. "I swear sometimes I hear voices."

"I wish those voices would tell you to get a better wardrobe." Roman tipped his chin to Nick's attire, not impressed by the more casual T-shirt and jeans his brother was wearing. "Alex here yet? He's still young and impressionable, there's hope I can save him."

"Yeah, he's here. Everyone is out back." Dave pointed to the hall. "By the way, Mom just stopped crying. Now you've brought a girl home, she's probably going to start again."

The revelation surprised me. I knew he wasn't big on relationships, but I assumed that one or two would have made the cut. I turned to face Roman. "You didn't bring girls home when you were in high school? Or college?"

"I brought girls home." A grin crept across his lips. "No one happened to be awake when they were there."

"Interesting." My finger tapped on my chin, picturing younger Roman smuggling women into his childhood home like contraband. "This is all so riveting."

"I'll bet." His hand pressed at my lower back. "Let's go meet people."

Nick and Dave led the way with Roman and I following out to the backyard. Tables and chairs were on top of a large hardwood temporary floor that had been laid over the grass. It looked as if a room had been dropped in the middle of the yard, the tables covered in white cloth with colorful floral centerpieces.

There were maybe twenty people—twenty-five tops—mingling and laughing against a soundtrack of music and the sizzle of a grill. The setting was missing the usual people in white uniforms, with Eric and his friend Ryan searing steaks on a BBQ the size of a Mini Cooper.

"Hey!" A familiar voice called from behind me. "Lauren, how cool of you to come." It was Tia, looking more radiant than should be humanly allowed.

I wasn't sure if we should handshake or hug since our last meeting had ended with an exchange of money. Not two grand like I'd asked Roman for, I had totally given Tia a discount and not told him.

Tia made the decision for me, grabbing my hand and giving it a quick squeeze before replacing her fingers with a champagne flute. Like a sideshow in Vegas, the move was so seamless I had no idea where the glass had come from.

"Thanks so much for having me." I lifted my magic glass. "Everything looks amazing."

"Roman." He got a regular hug with no beverage sleight of hand. "You should go help Eric with dinner, I'm sure he'd love to see you."

It seemed the Larsson charm had rubbed off on her or she had her own version of it. But I sensed her smile and suggestion that he go have a friendly brotherly reunion wasn't for anyone else's benefit other than her own.

"Nice try, Tia." He didn't move from my side. "But I'm not going to conveniently leave so you can ask inappropriate questions. So if you want to ask something, you'll have to do it with me here."

"Fine." She shrugged, not looking surprised her plan had been foiled. "Just an FYI, I totally *knew* you guys were together."

I wasn't sure how or what she knew, but it made me slightly uncomfortable. Maybe it was because I wasn't sure what *I* knew, the situation currently undefined other than we were spending a lot of time together even when we weren't having sex.

It wasn't that I was worried about Roman sleeping with anyone else either—unless you counted the couple of weekends that he wasn't with me, there hadn't been the time. He might not be the most virtuous man I knew, but I doubted he was a complete piece of shit.

"You know, maybe I'll go say hi to Eric." I gave Roman's arm a squeeze, deciding I should bite the bullet and get all the awkward out of the way all at once. And then I could leave Roman to deal with Tia's questions on what we were or weren't doing. I almost wanted to stick around to hear the answers, except I was worried I might not like them. "Feel free to grill him while I'm gone."

I gave them both a wave before Roman had a chance to stop

me, Tia grabbing his arm as I walked away and holding him hostage. I'd already decided I liked her, but the extra assist had definitely won her extra points.

Eric's eyes lifted as I strolled over, taking a swig of his beer as he handed a large pair of tongs to Ryan before he stepped away from the grill.

"Lauren." He nodded, giving me a warm smile. "Nice to see you again."

It still didn't feel normal to see him in an informal capacity, one that wasn't separated by a big screen or at the very least some barriers and a red carpet. But to his credit—and unlike his brother—his ego was missing in action, the look on his face lacking any hostility. If he wasn't happy about me being there, he was doing an excellent job of hiding it, the kindness seeming genuine.

"I want to apologize for Roman's insensitivity." I'd decided the direct approach would be for the best. "I hope me being here isn't a problem."

"Not at all," he grinned, taking another swig of his beer. "You don't think I would have let him invite any stranger to my house, do you? When he asked if he could bring a date, I knew it was you."

"Well, at least one of us knew." I tried to smile, still undecided on what I was going to do to punish Roman. "Has he always been such a selfish prick?"

He laughed, the trademark Larsson charm shining through. "He likes everyone to think so, but trust me, he isn't as bad as he pretends to be. He can be pretty considerate and easygoing too."

"We are talking about *Roman*, right?" I joked, only barely catching glimpses of his easygoing side. Last Friday had been the first real time, and previously at the bar, but then I had suspected it had been for ulterior motives.

"One and the same." He looked over at his brother who was still being held captive by my new favorite person, Tia. "He skews the truth to get what he wants, and he's pretty slick at it too. But he's not a complete degenerate, he won't outright lie or cheat. It's a fine line, but it's there. But you already know that or you wouldn't be here."

"I didn't really have a choice about being here," I laughed with a casual shrug. "He didn't tell me where we were going."

Eric shook his head, his blue eyes almost identical to his brother's gazing at me with more understanding than I would have liked. "I meant with *him*."

"With all your money, you could have hired someone to cook for us." Roman came up behind me, at some point having escaped from Tia's interrogation. "When did you get so cheap?"

"Since I am trying to avoid tipping off the press I'm getting married tomorrow." Eric grinned at his brother. "It's bad enough they already suspect, the less activity I have around the property, the better. Besides, I'm perfectly capable of handling my own grill, it gave me a chance to use that prenup you guys drew up as kindling." He raised his beer with a toast, grinning as he took a swallow.

Roman bit back his grin, slinging his hand around my waist. "You know burning it doesn't void it, moron."

"As far as I'm concerned, it does. You live your truth, I'll live mine." Eric tipped his chin to me. "Enjoy the rest of the night." He wandered back to the BBQ, leaving us alone.

Roman gave me a satisfied smile. "See, I told you he wouldn't give a shit. You should listen to me more often."

"You enjoy your time with Tia?" I ignored him and his smugness. "Seemed like you were having a nice chat."

He shook his head, barking out a laugh. "Let's go meet my mother and my younger brother. It's doubtful you'll get a chance after dinner, Eric's cooking skills are questionable at best and we'll probably all end up in the emergency room."

With his hand around my waist, he guided me over to a

stunning blonde woman who didn't look old enough or crazy enough to have given birth to five sons.

"Mom, this is Lauren Harper. We work together and she's also my date." He gave me a smile. "Harper, this is my mother, Kate."

"Oh, Roman." Kate sniffed into a tissue, trying to wipe up her tears and compose herself. "I'm so happy to meet you, Lauren."

"It's lovely to meet you too." I held out my hand, she grabbed it and gave it a quick squeeze.

"I'm not sure why you are crying." Roman rolled his eyes. "Eric's just getting married, they aren't even moving."

"You hush." She gave him a playful nudge. "I'm allowed to cry if I want to."

"Wow, you're Roman's date?" A tall but thinner and younger version of Eric and Roman appeared by his mother's side. "I thought Nick and Dave were kidding."

I wasn't sure how it was possible, but every single one of those boys was gorgeous. Surely one of them should have, by law of averages, been less handsome? Shorter at the very least. It seemed statistically impossible, but there it was in front of me.

"Lauren." I shook his hand. "You must be Alex."

"I am." A cheeky grin spread across his face. "Does he talk about me a lot?"

"I had such high hopes for you, Alex." Roman sighed, pretending to look annoyed. "*You* were my favorite."

After a few more back and forth between the brothers and some chiding from Kate, we settled into an easy conversation.

Roman introduced me to Tia's family, as well as her best friend, Lila who was also dating Ryan. And lastly he introduced me to his father, Jensen, who was as far removed from Hollywood as possible by being a biomedical engineer of all things.

Jensen was more reserved than his sons, happy to sit back and enjoy the evening with his wife Selena. He and Kate had been divorced for over a decade, but still maintained a very civil and amicable relationship. It was encouraging to see, honestly. In our line of work, people being friendly after they divorced wasn't the norm.

"If everyone can grab a seat, we're serving dinner." Eric called everyone to attention while he and Ryan carried over trays of food to the tables.

It was still weird being there, but after another couple of glasses of champagne, I embraced the strange and went with it.

"So, you're thinking of studying law?" I turned to Alex who had conveniently sat next to me. I think he'd been hoping to irritate Roman who was on my other side, but if he was annoyed by it, he wasn't showing it.

"Yeah, two more years of under grad." Alex sipped a beer, despite being just shy of turning twenty-one. "Hoping to stay at Berkeley for Law School, New England is too cold for me."

"He was coddled too much as a child," Roman weighed in. "Still, I guess it could be worse. He could be going into show business like the other clowns I'm related to." The disgust on his face would have been believable except for the smile he was wearing.

"Roman is just jealous because he has zero talent." Dave wandered over to our table, dragging over a chair with him. "He also has zero personality so it's just as well as he chooses to spend most of the time in an office." He took a seat near Alex.

Roman took it in stride, throwing a few clever barbs of his own back, but was surprisingly relaxed.

"Your family is pretty great." My shoulder nudged his. Everyone else had moved from the tables and was once again mingling, leaving us alone.

He looked over at his brothers, all of which were laughing. "They're okay, I guess. Which brings me to my next question. What are your plans for tomorrow?"

"Isn't tomorrow the day of your brother's wedding?" I asked, figuring that I wouldn't see him until probably later.

Roman rolled his eyes, his arm relaxing on the back of my chair. "I assume so, unless they both come to their senses in the next twenty-four hours and call the whole thing off."

My fist gave him a playful bump on the arm. "I know you said marriage isn't your thing, but you could try being happy for them." I gestured to Tia and Eric, both of them looking outrageously in love.

"Yeah, whatever." He ignored their loved-up display and turned back to me. "Tomorrow, are you free? I want to see you."

"What are you asking me?" I was careful not to assume anything because with Roman, you just couldn't tell.

He *might* have been inviting me to be his plus one to his brother's wedding, this time giving me the courtesy of a head's up before thrusting me into a family function. Or he *might* have been using me as an excuse to get out of it, in the same way a shady boyfriend asks you to be an alibi when he knocks over a liquor store.

I wasn't confident in guessing which one of those was more likely, and more to the point, which one gave me less anxiety.

His eyes connected with mine as the noise continued around us. "I'm asking you to come to the wedding with me."

I sighed, the conflict making my skin itch.

I wanted to say yes, to say that I would love to go as his plus one to what would probably be a beautiful wedding. Not to mention it wasn't every day—unless you counted right now—that I got to sneak into a movie star's private celebration. I imagined it would be an amazing day followed by an even more spectacular night.

But.

But.

But.

Deep down I knew I was inviting trouble.

Going to weddings was something you did with a boyfriend. Clutching the arm of that special someone while basking in the love around you. Maybe you imagined what it might be like when it's your turn, or even daydream about catching the bouquet. And while I knew this was the closest I'd been to a relationship in months—even if I had fallen into it accidentally—I was cautious about getting the wrong idea.

Not just me, but everyone else. His mother was already teary-eyed over Roman bringing home a girl and his brothers were too nice for words. Did they assume that one day that might be us? I had enough expectations of my own I needed to live up to, I wasn't sure I wanted to disappoint what was probably one of the nicest families I'd ever met.

"Roman, what are you doing?" I squeezed his hand, knowing I was possibly making a mistake.

"I'm asking you to be my date for my brother's wedding." He squeezed back. "It doesn't have to be a big deal."

Just go to the wedding, my subconscious screamed at me. *Like he said, it doesn't have to be a big deal.* "What if I say no?"

"Then I'll go by myself." He shrugged. "I'm not in the habit of having women bound and gagged, although, with you, I wouldn't rule it out." He tapped me on the nose.

There was a sincerity in his voice and in his eyes that tugged at my heart. It disarmed me, and for a second I'd forgotten everything that had come before that moment and what might come after. I forgot about what it might or could mean, and let go.

"Thank you, I'd love to come." I said it before I realized, the words surprising me as they left my lips.

"Good." He gave me a satisfied smile. "But if you want me to bind and gag you, I'm still up for that."

I shook my head feeling more thrilled than I probably should. "How about I bind and gag you instead?" I felt myself smile. "That might be fun actually."

He laughed, brushing my knuckle with a kiss before leaning in and whispering, "Not a chance, Harper."

CHAPTER #20

I HADN'T CAVED.

As tempting as it was to give into Roman and spend the night with him after we left the rehearsal dinner, I didn't.

Instead, I insisted he bring me home where I spent the night alone. Not because I was angry about his little stunt, springing his family on me unprepared. And it wasn't just to prove a point—although that was a nice fringe benefit. It was because I needed a night just to get my head around what the hell I was doing. And more to the point, what I wanted to do.

He made it clear my decision to spend the night alone displeased him, but he didn't fight me after he dropped me at home. Instead he kissed me goodbye and told me he'd be back in the afternoon, Tia and Eric's wedding was at dusk in the same backyard we had dinner in the night before.

"Isn't today your day off?" I looked up from painting my nails on the couch to see Morgan in her scrubs.

"Yeah, but they're short staffed so I'm going to go cover for a few hours." She grabbed her handbag and phone. "You spending the day with Roman?"

"Yes." I blew on my fingers, trying to look casual. "I'm going to his brother's wedding."

"Hmmm, brother's wedding, huh?" She didn't even try and hide the smugness. "But you're not dating or anything."

"I know, I know." I held up a hand. "Save the judgment, we can discuss my stupidity at lunch tomorrow. Roman is taking us out."

"Oooooo, Roman is taking us out." She gave a little shoulder shimmy with a silly look on her face, like she was enjoying making me squirm. "Can I be the concerned sister and ask him what his intentions are?"

My look of warning did nothing to wipe the grin off her face. "No, you cannot."

She groaned, pouting at the door. "Fine, be boring. Have fun at the wedding. I'll expect all the details tomorrow."

It was my turn to groan as I waved her goodbye.

While I had never intentionally broken privilege, if I didn't tell her about—what I dubbed—the Larsson connection soon, I was going to explode. It's not like I would tell her about my legal involvement, and it wasn't like she was going to tell anyone else.

Tomorrow. I would talk to Roman today and explain to him how important it was that I tell my sister. Assure him that we could trust her and his connection to his famous brother would never be revealed. At least not by us.

A long deep breath slowly eased out. It was one less thing to worry about so now I could have a nervous breakdown over a more pressing issue, like what the hell was I supposed to wear?

Was there a particular outfit that was suitable when going to the wedding of a famous person, you barely knew, whose brother you were sort of dating, and you'd handled the bride's prenup?

Little black dress maybe?

Or was it more a floral maxi dress?

Ugh, at least I had a few hours to stare blankly at my wardrobe before I needed to make a decision either way.

An emerald green cocktail dress was what I ended up deciding on. Not too flashy, not too formal and hopefully nothing that would draw any undue attention to myself.

Then there was the issue of a gift, not the easiest thing to organize when you had zero time and had no idea what to even get. I very much doubted they were registered at *Macy's,* but I couldn't go empty handed either. So, against my better judgment—the one that said they wouldn't need anything I could afford—I made a quick trip to *Target* and got a toaster oven. Because I didn't care how much money you had, when you got the munchies at two in the morning and the maid has gone home for the day, you were going to need a freaking toaster oven to heat up frozen pizza bites.

"You ready?" Roman walked through my door looking amazing in a charcoal suit that should have been illegal. I thought I'd seen everything in his designer arsenal, but clearly he'd been saving this one for a special occasion.

"I hate this suit," I lied, taking a minute to appreciate my view, the urge to play with his tie too strong as my fingers adjusted it. "It makes your ass look hideous."

He laughed, his hands settling on my hips. "Good, I'd hate for someone to be staring at my ass all night long especially with my mother around. What kind of sick pervert would do that anyway?"

It would have been easy to drag him into my bedroom and unwrap him one delicious designer label at a time, but I didn't want to make us late.

I tugged at his arm, moving him to my kitchen table where the present sat beautifully wrapped. "Can you help me get this into the car or are your muscles decorative?"

"What the hell is it?" He looked at the box with suspicion, turning it around even though it was covered in shiny silver paper and a big white bow.

"I got them a present." I figured it was self-explanatory but clearly it wasn't. "I wasn't going to your brother's wedding without getting them something."

He shook his head, looking amused. "You didn't have to do that, you're going as my guest and I already got them some investment bonds."

"Wow, investment bonds," I deadpanned, not at all shocked he would have gotten them a practical present. "Are you trying to bore them to death before their first anniversary?"

He picked up the box, weighing it in his hands. "And what did you get them?"

I straightened, feeling proud of myself. "It's a toaster oven and they are going to love it."

"You got them a toaster oven?" His smile mocked me as an eyebrow rose. "A kitchen appliance?"

His mocking did nothing to ruin my sense of achievement. "I sure did, it's a Cuisinart and fits a whole 12-inch pizza. And I loved it so much I even got one for myself." I pointed to the large box on the kitchen counter. "They can eat years worth of midnight snacks while they are waiting for your stupid bonds to mature. Now we better get out of here or we're going to be late."

He rolled his eyes, holding the box as I gave him a friendly shove to the door. We took the elevator this time, his eyes restless as they roamed on me until we got to the bottom floor and walked out to his car. The lack of trunk space in the Ferrari meant I had to balance the box on my knee until we got to Eric's huge mansion. It was useful for making sure I kept my hands to myself, so at least we weren't late.

Roman parked at the front like we had the night before, his brother Dave greeting us as we stepped out of the car.

"What's in the box?" He took it from my hands, giving me the chance to climb out of the passenger seat as Roman came around to my side.

He tapped the present in Dave's hand before putting his arm around me, "A toaster oven."

"Sweet." He nodded, grinning as he carried it into the house.

I elbowed Roman in the ribs as we followed Dave up the stairs. "See, someone appreciates my genius."

Roman gripped me tighter as he leaned in. "That's because he still lives like he's in a frat house."

"I heard that, asshole," Dave called from over his shoulder.

"And yet," Roman laughed, "you didn't deny it."

Dave pointed us out to the backyard while he disappeared with the present.

In the short time since we'd last been at Eric's house, it had been transformed from a beautiful backyard into a stunning outdoor venue. Large white canopies had been erected with more of that polished wooden floor being placed on the grass, the area covered in pastel-colored roses and large white calla lilies.

White chairs had been set up in two neat rows with a white aisle runner separating to two halves that lead to a huge fairy light lit arch.

"Wow, it looks beautiful." My eyes floated as they absorbed every tiny detail of the storybook scene.

Roman's hand pressed on the small of my back as we moved to the chairs, people already sitting down and talking as soft music played. "You want to take a seat? I'm just going to check on Eric."

"Yes, yes, of course." I waved him off, too busy looking at all the tiny details to worry about whether he was sitting next to me right then. "Tell him to break a leg or whatever. Oh, look what they did to the pool!" I pointed to the tiny floating lanterns that bobbed on the dark blue surface.

He glanced over, shaking his head he gave me a quick kiss. "I'll be back."

As he left, I settled into my seat, amazed by how at ease I

felt. It could possibly be the two glasses of wine I'd had between my mercy dash to Target and getting ready for the wedding. *Or* maybe I was becoming desensitized to being around Roman and how crazy it seemed.

He wasn't as terrible any more. His arrogance, no longer abrasive. And even some of the traits I'd once found obnoxious and annoying, now seemed endearing and sort of cute.

I liked spending time with him, was excited by the way he challenged me, and loved that he didn't treat me like a glass doll that needed to be set on a pedestal. If I didn't know better—I wasn't sure how much of my feelings were wine related—I would assume I was starting to have feelings for Roman.

Feelings where I didn't want to kill or maim him.

Boyfriend feelings.

Shit.

I tried to distract myself, looking around at the people sitting down and seeing if I recognized anyone. There were a few familiar faces, people I'd seen from the night before. Tia's Brother-in-law was chatting to Tia's younger sister who had flown in from Paris, both of them oblivious to my staring.

Roman came back to sit beside me. "Did I miss anything?"

"The blonde—who I'm positive is famous—is pregnant. She keeps brushing her hand over her belly and her man is hovering over her like a bodyguard." I discreetly pointed to the blond couple who looked photo shopped before continuing. "That guy toward the back is security but pretending to be a guest, he has an earpiece and a bulge in his back that is possibly a gun. That woman beside your mom, who I assume is your aunt, is annoyed she didn't wear her waterproof mascara and has been dabbing her eyes and retouching her foundation every few minutes. And I think your brother Alex is trying to hit on Tia's younger sister, she's being polite but isn't interested."

That was all I had for now, but I was sure that I might get a few other interesting bits and pieces before the bride made an appearance.

"And did you find out if it was Professor Plum who killed Mrs. Peacock in the library with the candle stick?" Roman laughed, resting his arm on the back of my chair. "You're here for a wedding, not to assess a jury pool."

"Sorry, old habits." I turned to him, sidelining my people watching for a while. "How's your brother doing? Is he nervous?"

Roman shook his head. "Nope, he's been waiting for this for a while. Tia, on the other hand, is in a bathroom upstairs throwing up. I think Lila has given her a Xanax."

"Well, it's a big deal, walking out in front of all these people." I pointed to the fifty or sixty gathered friends and family. "I'm pretty sure I'd be throwing up too."

"Funny, I didn't take you for the marrying type." He rubbed his chin like he was deep in thought. "You're not getting sentimental on me are you, Harper?"

"No," I scoffed, waving my hand like he had said the most ridiculous thing ever. Because it *was* the most ridiculous thing ever.

I didn't even want a serious relationship, let alone get married. A husband was the last thing I needed, not if I intended to make partner at some point. Marriage would only complicate things.

So, why was it that the idea didn't seem so bad anymore? Like *maybe*, if I found someone who was likeminded and supportive, that it would be possible to have both. I don't know, it might work out, right?

"Nope, no marriage for me," I assured him, the words for the first time ever sounding uncomfortable in my mouth. "I just meant, if I was to lose my mind and agree to spend the rest of my life with one guy that it might be nerve wracking to promise that in front of an audience of people."

He looked like he was about to say something but as his mouth opened, the music got louder. An excited hush fell over the crowd as people hustled to their seats. Eric's parents and Tia's mother made their way down the aisle, saying quiet and excited hellos as they shuffled to their chairs.

Next came Eric and his best man, Ryan, both of them looking breathtaking in matching black suits. They walked casually to the front of the arch where they chatted to the waiting celebrant, Eric occasionally turning and flashing one of his movie star heartthrob grins.

Then the music stopped, the break only for a minute before the familiar strains of "Cannon in D" were piped through the speakers.

Tia's niece and nephew walked out first, both looking adorable as they almost ran to where their parents were sitting. And then came Lila, Tia's best friend and maid of honor, floating down the aisle in a gorgeous lavender gown.

There was a collective gasp as Tia stepped out.

Wearing a simple but stunning lace dress, she looked like a princess on the arm of her dad. She smiled as she walked past, slowly edging her way to Eric who hadn't taken his eyes off her. She was probably the most beautiful bride I'd ever seen, radiant and in love, and Eric looked like a man who would wage a war just to make her happy.

I never cried at weddings.

Never felt that tug at my heart.

But as the service started, I felt my eyes water with a constant flutter in my belly as they exchanged vows and promised each other forever.

I hadn't wanted that for myself, so why did it make me so goddamn emotional?

Roman looked over, but I forced a grin and pretended to be as unaffected as he seemed to be, keeping my feelings locked down until Eric finally kissed his bride.

A sigh of relief spilled from my body as they walked back up the aisle as husband and wife. The happy couple heading off to take some photos while waiters circled with large silver trays of drinks and canapés. And if there was ever a time I needed a drink, it was right now—the effects of those two wines had long diminished.

"Thirsty?" Roman nodded to my hands, a champagne flute housed in each.

"It's hot out and I don't want to dehydrate." I took a gulp from one, hoping the alcohol might do something about this affliction making me feel things.

Nope.

I still felt weepy and emotional.

Better take another gulp.

Roman took one of the empty glasses from my hand and replaced it with some water. "You might want to slow down if you want to make it to dinner. I would hate to find you floating in the pool with all the pretty lights."

My head nodded, knowing that getting drunk wouldn't be wise when I was feeling so unpredictable. "I think I might find a bathroom and freshen up a little. The heat." I waved lamely as I excused myself.

The furrow of his brow told me he was suspicious, but he didn't stop me. I left him and the majority of the guests outside, and wandered into the back of the house. There were a few people in the kitchen, mainly in white outfits relining their trays with more food and drink. While a few guests loitered in the large open area I assumed was a casual living room.

A helpful man—who I was positive was security—directed me to a bathroom toward the back of the hall, my heels clicking on the floor as I powerwalked to it.

I'd barely got the door closed when I turned and threw up.

Heat traveled up my body as I sunk to my knees and retched again. It was the second time Roman Pierce had evoked that kind of reaction, and only one of those times did I know it was because I didn't hate him.

No, this was so much worse than hate.

Oh my God.

Was I falling in love with him?

My body shook as I gripped the edges of the porcelain, trying to fight the urge to be sick again as feelings and thoughts tumbled in my head.

This wasn't supposed to happen, and more to the point, how did I *let* it happen.

I had to stop it, had to find a way to go back to hating him. Or at the very least, figure out a way to calm my fucking idiot heart that had somehow decided he was the guy I wanted a future with.

"Just take me now, Lord," I whispered in the dark. *"Let's just end it here so I don't have to go out there and face him."*

He would know.

He would take one look at me and *know* exactly what I was feeling.

And there was no way I could risk that.

I stood slowly, looking at myself in the mirror as I cupped water from the facet and brought it to my mouth. I had some mints in my purse and was able to fix my makeup so at least it wouldn't be obvious the thought of being in love with Roman Pierce had driven me to puke.

"Just go out there, laugh and then go home and screw his brains out." I nodded to myself in the mirror. "Remind yourself you are just having sex, and being in love is for suckers."

I flipped myself off, believing none of the words. Not the ones I'd spoken out loud at the mirror nor the ones that were looping around in my head trying to convince myself that I didn't have feelings.

Of all the terrible times to have an epiphany, a bathroom at the wedding of people you barely knew was probably the worst.

I had psyched myself up enough to leave and stepped back into the hall when I heard voices coming toward me.

"Pray to the Viking Gods, Lila. Pray to all of them." The bride, not looking so radiant, came storming toward me.

"Oh, hey." Lila waved, carrying Tia's veil as she trailed behind. "We just need the bathroom real quick. Bride emergency and all that."

They shuffled past me, locking themselves in the bathroom as I stood outside slightly puzzled.

The familiar sound of vomit followed soon after.

Hmmm. You would think the nerves would have ended once the formalities were over, right? But if the activity in the bathroom was anything to go by, someone was still feeling stressed.

I had a terrible track record with bathrooms I'd decided.

"Are you okay?" I knocked on the door. Once again, divine intervention had thrown me a distraction when I was having my crisis.

"Yep, all good." Lila's voice floated from inside; Tia too busy being sick to answer for herself.

I didn't care what Lila was saying, there was nothing about this situation that was *all good*.

Me having feelings for Roman—not good.

Tia puking in a bathroom after she married the man of her dreams—not good.

Which was why instead of minding my own business and going back to the party where I would have to pretend I wasn't falling in love with a man, I was staying right where I was, talking to two women I barely knew through a bathroom door.

The door slowly opened, Lila stepping out holding Tia's veil in her hand with the pale veil-less bride following her out.

"Stomach flu?" I offered, even though I was almost positive it wasn't.

"You can't say one word." Tia's head shook. "Not one word, especially to Roman."

Yeah, I thought so.

I took a deep breath, my back straightening as I looked at her in the eyes. "Tia, you seem to have forgotten that I'm your lawyer. Even if I wanted to—which I don't—I couldn't say anything to anyone. Not to Roman, not to Eric, and not to those Viking Gods you were praying to when you stormed in."

Lila and Tia glanced at each other, the unspoken *I think we can trust her* being debated as we stood there in silence.

Tia nodded to the hallway. "We need to take this upstairs."

I followed wordlessly, climbing the stairs while the noise of the wedding got further away as we made it to the second floor. Tia led us to a bedroom, closing the door once we were all inside.

"I'm two weeks late, I think I'm pregnant, and I'm freaking the fuck out." She paced, her fingers holding the hem of her dress so she didn't step on the lace.

Cue my complete lack of surprise.

Vomiting.

Looking pale.

Secret meeting with your bestie in a bathroom.

It had been my first guess even without her confirmation.

"Okay, and are you worried about what Eric is going to say?" I asked as I watched her wring her hands.

Part of my job was to ask questions, to find out the problem and the best possible defense. And while this wasn't a court case, if I understood exactly what was worrying her, I was confident we could find a solution.

"I know what you're thinking." She waved her hands in the air.

"What's the big deal, we love each other, we're married, so maybe the timing is off but it's not the end of the world. But it is a big deal, it's a *huge* deal, and I didn't plan this." She took a gasp of air, her breath running out as she spoke with limited pauses. "Eric just signed on to do a movie that will have him away for months, and they are shooting in remote locations that I couldn't go to even if I wanted to. This movie, it's his chance for an Oscar." She took another breath. "And I know he will turn it down if he can't be here during the pregnancy or possibly miss the birth of his first child. The timing is all wrong and he will end up hating me forever."

"Tia, he won't hate you." Lila tried to find some reason. "Maybe he can work something out with the director, maybe he can work the filming schedule and fly back in between."

Tia shook her head, shooting down every scenario. "You know him. He will tell me there is nothing more important than his family, which is exactly what I'd want to hear. But I know that there will be a part of him that will fester because of it."

"Have you done a pregnancy test?" My question made them stop and look at me. "Because you could be worrying for no reason."

Tia spoke slowly. "I'm late, and I've been throwing up. I'm on the pill, but I know that thing isn't foolproof." She started pacing again. "I mean, look at him. The man has a smile that could get you pregnant. Honestly, I'm surprised it's taken this long."

I was with her on that. I'd known those Larsson boys were trouble. And as horrible as it was to think, I was glad it wasn't my uterus that had been the casualty. Roman's smile was just as potent, it's a wonder we all weren't sporting matching bumps.

"Okay, we're going to do a test and find out." I grabbed her hands and tried to coax her to sit down on the bed.

"What, like *now*?" Tia's eyes got wide, flashing with panic. "If I don't go down there soon, Eric is going to know something is up. I can't disappear on my wedding day. And what are we supposed to do? Send someone to run to *CVS* and get a test? You guys can't leave either; it will look suspicious. He'll find out."

"Breathe, Tia." Lila held her hand, sucking in air and blowing out slowly in an effort to get her friend to do the same.

"You go down there, act normal." I pulled out my phone from my purse. "I'm going to call my sister, she's a nurse and we can trust her." Not to mention that if Tia's suspicions were correct, she could help me talk her off the ledge. Morgan was amazing like that, which was why she was so good at her job.

"She can bring us the test, no one has to leave, and we'll arouse as little suspicion as possible. When she gets here, you excuse yourself, we meet up back in your bedroom and find out once and for all."

It was the perfect plan, and more importantly all we could do right now considering we were in the middle of a wedding and options were limited.

Tia shook her head, not looking convinced. "I don't know."

"Trust me, this is what we need to do." I delegated as I hesitated on Morgan's number. "Lila, help clean her up and get her back to the party. I'll come find you both when we are ready."

I stepped out into the hall to give them some privacy and found another room, the door closing.

Please Morgan, be home.

"HEY LO, EVERYTHING okay? I thought you were at a wedding with Roman?" My ever-dependable sister answered right away.

"Morgan, listen, I need you to do something and not ask questions." It was my turn to pace, not only needing to deal with the possibility of Tia's pregnancy but that Roman was probably starting wonder where I was.

This was the longest bathroom break in history.

"Lo, this isn't the call where you ask me to hide a body or something?" Morgan laughed. "I know we took that blood oath, but I'm out of scrubs until I do laundry."

"No, you don't need to hide a body." Though it might have been easier than smuggling a pregnancy test into a movie star's wedding with the amount of security and people walking around. "I need you to get me a pregnancy test, actually get a couple just to be sure, and I'm going to need you to bring them to me."

"You're pregnant?" my usually cool and calm sister almost screamed into the phone.

"No, it's not for me," I said, quickly dismissing her fears of her younger sister being knocked up. "But I can't tell you much more other than ask you to trust me and not tell anyone about it."

"Lo, it's a pregnancy test. I'm not going down to the corner and buying a dime bag. No one is going to question me."

Well, at least we had that going for us.

I gave her some last-minute instructions and the address. Then I told her to call me when she got to the gate and I would work out a way to get her inside. And like an absolute rock star, she didn't ask me whose house it was or why she just couldn't walk up to the front door. Instead, she promised to see me soon with a variety of pregnancy testing items and ended the call.

My cell promptly rang the minute we'd hung up.

"Hello." I tried to sound surprised, causal, even though I had seen from the caller ID it was Roman.

"Did you leave?" he asked, not bothering with the greeting. "Where the hell did you go?"

"Hey, Roman." I hoped he hadn't decided to search the house and was standing outside the door. "I had a client call me and it was an emergency. I had to take it. I'm just dealing with it now."

"What client?" he asked, because he couldn't just take my word for it and mind his own business.

I shook my head and said the first name that came to mind. "Chase Anderson."

Shit.

"What the fuck does that asshole want?" he growled into the phone. "You're vetting an acquisition, not his personal counsel. Tell him to call Daniel or Carter if he needs fucking legal advice."

I hated lying to him, and hated even more that the one name I had picked was the client he'd been telling me to dump.

Why hadn't I said someone else? *Anyone* else! Not that I could do much now, my stupid mouth committing me to my bogus excuse.

"I am not going to tell a client to call a partner when I can deal with it myself. And who are you to tell me otherwise?"

For the first time ever, I didn't want to argue with him. I wanted to just tell him that it was something I needed to deal with and I would see him soon.

But I couldn't.

I had given Tia my word.

And even though I knew that regardless of the result of the pregnancy test, everything would work out, my word was my word.

I wouldn't break it, even if it meant a little personal hardship.

"Lauren, I know we both get off on the argument, but he has no business with you." He huffed into the phone. "So, if he is calling you, it's for *other* reasons and not because of your amazing legal mind."

"Just let it go, Roman." I silently begged him to just drop it. "I'll be back in a few minutes and we can enjoy the rest of the wedding."

"So, what does he want?"

I held my breath, wondering if he could tell I was full of shit. "Roman, you know I can't tell you that."

He barked out a humorless laugh. "Bullshit, we work for the same firm, it's called authorized disclosure."

I was grasping at straws, digging myself into a hole I wasn't easily going to be able to climb out of.

"Chase Anderson instructed that this particular information be confided to specified lawyers, so authorized disclosure doesn't extend to you in this case."

His voice dropped to almost a growl. "Why would he do *that*?"

"I don't know, Roman." I shrugged, wondering if it was just male posturing or he had a reason for giving me a hard time. "Why does anyone do anything? Because they can. I'll be back soon." I hung up before he could argue.

My phone promptly lit up again, Roman's name flashing across the screen, but I ignored it and switched my phone to silent while I waited for Morgan to arrive.

I had debated going back to the party until she got there but decided it would just invite more questions. Roman would no doubt give me the third degree, pissed I'd hung up on him and ignored his calls, only to have him grill me further when I had to "take another call" when she arrived. So instead, I decided to sit up in what I assumed was a guest bedroom, to avoid any further questions until my sister got there. I'd deal with whatever mood Roman was in later; hopefully he'd have cooled down by then.

It seemed like forever before Morgan messaged me. She'd been denied entry—unsurprisingly—and waved on by security that hadn't been there initially but was now attending the gate. She was waiting for me outside, loitering in front of one of the neighbor's properties.

Short of dressing her in a police outfit and falsifying a warrant, sneaking Morgan in would be impossible. So instead, I was going to have to go out—without being seen by Roman or anyone else who would ask questions—get the loot and bring it back inside. Oh, and then find the bride and get her to discreetly pee on the stick so we could see if she was with child. *No sweat, right?* Ugh.

I cracked open the door, checking the coast was clear before I stepped out. My eyes darted left and right as I descended the stairs and walked in the direction I vaguely remembered led to the front door.

Turns out I knew the layout of the house better than I first thought, finding my way easily. And after assuring the scary looking man at the door that I was just stepping out for a few minutes and would be right back—it would suck if an overzealous security guard denied my reentry—I slipped out and walked down the driveway to the front gate.

It had been easier when the trip had been in a car and not in stilettos.

"Morgan," I whispered in the dark, my heels sinking into the dirt as I wandered to where her car was conspicuously idling.

She would have sucked as a wheelman.

"Roman's brother lives there?" Morgan pointed to the gate where she'd been denied entry. "What the hell does he do?"

I leaned against the car door, my hand reaching through the open driver's side window. "Drug dealer. I'm just as shocked as you are, but we can't choose our family."

She shook her head, tossing me a bag, the exchange looking more suspicious by the second. "Here you go, there are a couple of different ones in there, call me if you need anything else."

"Thanks, Morgan, I really appreciate this." I clutched the bag to my chest, thankful I had the greatest sister known to man. "I owe you one."

"Meh, you're fine." She shrugged. "I know you pretend to be a badass, Lo, but you have a good heart. You would have done the same for me."

It seemed to be the night for pesky emotions, the words getting stuck in my throat as I nodded. "I need to go, I'll call you later."

She waved, driving off as I returned to Eric's front gate and further ruining the shoes I was wearing. Strangely, I didn't care, shrugging it off as I passed the disgruntled man at the door again, and made my way back into the house.

So far, so good—and other than the security, who was eyeing me suspiciously, I hadn't caught anyone else's attention.

As I got closer to the backyard, I was able to see Roman. He was sitting at a table, clutching his phone so tight I was surprised the thing hadn't been reduced to dust. He had called me a few times, but I hadn't answered, and I could tell that when I finally did talk to him, it was going to be heated.

Still, I had bigger issues right now. Like how I was going to get the bride's attention so she could take the test while her new husband and invited guests remained none the wiser.

"Did you get it?" I turned around, finding Lila creeping up behind me.

I nodded, my chin tipping to the white bag I was hiding behind my purse. "Can you get her back upstairs without anyone noticing?"

"Yeah, I can manage that." She smirked, both of us gazing out at Tia who was currently wrapped in her husband's arms. "Roman is going to be a problem though, he's been looking for you."

"I'll take care of Roman as soon as we're done with this." Not sure how I was going to do that exactly, but I'd work it out. "I'm going to go upstairs to wait for you. If they see the three of us going up there together it will look suspicious."

Lila agreed, walking out to the backyard while I followed my earlier path and found the bedroom I had been in before. I opened the door to the connecting bathroom and quickly read through the instructions. I doubted peeing on a stick was a complicated venture, but it was better to cover all our bases and not make a stupid mistake like peeing on the wrong end.

It didn't take long before Lila and Tia came in, finding me in the bathroom.

"We've got like twenty minutes tops." Tia glanced at the door like she was expecting someone to walk through. "I really appreciate you doing this for me, Lauren."

"Hey, what are lawyers for?" I nodded to the sticks on the bathroom counter. "Pee here and then recap it. There are two windows, one so we know the test worked and one for the result. The one with a blue cap is an early detection test, so do them both. We'll know in a couple of minutes either way."

She looked nervously at the tests, taking a deep breath as we cleared out of the room to give her some privacy.

"Did your sister ask questions?" Lila sat on the bed as we waited.

I shook my head. "We took a blood oath, anytime one of us

needs something, we call. No questions asked."

"Tia and I have a similar arrangement." She laughed. "It's only recently that I've relaxed when I see her number come up on my phone. I never had a sister."

"It's done." Tia exited the bathroom, wiping her hands on a small towel. "Now we wait." She joined Lila on the bed.

"How's the nausea?" I asked, noticing her color had come back. That had to be a good sign.

She shrugged. "Okay, I guess. I didn't eat much dinner so there's not a lot to come up." Her hand flew to her mouth. "Oh, shit, you missed the main course."

"It's fine, this was more important," I reassured her, not feeling very hungry anyway.

We sat in silence, the minutes ticking unnaturally slow while we waited. I could feel the tension in the air, but no one felt the need to talk. It wasn't the sort of thing that required conversation, and we were well past the point of making small talk.

I pulled out my phone and glanced at the time. "I think we can look now. Do you want me to leave? Or would you like me to stay?" I asked, realizing she might not want to share the moment with someone she barely knew.

"Stay." She stood up and gave Lila's hand a squeeze. "You've gone to all this trouble to help me, the least I can do is allow you to share in the result."

Slowly she walked into the bathroom, picking up the first test while Lila and I waited at the door.

"Oh thank God." Her knees gave way under her as she sat on the toilet. "It's negative."

"See, nothing to worry about. The nausea is probably stress, or maybe it really is the stomach flu. I'd still check in with a doctor in the next few days, just to be sure. And maybe get him to run a blood test to rule out anything else funky going on."

"These test are pretty accurate, right?" She looked at the other test, which was also negative. "I'm not going to find out in a couple of weeks that I was knocked up and got faked out by *Clear Blue* am I?"

"I read the instructions." I pointed to the folded up piece of paper with lines of tiny writing I was positive almost nobody read. "Even if your cycle was slightly off, at two weeks there would be enough of the pregnancy hormone for the test to detect. Especially the early one. False negatives are rare, and I think in this case we can safely rule it out."

"Okay, okay." Tia visibly relaxed. "So, it was a false alarm."

I bagged up the used test, disposing of the evidence. "I'd say the stress of the wedding, arguing about the prenup, knowing that Eric is going away soon to a remote location—all contributed. But it's fine now. You should get back to the wedding though before anyone starts asking questions. I'll get rid of this."

After all, the last thing she needed was someone walking in and finding a pregnancy test in the trash.

"I'll tell, Eric," she assured me. "Just obviously not tonight. I mean, there is no reason to say anything right now considering it was a false alarm, right?"

"Tia, it's your business and it's not my place to judge you either way." I checked the bench making sure nothing had slipped my attention and it was clear of any pregnancy testing equipment and/or packaging. "I think he will understand your panic, but if you want to just forget the whole thing, then that's your right too."

"I think you should tell him, Tia," Lila weighed in. "Just wait until your Italian honeymoon. He'll be relaxed, soaking up the sun and you guys can just talk."

"Agreed." Tia nodded, before reaching out and giving my hand a squeeze. "Lauren, I know I said this before, but I really appreciate this. Organizing the tests, not saying anything—it was a lot to ask."

"It's fine." I squeezed back. "Now, go back and enjoy your wedding."

She nodded, both of them leaving me to head back to the party. Meanwhile, I had to think up what the hell I was going to tell Roman.

It had been an hour at least, maybe closer to two, I couldn't be sure.

The appetizer and main course had already been served, and he'd been sitting there alone while I was ignoring his calls.

He was going to be furious.

That wasn't even taking into consideration the reason I initially gave him for disappearing was to assist a client he'd convinced himself had ulterior motives.

Taking a deep breath and grabbing the stash of smuggled goods, I left the bathroom, cursing my purse wasn't big enough to hide the evidence as I descended down the stairs.

"Lose your way?" Roman was standing there waiting with his arms folded tightly across his chest.

"Hey, someone was in the other bathroom, and one of the waiters told me there was one upstairs." I tried to keep my voice neutral, doing my best to camouflage my bag of contraband.

His eyebrow rose, seeming unreasonably calm. "Well, I'm glad for you. I, on the other hand, have been sitting beside an empty chair wondering why I bothered to bring a date at all."

He didn't yell, didn't raise his voice either, but I could tell he was furious.

"Roman—"

He held his hand up, not giving me a chance to explain.

"Do you know how many times someone asked me where you were? Or one of my brothers gave me shit about you coming to your senses and leaving?"

I opened my mouth and tried again. "I'm sorry, I just had

something I needed to take care of."

"Bullshit." He moved closer. "Unless Chase Anderson was in jail or his business was suddenly involved in a hostile takeover, there was no reason to take his call. But whatever." He waved his hand dismissively. "You can't tell me. I'm not in the loop."

"You have to trust me." I met his eyes, hoping he would see that I was sincere.

"Trust you?" He threw his head back and laughed. "You know how many women I have introduced to my family? How many times I've brought a date home? And the one fucking time I thought it was a good idea—because I stupidly believed we were cool—you embarrassed me. Fuck that, Harper. Fuck that, and fuck whatever you *had* to do."

"Roman."

"Don't fucking *Roman* me either." He leaned in, his lip curling into a sneer. "I'm giving you one chance to tell me exactly what was so important that you left me to sit there looking like a fucking chump, and I want the truth."

I had no idea what to say, what I could possibly tell him that would make it better. But I knew the truth wasn't it.

It didn't matter that Tia ended up not being pregnant; it wasn't my news to share, especially not with a man who was acting so hostile even if he felt he was justified.

"You are obviously upset, and I get it." It had been the last thing I wanted to do. "I am sorry that I had to step away, and I'm sorry because of that you were embarrassed or hurt." I reached out to his arm, needing to touch him, and by some miracle he didn't pull away. "Please know that the only reason I was gone was because it was important."

It was at that moment that the stupid CVS bag I'd been clutching dropped to the floor. The contents spilled out at our feet.

"What the fuck?" He bent down and grabbed it before I had

a chance. "Why the hell do you have a pregnancy test?"

Crap. However bad I'd thought it had been, it got so much worse.

I scooped what was left on the floor, bundling it back in the bag without answering him, unsure of what I was going to say.

"Is this yours?" He waved the wand in the air in front of me, not giving me a chance to answer before continuing. "Why the hell am I even asking you, of course it's yours, why else would you have it."

"It's not what it looks like."

Even though that statement was one hundred percent true, it was the exact same statement someone said when they were guilty. As lawyers we'd heard it a thousand times, and almost always it was *exactly* what it looked like.

"Well, at least it's negative." He tilted the test to the side before holding it out for me. "Must be a relief for you and whoever you thought impregnated you. We both know it couldn't have been me."

"How dare you!" I snatched the test from his hand and stuffed it in the bag with the others. He could be as mad as he wanted, but it didn't give him permission to assume the worst about me, and talk to me like I was nothing.

"How dare I?" His eyes widened in disbelief as he stood over me. "Are you fucking kidding me right now? If it pleases the court, allow me to build the scenario for you. You agree to come with me to my brother's wedding and then mysteriously disappear. Suspecting you are carrying some other sucker's kid, the guilt tears you up inside so much that you decide you can't wait a second longer and take the fucking test. Why you didn't do it at home is beyond me, but I haven't had time to get to a motive just yet. Then you find out it's negative and you miraculously reappear. What I want to know, Harper, is two things. First, why the sudden phone call with Chase Anderson and the appearance of a pregnancy test? And if that thing was positive, were you going to play me for a moron and pretend it was mine?"

"Are you serious?" My eyes almost bulged out of my head. "You do realize that you are not only challenging my character but my professional standing."

"I'm only analyzing the evidence I have in front of me," he responded coolly. "And wondering what those billable hours were used for?"

"You make me sick." My fist tightened either side of me as my body shook. "How dare you call into question my integrity?"

I wanted to scream, to claw his eyes out, but I also wanted to cry. That he could assume the worst in me so easily was horrifying.

"Deflection isn't a defense, sweetheart." The words bit out through his clenched jaw. "Surely, you know better."

"That's enough." I pushed him to the side, not willing to have him draw multiple incorrect conclusions and paint me as an evil and manipulative bitch. Not to mention a whore who slept with clients, because obviously it was what was between my legs that had gotten me my law degree. "You can be mad that I left and not be a heartless offensive asshole. You disgust me. That you would sink so freaking low. Unlike you, the last thing I wanted was to hurt you."

He threw his head back, the laugh echoing down the empty hall. "For me to be hurt, I'd have to care about you. Which I don't."

A knife through my heart would have hurt less. Each one of his words stung more than the last as everything he said to me echoed in my mind. The things he thought, the things he believed—that he'd been so easily convinced. I couldn't believe that less than a few hours ago I believed I was in love with him.

Thank God I hadn't said anything, saving myself from even further hurt, and how funny he would have found it.

"Well, then." I kicked up my chin not willing to subject myself to him and his cruelty any longer. "You enjoy being an evil bastard. I hope that works out for you. But I am going to go now, because I don't deserve *your shit* or have to listen to your vicious *and* inaccurate lies. So long, you horrible asshole." I tossed him a wave as I marched down the hall to the front door.

I was so *mad*, so mad and hurt and—ugh, it was like every human emotion I had turned on simultaneously and was jostling for dominance.

Screw him.

Screw love and relationships and everything else.

I stormed out of the house, and thank God he didn't follow. I wasn't sure I would have been able to restrain myself and not beat him to death with the bag of pregnancy tests that weren't mine. Too many witnesses, the security giving me suspicious glances as I powerwalked down the driveway would have been the first ones to turn me in.

My feet kept moving, and by some miracle I remained upright as I navigated the long stretch of concrete in heels until I reached the gate.

Hitting the button on the side, the large metal monstrosity slid open allowing me my freedom. I didn't bother turning around, just kept walking as my shoes sunk into the grass—the pumps were already ruined anyway—and I made my way further up the road that had no sidewalk.

I guess people around there didn't do a lot of walking; I didn't expect to see a cab coming cruising by either. As I pulled out my phone to once again call my sister, I decided I hated Beverly Hills.

I hated weddings too, my shoes and my stupid outfit.

But of all the things I hated, the thing that had the number one position was Roman.

So. Much. Hate.

"Hello?" Morgan's voice sounded funny when she answered

the phone and I hoped she wasn't sleeping.

"Morgan." Her name the only thing I was able to say before a sob tore at my throat. "I need you to come get me."

"I'll be right there, Lo." She didn't ask questions as I heard rustling in the background. "I'm putting on my shoes right now. Just hang on, okay."

"Okay." I nodded under the security light of some other rich person I probably hated too. "Thank you."

After giving her instructions on where to find me, I ended the call and stood on the side of the road waiting.

Even though I didn't want to see Roman, I half expected him to come looking. Possibly having a moment of behaving like a *regular* human, and being concerned about whether I had a way to get home or if I was safe. But that was just me being delusional again, because he'd told me exactly how much he didn't care about me.

What an idiot.

Me, not him.

He was something else—all of which were horrible with a string of curse words attached—but I had been the idiot.

It felt like forever before I finally saw my sister's car, the headlights making me so relieved I almost cried.

"Did he hurt you?" She gripped the steering wheel tight as I hopped into the passenger seat. "Because if he hurt you, Lo, I *will* hurt him."

"Not physically." My head shook as I kicked off my ruined pumps. "Please . . . just take me home."

I could tell she didn't want to. That she wanted to turn her Subaru Forrester around, ram the damn gate and then possibly run over Roman.

Morgan was the least violent person I knew. She saw the horrors of it at her work and actively tried to save people even if they didn't deserve it.

She was a much better person than I was.

But you hurt her family, and she turned into Uma Thurman in *Kill Bill*.

"Okay, let's get you home."

She didn't ask any more questions and just drove until we got to our apartment.

I didn't even cry, my brain and body too numb to even know what to feel.

The worst part of it all was the loss I felt.

Roman and I—for whatever reason—worked. Or at least we had, and I never in a million years would have thought he could have been so horrible and cruel. Arrogant, cocky, bossy, annoying—sure, but *not* downright mean.

I guess I didn't know him as well as I thought I did.

Things had been a lot easier when the only thing I felt was dislike and hate.

I needed to go back to that.

CHAPTER 22

"OKAY, SO I didn't pressure you yesterday, but now you *need* to talk to me." Morgan sat down on my bed where I had been curled up under my comforter since getting home last night. There had been a shower in between, but I hadn't eaten, something my stomach was reminding me of this morning as it growled in protest.

I flopped over onto my back with little enthusiasm for actually getting out of bed, but she was right about me needing to talk to her. I needed to tell someone if for no other reason than so I could get it straight in my own head.

"I was starting to have feelings for him." I groaned, covering my face with my hands. "Not just *we're having sex* feelings, like maybe it could be more feelings."

"You think I didn't know that?" She yanked at my hands, giving me a warm smile. "Lo, you might think you're pretty smooth, but you're my sister and I know you. Besides, you haven't dated anyone for longer than two dates in what? A year or more? It was pretty obvious it was more than just sex."

I shook my head, wondering if I had genuinely been blind or just stupid. "It wasn't obvious to me. It just grew into more, and what's worse is, that I didn't realize how much I'd really wanted it."

"So, did you tell him and he didn't feel the same way? And why the hell did you need a pregnancy test? I get the feeling the two are somehow connected."

Morgan was right, ironically they were.

So, I started to recount the whole tale of how I went from realizing I was falling in love with Roman, to throwing up in the bathroom, to running into the bride who suspected she was in the family way.

I left out names, Morgan not knowing that *Eric Larsson* was Roman's brother and the groom, and *Tia Larsson* was the possibly knocked-up bride. It wasn't because I was worried about her saying anything; it just didn't change the situation regardless of who they were.

So, the bride was worried that an unplanned pregnancy would possibly screw up her new husband's job offer—the possibility of a future Oscar left unmentioned—and so I'd offered to help. My involvement kept me away from Roman, which prompted a stupid lie about Chase Anderson, followed by the spectacular finale of him finding the pregnancy test and assuming it was mine.

"Where does he live?" she demanded, rising off the mattress with a face full of fury. "Tell me exactly where to find him. How dare he assume anything about you? And even if you were pregnant, he wasn't exactly sitting at home playing *Magic: The Gathering* before you two got together. He's probably been involved in a few pregnancy tests of his own."

Ugh, funnily enough, hearing about Roman and his past didn't make me feel better.

When he was with me, his past didn't matter.

Neither did mine.

We only cared about what was in front of us.

"It doesn't matter anymore." I tried like hell to find the silver lining. "At least I found out how horrible he was *before* I spilled my guts and made a fool out of myself. It could have been so much worse."

I wasn't sure if I believed that; it didn't feel like it could get more painful than it already felt. And to make matters more horrible, I was going to have to see him tomorrow when I went back to work.

That was why office dating was frowned upon. Because only an idiot would believe you could go back to be friendly after an asshole had crushed your heart. In this case, I was the idiot.

I'm sure he didn't care.

He was probably looking forward to it, thinking up new ways to torment me. It would be like old times only one thousand times worse because unlike before, I knew he could be sweet and loving and be so goddamn kind.

"He can't honestly believe you would have slept with a client, Lauren." My sister tugged on my arm, shaking her head. "He has to know that you would never—"

"He clearly knows nothing." A breath hitched, my chest tight. "And it doesn't matter if he believes it, he freaking said it. Out loud. To my face. He said it like it could be a possibility, like I would ever use my body like that. It was more than just hurtful; it was malicious. And if he doesn't believe it and said it anyway, then that's almost worse."

Morgan nodded, her hand rubbing against the length of my arm. "I know, and you deserved better. He is going to have to live with that, having said those words to you. And even though he backed you into a corner, you took the high road. I'm so proud of you." Her hand squeezed. "You have more integrity in your little finger than most people do in their whole body."

"I can't believe I have to see him tomorrow," I groaned, fantasizing about getting a doctor's note excusing me from work. As tempting as it was, I'd already faked being sick to avoid him once, and I wasn't doing that again.

"I know it feels horrible, Lo." Morgan gently rubbed my back. "But I promise you, you are stronger than you think. You will go back in there tomorrow and you are going to kick ass, because you are one of the best damn lawyers the firm has ever seen. And he doesn't get to take that away from you, not him and his narrow-minded macho bullshit. You did the right thing, and someday he is going to regret walking away from the best damn woman that he's ever met."

A soft laugh escaped my lips. "You're my sister, you have to think I'm awesome, but *the best damn woman he's ever* met is a pretty big call."

Right then I would have settled for being someone he didn't hate and who he didn't want to hurt. I was pretty sure I was so far from the top of his list, I'd barely get a mention.

"For someone so smart, Lo, you can act super dumb." She shoved my shoulder gently. "He might have said all that other stuff, but he was in love with you too. Or starting to be. Why else would he have taken you to his brother's wedding? The ride on the bike, that isn't stuff you just do to get a woman into bed. After all, you guys were already sleeping together, right?"

Her words didn't give me comfort, possibly just confusing me more. "Is that you being kind and telling me I was a sure thing?"

"You were never a sure thing, sweetie, but all that effort, it had to mean *something.*" She wrapped her arms around me, the comfort they gave me immeasurable.

It was like I was sixteen again and this was my first heartbreak, she had always known exactly what to say.

"And the way he overreacted? Because every man assumes you're having sex with a client when you need to take a call." She rolled her eyes sarcastically. "It's completely illogical, there was nothing to even hint that. And if he didn't *care,*" she made quotation marks with her fingers, "would he care which client you were talking to, or how long you were powdering your nose. He cared *because* he was jealous, because maybe he was scared of what *he* was feeling. And I can almost bet that is the same as what you're feeling. If he honestly believed you'd acted inappropriately he wouldn't have bothered to confront you, he would have taken it to the bar. When have you ever known him to be compassionate in business?"

She was right about that.

I'd just recently seen a kinder side, but at work he was ruthless. And if he suspected someone was up to something, the last thing he'd do was talk about it. Instead, he would systematically plot their downfall. Not sure what it said about the situation, that he confronted me. Did he honestly not believe it? Or was that his version of throwing me a bone, giving me a "heads up" out of the kindness of his heart—my reward for time served or some other bullshit.

Neither gave me comfort.

"He didn't give me a chance." The sob got stuck in my throat. "He didn't even want to listen. He just assumed the worst and allowed himself to believe it. He should have known me better."

If the situation were reversed, I hoped I would have given him the benefit of the doubt. That the time we had spent and gotten to know each other counted more than a misunderstanding. That I *knew* him better than to assume all those horrible things he'd thought about me.

"I don't know if I'll ever forget the way he looked at me." My arms wrapped around my chest. "So cold, so detached. When he said he didn't care, Morgan, he meant *that*. I don't think I can ever forget or forgive how he made me feel."

"Forgive him?" Morgan scoffed. "That man needs to come back crawling on his hands and knees, saying sorry in at least four languages before you even consider it. But I am telling you, that dumbass was in love with you as much as you are him. Probably more, because let's face it, you're a hundred times better."

I didn't know what to believe, but Roman being in love with me didn't seem likely. I'm sure Morgan thought she knew what she was talking about, and if we were talking about a regular guy, she'd have probably been right. But there was nothing about Roman or the situation that was *regular*.

No, he wasn't in love with me; I doubted he had the ability to love *anyone* but himself. He was amused by me, possibly even fascinated, but that's where his feelings ended. And I wounded his ego, hurt his pride in front of an audience, so he decided that I needed to be hurt and punished too.

"I really liked him, Morgan." The pain cut deep and even still, I couldn't hate him. "*Really* liked him, and he hurt me so much."

"Oh, Lo." She gave me a squeeze. "It will get better, I promise."

God, I hoped she was right, because I never wanted to feel that way ever again.

CHAPTER #23

HE WAS ALREADY there when I got to work. He'd left his door open so I made sure I kept my steps measured and my head up as I walked past, but I didn't look inside.

I knew it was only a matter of time before I had to face him.

It was Monday, and we had our usual scheduled meeting with Daniel. There was no way I could avoid him, which was a shame because the last thing I wanted was to see his smug, beautiful face.

I'd spent the weekend absorbing the hurt, letting it consume me.

But I wasn't going to do that anymore.

Oh, it still hurt. Stung me like no other. But I had a job to do, and I wasn't going to let him or my previous bad decisions stop me from doing it.

There would be a cold day in hell before I would let him bring my integrity into question again. And if he even dared to breath a word of it, I would make sure it was his name that was destroyed and not mine.

But I wouldn't retaliate without just cause.

I wouldn't allow myself to sink to his level.

That was the difference between us. That, despite him, I would remain a decent person.

I was going to be better. Stronger. More proficient. And he, and those past few weeks, would fade into a memory of the time where I had been stupid.

Daniel Moss insisted there were wall clocks mounted in every single office. It made the "oh, I didn't realize the time," excuse redundant. So when I looked up on the wall and saw it was five minutes to nine, I rose out of my chair and walked to my door.

He must have had the same idea.

"Pierce." I nodded my hello, stepping out into the hall.

My pulse was racing even though I had thought I was prepared for this, seeing him two minutes before I had planned throwing me off my game.

But I wouldn't show it though.

Nope. I was rock solid.

"Harper." He looked surprised, but followed me to Daniel's office. I felt his strides just a half step behind me, his shadow looming like my dark mood had all weekend.

I reached Daniel's office first, pulling the door open and taking my usual spot at his meeting table. Roman—just saying his name made my skin crawl, which is why I had been avoiding it—did the same.

"Lauren, Roman." Daniel nodded, drumming his fingers on the desk. "Where are we on the Cane divorce?"

"It is signed by both parties," Roman answered, "I'm putting it in front of a judge today."

Daniel sighed. "And you're sure it will remain uncontested? I don't want one of our biggest clients saddled to this asshole for the next twelve months because someone decided they wanted a bigger piece of the pie."

"The terms of the settlement were that he sign a postnuptial agreement," I added, thankful I didn't sound either scared or like I was about to cry. "There would be no financial gain to stalling the divorce now, if anything, it will cost him money. Once the official waiting period is over, it will be finalized."

"Good." Daniel nodded, leaning back in his chair. "Then make it so." He waved his hand in the air. "I'll expect the two of you to continue to work with me on her account. With the patent and her new products, the workload is going to be heavy, so the two of you are going to be spending lots of quality time together." He smiled before adding, "I'm sure everyone is going to enjoy that."

Great. I forced my face to remain neutral even though I wanted to cringe.

It wasn't a surprise and I knew if I wanted to keep my job, working with Roman was going to have to continue. Even though my heart and my spirit were broken, I wouldn't let him see.

I wouldn't allow it.

"Excited to come up with some new ideas for Ms. Cane." The words were like acid in my mouth as I continued the smile. "Pierce and I won't let you down."

I felt him stiffen beside me, my response not one he was expecting but surprisingly he remained quiet.

"Good." Daniel nodded, taking Roman's silence as compliance and flipped open a folder in front of him. "Next, Lauren, the ITP fiber optics acquisition. I had a call from Anderson this morning, he wants to go over your prospects again."

Shit.

Currently, I hated Chase Anderson only slightly less than Roman Pierce. Not through any fault of his own, we had never met, and only had one brief conversation. But that man had caused nothing but trouble since the day Roman tossed him on my desk.

"I'll call his secretary and schedule a meeting." I forced the smile, wondering if I'd imagined the temperature drop in the room or it was Roman being frosty.

"Excellent." Daniel didn't seem to notice the sudden arctic chill and continued. "I have a couple of new cases we need to start by this afternoon. I'll email you both the details."

The meeting was shorter than usual for once, which meant I got a reprieve. I had no doubt it wasn't always going to be this easy, but for now, I was thankful. I'd deal with later's problems, later.

Not waiting for Roman, I was the first to leave my seat, walking out of Daniel's office without saying goodbye to either of them. My attempt at making it look like I was "all good" with the situation was failing miserably, but at least I wasn't crying and rocking in a corner. And I'd take the victories where I could get them.

"His secretary?" Roman's voice came from behind me.

Damn it. I'd almost made it to my door.

"Yes, Roman." I turned against my better judgment. I should have just ignored him. "It is customary when setting an appointment with a client that you call his or her secretary. It's actually a very old practice, I'm positive they would have covered it during your time at Yale."

He put his hands together and clapped, his grin a little less smug but still there. "Well done, Harper." His head tilted to the side. "But yes, I was aware of the process. I just figured since you two were calling each other during personal hours you'd bypass the whole formality. You two being so *close*, and all that."

I should have ignored him.

Should being the operative word in that sentence.

"Do you ever get tired of it?" I planted my hands on my hips, the anger bubbling inside of me with no way of containing it. "Being so interested in everything I do. I mean, I get it—I'm your biggest competition. And in the history of the firm, they have never offered two associates junior partner at the same time. One of us will have to go first, and it scares the hell out of you it *might* be me."

I expected him to laugh. To throw his head back, and for

those blue eyes to light up the way they always did, and tell me I was wrong. Because as much as I was saying all that stuff, I didn't believe Roman was worried about any of it.

But he didn't.

Instead he moved closer, narrowing his eyes as he leaned in. "You really think I'm worried about losing out junior partner to you?"

I couldn't decide if the sentence was loaded with sarcasm or distaste. Or maybe disbelief that I'd called out his bullshit instead of ignoring it.

"You *should* be." I stood my ground. "Because I'm a damn good lawyer, and you know it."

And without the theatrics of slamming the door—which was what I'd wanted to do—I walked into my office and calmly closed it.

It killed me.

I'd been gripping the handle so tight I was surprised it didn't come apart in my hand. But I'd done it.

Unlike him, I'd kept our rivalry professional even though there was so much more I could have said. I wouldn't allow myself to stoop to his level, deciding I needed to focus on work. He was being a schoolyard bully, taunting me into a reaction because nothing he said had any truth. And if me being the best associate Moss, Byrne and Carter had ever seen threatened him, then so be it. What had he said to me when we first met? He didn't need any more friends. Yeah, well neither did I.

With purpose driving me instead of pain—it was still there but it was going to be dealt with after hours—I picked up the phone and dialed Chase Anderson's secretary. The sooner I was done with his mind-numbing account, the better.

"Chase Anderson's office, this is Holly."

"Hi Holly, this is Lauren Harper from Moss, Byrne and Carter." I took a deep breath and slowly let it out. "I believe Mr. Anderson wanted to discuss the candidates I vetted for him."

"Oh yes, Ms. Harper. He's been waiting for your call, let me put you through."

Well, hopefully that meant he'd made a decision; I could think of little else that would make him want to talk to me.

"Lauren." My name used in place of a hello.

"Mr. Anderson."

"Uh-uh, I told you, it's Chase." He didn't do the last name thing, saying it messed with his Chi or some other shit.

"My apologies, *Chase*." I was glad he couldn't see me roll my eyes. "I take it that Anita has gone over the options I presented."

"Yeah, she did." I heard the rustling of papers. "It was very detailed."

We were only minutes into the conversation and I was on my second eye roll. "Well, Chase, it's my job to be detailed. Are you any closer to making a decision?"

It was pushier than I usually was, but I wanted anything associated with Roman Pierce eradicated from my life. And that included the stupid account he'd given me when I'd lost the bet, and the implication that had come with it. Besides, Chase had been dragging his feet for months on this, with three other associates previously vetting for him before he "shelved" the idea for another time.

I wanted to be the one to close him after all of them had failed.

"I have." His answer almost knocked me off my chair. "I want to go with *Focus Solutions*, have the paperwork drawn up and make them an offer. And no offense, Lauren, but I only deal with partners when I sign."

"Of course, if that is what you prefer." I fought the urge to cheer, just stopping short of getting on my knees and giving thanks. "I'll speak to Mr. Carter and schedule a meeting once Focus accepts the offer."

"Good." I was ready for his goodbye when he added. "By

the way, Anita was really impressed by you and she doesn't get impressed easily."

"Well, thank you, please extend my thanks and best wishes to her."

Anita had barely cracked a smile during the whole meeting so it was surprising to hear she was impressed. It had been strictly business, refreshing considering most meetings were filled with the usual male posturing.

"Is there anything else?" I added when he hadn't ended the call.

He cleared his throat. "Actually, yes there is. This is . . ." Pause. "Well, it's kind of a delicate matter and I'm not very comfortable discussing it to be honest."

My eyes lifted to the celling and asked God why.

What was it about me and sensitive matters? And how did I always find myself in the middle of them? First, it had been Roman with Eric and Tia's prenup, then there was Tia's pregnancy scare at her wedding, and now it was Chase Anderson's who knows what.

Maybe I smiled too much, or there was something overly friendly about my face. But the last time I checked I didn't have an advice column.

"Chase." I shook my head cursing myself for not ending this conversation when I had the chance. "Anything you tell me is confidential. Whatever it is, it's privileged information that I can't and won't share."

He took a deep breath. "And how does that work with sharing information in your firm? Especially sharing what I tell you with other lawyers?"

What?

While it wasn't a question we got asked a lot, a few of our more seasoned clients didn't like their information shared. Some were delusional, believing California law offices were rife with corporate espionage. Others had legitimate reasons, like they played golf with one of the partners and didn't want their dirty laundry aired.

But Chase Anderson talking about limiting authorized disclosure was the *exact* thing I'd lied about to Roman at Eric and Tia's wedding.

This had to be some kind sick of joke.

"Lauren?"

Shit.

"I'm sorry, Chase, yes, I'm here." I shook my head, still not believing the coincidence. "Of course you can limit how your information is shared in the firm and that includes with who. So, yes, anything you say to me will be kept confidential even with members of my firm."

"Good. Good." He blew out a breath. "Because it is about Roman Pierce."

And just when I thought this day couldn't get any worse.

"Okay, Chase." There weren't enough middle fingers to deal with this conversation. "Tell me about Roman."

THE PHONE CALL with Chase Anderson was extremely enlightening. Answered a lot of questions too. Like why the hell Roman seemed to dislike him so much, and why he had been so eager to palm it off on me.

Anita Anderson.

Roman and the COO of ITP had met a little over a year ago before he'd started with Moss, Byrne and Carter. And apparently one drunken night was all she needed to fall in love with him.

Roman Pierce didn't share the sentiment.

So, while Anita accepted they weren't destined for a life of eternal happiness, she still harbored feelings of wanting to rip his balls off.

I totally understood the compulsion.

And while yes, she'll admit he never led her on, and she had mistook their one-night stand for more than it was, she refused to work with a man who, in her mind, broke her heart. And the mystery of ITP dragging their feet on the fiber options acquisition was solved.

Anita wanted nothing to do with Moss, Byrne and Carter as long as Roman was part of the firm. And our initial meeting had been set so she could string me along like she had the other associates who had come before me with no intention of us ever closing. But for some reason during our meeting she changed her mind.

Chase hated Roman because he hurt—however unintentionally—his sister. And from what I'd learned about him, he probably saw a lot of himself in the situation. His string of flings with young, smart and beautiful women was well documented, which was why Roman would wrongly assume he'd be interested in me. I wasn't sure if that was a compliment or an insult, but unlike Roman, Chase Anderson didn't date women he worked with. Smart man.

Instead, he allowed Anita to have her fun, torturing whoever Moss, Byrne and Carter sent over, even if it did mean they were slow on an acquisition. I think she was secretly hoping Roman would one day show up. I couldn't even guess what the outcome would have been.

Millionaires, what's a few hundred thousand dollars lost when you had a grudge to settle?

But now the deal was almost done, and with Anita no longer interested in playing the game, ITP was out. And what Chase needed was me—because I had nothing better to do than be dragged into everyone else's problems—to find an amicable dissolution of the professional relationship. Because obviously he didn't want to admit he was wasting the firm's time, or advertise that his sister was slightly vindictive and emotional when it came to a certain someone.

It took me most of the day.

I'd told Moss and Carter the great news about the ITP acquisition, and made an offer to Focus. Of course, they accepted because it was either be welcomed into the ITP family or be taken over by administrators. The lesser of the two evils it seemed, was to get into bed with Chase.

Next point of business was finding a way to sever ties with ITP, but not have it be obvious. At least it wasn't as boring as the data I had previously digested for them, and it gave me a reason to be stuck in my office all day.

Roman, and all the things he made me feel, were avoided as I buried myself in work. The hurt, the anger—how easily I'd fallen for him, all got brushed aside. It was easier to be good at my job than to accept how much I sucked at choosing someone to love me.

And unlike what he'd had with Anita, Roman let me believe we'd been more.

I was still hunched over my desk even though the clock on the wall said seven o'clock. I was secretly hoping that when I did eventually leave, Roman would be long gone and I'd be spared seeing his stupid, gorgeous face.

My ITP file was open on my computer as my fingers curled around my phone. "You need to buy Mack Media."

"The app developers who had that game Crazy Fish and haven't done anything since?" Chase asked, who was also still at his desk. "Why the hell would I buy them?"

"Because we have MicroTech as clients. And they are the parent company of Dime Time, the developers of Fish Frenzy, which is the direct competition to Mack Media's game. It would be a conflict of interest for us, and MicroTech was one of Carter's original clients. There is no way he'd let them go, which means—"

"I would gracefully bow out, thank Moss, Byrne and Cater for their service, and take my business to a new firm who doesn't represent a shitty app about fish." He took a deep breath. "Anita was right, you really are something."

"Crazy Fish is still making money, there are worse things to have in your portfolio. Who knows, maybe you can inject some new ideas into their development team and launch the next addictive app."

It was the best solution and one that meant no one had to know anything about anything.

Except for me, who lately had become the keeper of all secrets.

Pity it hadn't worked out to be a good thing.

"I'll get Anita to start the ball rolling, contact the firm once we're in final talks and let one of the partners break the bad news to me. There's no need for you to get your hands dirty on this."

"Thank you." I'm sure the partners wouldn't have been thrilled at the loss of ITP's business, but it did mean we were able to pursue some other clients in the same industry. And after the loss of company time in recent months, I'm sure no one would be too sad to see them go.

We said our goodbyes, with Chase letting me know if I ever wanted to leave and become their in-house counsel, there was a place for me at ITP. I politely declined, not wanting to sentence myself to Tech Hell for all eternity.

Plus, there wasn't a chance in hell I was moving to Palo Alto.

I shut down my computer and grabbed my handbag, breathing a sigh of relief as I looked at the clock.

I'd survived.

It still hurt just as much, and I was still just as angry, but I'd made it an entire day. I didn't crumble or cry, and from the outside looking in, I had my shit together.

Much to my disgust, my body still ached for him, still wanted to feel his kisses. Trust me, I was just as appalled as any sane person would be. But while my heart was shattered, thankfully my mind was still intact, which reminded me why I would never allow him to get close to us again.

In any capacity—body, mind or heart.

As I left my office, I noticed his door was closed with the light spilling between the gap on the floor.

He was still there.

Shit.

Shaking my head and thankful at least I didn't have to see him, I flipped off the closed door and took the elevator down to the lobby. If I hadn't seen him by now, the chances of running into him tonight were slim.

Thank God for small mercies.

"Hi!"

It seemed my thanks to God were somewhat premature.

Standing in front of me was a tall blond with large breasts. I couldn't even call her cute because she was so far removed from that. She was beautiful, stunning, and gorgeous in ways I didn't think were possible.

And unfortunately, I had seen her before.

"Hi Carla, how are you?" I managed to force the words out, knowing none of this was her fault and yet hating her all the same.

Her pouty pink lips spread into a smile. "Great thank you, Lauren. Is Roman still upstairs? We're supposed to meet down here but I'm a little early."

"Yeah, I think so." I shrugged trying to sound like I really didn't care.

Walk away, Lauren.

Leave him and his whatever and go home.

"I thought you guys got together on Tuesdays."

Shit, it came out of my mouth before I'd had a chance to stop it.

"Ha, yeah." She laughed, her nose wrinkling. "But it's been a while, so I guess he couldn't wait."

Yeah, I guessed so.

"Well, it was good seeing you again," I lied as the pain throbbed in my chest. "Have a good night." I waved, nodding to the security guard as he let me out.

It had been two days.

Two days since the wedding and two days since . . . Roman and I broke up. And even though I knew we were no longer together and he had every right to be with whoever he wanted, I still couldn't believe he'd called her so soon.

Like I'd been nothing, replaced without a second thought.

And all the ways I'd told myself I'd been a badass all day unraveled as I cried the whole way home.

CHAPTER #24

SUCCESS AND LIVING a good life was the best revenge.

The person or people who had wronged you would suffer more from seeing you rise above than they ever would from whatever petty retribution you had planned.

So, as hard as it was, I put on my sexiest work outfit, made sure my makeup was on point. And I went to work looking like I didn't want to murder the man who tore my heart into a million tiny pieces.

I made sure I said hello to everyone, cheerily waving as I floated down the hall, and even stopped right outside Roman's open doorway.

"Hey, Pierce." I smiled, leaning against the jamb. "I hope Carla found you okay last night. I would have walked her up here myself, but I was in a hurry."

I wanted him to know that I knew.

I didn't care if Carla had mentioned our little meeting or not, I wasn't going to pretend I hadn't seen or known what her reappearance meant. And while he probably didn't care either way, it made me feel empowered to stand there and tell him, and force him to look at me when I did.

"Harper." His eyes rolled over the length of my body, slowly making their way back to my eyes. "I—"

It was the first time I'd ever seen Roman Pierce speechless.

I wasn't sure if it was the outfit, my attitude or being called out for being a piece of shit. Maybe it was a combination of all three. And it felt awesome to toss him a wave and tell him, "I'll see you later, I have work to do," and stride to my office like a conqueror.

For the whole day I held tight to the fake-it-until-you-make-it mentality. Looking him the eye every single time our paths crossed and acknowledging his presence. And by mid afternoon the smiles were no longer forced, my mouth spreading into a grin at the sight of him and knowing he didn't break me.

By the next day it was even easier.

Another killer outfit—I was pushing the boundaries of my corporate wear but nothing to get me hauled in by HR—and an even bigger killer attitude.

Daniel had even designated a new case, calling us into his office for another meeting and I hadn't backed down once. Showing both of them exactly what kind of lawyer I was.

But later that Wednesday, everything changed.

The door slammed behind him. "We need to talk."

I looked up from my computer, not expecting him but not all that surprised either. He might have the most amazing poker face I'd ever seen, but I could sense he was cracking.

"About what, Roman? I have a mountain of work to get through and I don't have time to chat." My hand waved to the pile of files sitting beside me.

His jaw tightened as he took the few steps from my door to the desk. "You *know* about what."

Unfortunately, I didn't.

The topic of conversation could have been anything, starting with him being a dick. Or it might have been about the Anderson account that soon would no longer be ours. Or it could have been about the ChemCal suit we'd been given two days ago, where I'd argued and proven that my direction for our defense was by far superior to his.

Or possibly, that he was a dick.

"Roman," I sighed, shaking my head like I pitied him. "As much as I would like the ability to possess mind-reading skills, I don't. It's something I thank God daily for, considering I work so closely to you." I leaned back into my chair. "I think I'd go blind with all those tits and ass floating around in my head. How do you get anything done?"

Just like old times, only this time around I was smarter, sharper and about one thousand times more prepared for his bullshit. I'd almost built a wall around my heart he would never penetrate again, the security it gave me making me feel brave.

His eyes caught on mine with no hint of a smile. "I had dinner with Tia and Eric last night."

Oh, so *that* was the conversation he wanted to have. The one where he found out the truth and realized what a horrible and hurtful prick he'd been. Funny how I knew it would eventually come, I just wasn't sure he had the balls to face me when it did. Especially not come into my office and demand anything from me considering what had happened.

"Are they well, Roman?" I gave him *nothing*, not even an inch of an opening. "How's married life treating them?"

He had the nerve to look sorry. "Lauren—"

"Don't fucking, *Lauren* me." I slammed my hands down on the desk, the sound of my name making me snap. "Walk out the door, Roman. Turn around and go back to where you came from because we have nothing more to say to each other."

I'd been doing so well and holding it together, but him calling me Lauren was not something I would allow. He didn't get to do that anymore. He'd given up that right.

"Why didn't you tell me?" He raked his hand through his hair in frustration. "Why the hell did you let me believe—"

"I didn't *let* you do anything." I couldn't stand it anymore. "You controlled what you thought and what you believed. And if those conclusions were so easy to come to, then you never knew me at all. And you already told me that you hadn't cared about me. So it's not like we could argue that someone who gave a shit might give another person the benefit of the doubt." The laugh ironic as it made its way up my throat. "There are times in life when you have to make choices, Roman. I made mine that day. I chose to help someone else, and I don't regret it. It's not my place for me to make yours."

He stepped back, eyes peeled open in surprise like I'd punched him right in the gut.

I'm sure he wasn't expecting me to fall to my feet and forgive him the minute he walked through the door, but I think deep down he hoped for it. Maybe for me to leap out of my chair and gasping between kisses how much I missed him. Funny thing was, I did miss him, and the ache to kiss him was so real on my lips that I had to beg myself not to.

Because right now I hated him more than I loved him.

Or at least, I *hoped* I did.

"It was a mistake, Lauren." He refused to leave, his feet making up the space they'd lost seconds before as he came closer. "I'm sor—"

"Get out." I didn't let him finish the word, pointing to the door.

Sorry didn't make things all right. It didn't change anything, and it sure as hell didn't communicate to me that he was genuinely apologetic.

It meant nothing.

Nothing.

It was something to say when you screwed up that you hoped would make it better, and it got tossed around waaaaaaay too easily.

He stood still, not leaving like I'd asked and looked at me with defiance. "You really want me to leave?"

"Yes." I didn't hesitate, refusing to do this on his terms.

"Fine." He took a step back, keeping his eyes on me the entire time. "But we're not done here."

I didn't bother dignifying his statement with a response, watching him leave and close the door before I slumped into my chair.

It's what I had wanted since Saturday.

Since I'd walked out Eric's door and called my sister to come get me. I'd dreamt about him finding out the truth, about looking at me and knowing that while he might not have agreed with them, I had my reasons.

And in all those times I'd imagined and played it in my mind, it had never felt as horrible as it did just then.

There was no vindication, no relief, and if I was honest, it almost felt worse. Because despite him finding out, we'd both still lost.

My head dropped into my hands and I took slow, deep, breaths.

I thought I was stronger than this, that I wouldn't still want him. And even though I wasn't stupid enough to let it happen, it didn't stop the pang in my heart.

Goddamn it.

HE DIDN'T RETURN to my office or revisit our conversation. I wasn't sure how I felt about it, but at least I was able to get through the rest of my day without having a nervous breakdown at work. Got to take the win when you can.

And as I walked past his office as I was leaving for the day, I'd noticed the door was open and the room was empty.

Everything was immaculate as usual—he hadn't come in

after talking to me and trashed the place—but it was rare for him to leave early. I checked my phone, noticing it was only six p.m., and while regular office hours didn't really apply to us, it seemed weird that he was gone.

Ignoring the anomaly while silently contemplating its significance, I drove home, thankful Morgan was back to working day shifts and was there to welcome me.

"Did he get on his knees and beg?" she asked, the idea of a healthy dinner shelved. Instead, she insisted we get into our PJs, order pizza and break out the biggest bottle of wine she could find.

"No, he tried to say sorry, like one stupid word is going to fix it," I slurred, possibly drinking most of the bottle on my own. "Like did he not remember what the hell he'd said? In what universe is an apology going to fix that?"

Morgan took a sip of her wine, wisely not gulping it like I had. "Such a jackass. We already agreed he needed to say sorry in at least four languages, he could have at least groveled a little."

Roman groveling wasn't something I ever expected to see. I doubted he even knew how. But the thought of him on his knees, scuffing the fabric of his precious expensive suit did make me smile a little. Though chances were, it might have been the wine that was responsible for the smile.

We were mostly done with dinner and already into our second bottle of wine when there was a knock at the door. My heart skipped a beat or two as I looked over at my sister. I just *knew* it was him.

"I don't want to see him." I dropped my voice to a whisper, shaking my head as my eyes stayed glued to the door. "I don't want him here."

She reached out and gave my hand a reassuring squeeze. "Then I'll tell him to leave. Just sit tight and I'll go get it."

I wasn't going to leave the room and hide, even though it would have been the easier option. Instead, I shuffled back onto the couch and watched as Morgan opened the front door.

She stood at the threshold, her arm bracing the wood as she turned around, looking mildly spooked. "Any idea why Eric Larsson is at our apartment?"

"Hey, you must be Lauren's sister, Morgan." He held out his hand, blinding her with his Hollywood smile.

It would have been easier if it had just been Roman, the intricacies of his family tree not yet explained to Morgan. There had been other things on my mind, like having my heart broken.

"Wow, you know our names." She shook his hand a little too enthusiastically. "Did Lauren do some legal work for you?" She caught herself, her hand flying up to her mouth. "I mean, you don't have to answer that, it's none of my business. I'm just . . . well, it's not every day a movie star lands on your doorstep." A nervous laugh escaped her lips.

"Thanks, mind if I come in?" he asked her but looked over at me, his eyebrow rose as he waited for permission.

"Yes, yes of course." Morgan pulled him through the doorway, missing the whole exchange. "How rude of me, you are very welcome. Come in."

It wasn't often that Morgan was reduced to a babbling mess, but springing a celebrity on her when we were wearing pajamas and drinking seemed to be the tipping point.

"Hey, Eric." I rose from the couch. "Something we can do for you?" I asked causally, ignoring the obvious reason he was here.

It wasn't like Roman to ask someone to play interference on his behalf, but then again, I wouldn't put it past him either. "I was hoping to have a chat." He looked over at Morgan and then back to me. "That is, if you can make the time."

I wondered if charisma and charm were hardwired to the Larsson DNA or if it was something they picked up after they came out of the uterus. That and a smile that could simultaneously melt panties, disengage brain cells, and render intelligent woman stupid. Because that lethal combination had a lot to answer for.

"Sure, we can chat." I ignored that I wasn't dressed appropriately, and while not drunk, had questionable sobriety. "Morgan, can you—"

"I have something to do." She grabbed the empty bottle of wine and the half full one and bundled them into her hands. "It was nice meeting you, Eric." She disappeared without being asked.

"She didn't know?" Eric nodded in the direction my sister had scampered as I invited him to take a seat.

"That you're Roman's brother or that I know you?" I asked, shrugging because both the answers were the same. "No, she didn't know anything other than I work with a jerk that I was stupid enough to date."

"Tia told me everything." He shook his head, having the same tendency as his brother to run his hand through his hair when frustrated. "That she thought she was pregnant and that you talked her off the ledge."

"Lila was doing most of the heavy lifting," I offered, my involvement more in procurement and evidence collection. "I just figured speculating wasn't doing anyone any good, and I was in a position to change that."

"She was right, you know." He laughed, before correcting himself. "Well, *half right*. I would have turned down the movie if she'd been pregnant. There was no way I would have left and missed a second of any of it. And her coming with me isn't an option, so it would have been my only choice." He turned and focused on me. "But I would *never* have regretted it, or ever blamed her for some perceived missed opportunity."

"Well, people can't think clearly when they are emotional," I offered, knowing the last thing Tia would have wanted was for him to be forced to make the choice.

"Yeah, emotions can really screw with someone's head. Makes you do all kinds of things that aren't rational and/or smart." He nodded, and it was clear we were no longer talking about his wife.

"Eric, he's your brother." The bias not needed to be clarified. "But the way he acted . . ." I shook my head, not even able to finish the sentence.

"I know you don't know me, but I know him." He continued when I didn't speak. "And he is the most level-headed man I've ever met. He's analytical and systematic, and when he makes a decision, he takes emotion out of it completely."

He held his hand up, stopping me from interrupting.

"But he was different with you."

I took a deep breath. "What do you want me to say, Eric? He looked me right in the eye and told me he didn't even care about me. That I embarrassed him, and that's not even taking into account the shit he assumed when he found the pregnancy test. I mean, why the hell would I take a pregnancy test at someone else's house? I know I wasn't giving him a lot to go on, but come on. Not to mention that he assumed it was someone else's kid. A *client's* no less. Because calling me a shitty person wasn't good enough for him, he had to attack my integrity and morality too. Like I'm the kind of person who would not only be manipulative, but have no honor either. It takes real talent to be that offensive, and it isn't something he should be proud of."

"So . . ." He rubbed the back of his neck. "Do you know all the loopholes to get us off the murder charge if we kill him? That sounds like it might be our only option."

A laugh bubbled up my throat, the situation too weird not to be funny. I was glad he wasn't giving me the he-made-a-mistake-stop-being-such-a-bitch speech I was expecting. "We can make it look like an accident, simpler than worrying about arguing justifiable cause."

"I have a bunch of meds that can make it look like natural causes." Morgan emerged from the kitchen, the glass of wine in her hand looking suspiciously full. "Sorry, I was eavesdropping." She didn't even try to hide it. "I'm willing to overlook that my sister has been dating a movie star's brother for weeks and didn't tell me, if you let me in on this action." She took another swallow. "Plus, I was already involved in both obtaining the pregnancy test that I now know was for your wife, and picking up my sister when your brother acted like an ass. He's lucky I have been biding my time up until this point."

"Morgan is a little protective." I grabbed the wine from her hand, trying to minimize the damage. "Older siblings." I laughed, as I pulled her down onto the couch.

"Yeah, they're funny like that." He winked as he stood up. "I know nothing I say is going to change anything, but for what it's worth he left our wedding shortly after you did. We assumed you had left together, and didn't know different until Nick found him obnoxiously drunk at his apartment the next morning. Then he and Dave took turns babysitting him to make sure he didn't end up drinking himself into a coma or doing something even more stupid."

"I didn't know." I shook my head, not even imagining he would have left his own brother's wedding. "He seemed fine on Monday."

"Yeah, that was after he managed to pull his shit together and before he'd found out. He'd come clean about the two of you going your separate ways to Nick, but had been cagy about the details. It wasn't until they told me that we put two and two together and told him the truth. It's the closest I've ever seen him to looking destroyed."

"I'm not heartless, Eric." I sighed, joining him as I stood. "I take no pleasure in any of it. I don't want to hurt him."

"All I'm saying is, if there is even the slightest chance," he sunk his hands into his pockets, "talk to him. That's all I'm asking. And in case you were wondering, he didn't send me. He doesn't even know I'm here, and will probably be pissed off I got involved." He shrugged. "Someone has to save him from himself."

"Well, thanks for coming." I stuck out my hand, feeling more confused now about Roman, and my feelings, than before he walked in. "I'm not making any promises."

"Not asking for any." He shook my hand before turning to Morgan. "Nice meeting you."

"Movie star or not, if Lo decides we kill him, we're sticking with that plan." Morgan eyed him hard, no longer awestruck.

He nodded as I walked him out. "I'll help you hide the body."

We said our goodbyes and I shut the door. I didn't even need to turn around to know Morgan was standing right behind me.

"I was going to tell you." I lifted my hands in defense. "Honestly."

She pulled me into a hug. "I know. I'm not mad. Maybe a little jealous your life is more exciting than mine, but never mad."

"I just don't know, Morgan." My head rested on her shoulder. "It's a lot, and then two days later he was with someone else."

"Hey, you don't have to decide anything tonight. Why don't you sleep on it and see how you feel about it in the morning. Then if you feel like talking to him, just talk."

She made a good point. Nothing was going to be achieved tonight, and I had a lot to think about. At least one positive thing had come out of the whole mess. There were no more secrets and everyone knew the truth.

Only thing left to figure out was, was it too late?

CHAPTER #25

THERE WAS A reason I avoided heavy drinking on a weeknight. And at six a.m. when my alarm announced with great joy that it was time to get my sorry butt out of bed, there weren't enough middle fingers or cups of coffee to make me okay with it.

By some miracle I'd made it to work on time. Still worried I might have the remnants of a higher-than-legal blood alcohol level, I decided to catch a cab to work and leave my car at home. Morgan, who didn't start until later in the day, was confident she'd be okay and offered to pick me up after we both finished.

But Roman wasn't there.

First, I assumed he was running late—out of character but anything was possible—or had a morning meeting. But when he hadn't arrived by lunchtime, I knew something was off.

"Hey." I stepped into Daniel's office, his head buried in a file as usual. "Where's Pierce this morning? Did the Mothership finally come and take him back home?"

"He's taken a personal day." He didn't look up. "Charlotte can help you this afternoon if you need it."

A personal day?

"Is he sick?" I asked, knowing that unless some freak virus

took hold in the last twenty-four hours, he wasn't.

"I didn't ask." Daniel lowered his pen and raised his eyes. "Is there anything else you needed?"

"Nope, all good." I smiled, slowly backing away. "I'll get back to work, one of us has to if the other one is slacking."

The discomfort churned in my gut as I shut Daniel's door and walked back to my office.

In all the time I'd know Roman, he'd never taken a day off. Never taken a sick day, and would probably still find a way to come into work if he was bleeding out of his eyeballs.

It was too much of a coincidence that yesterday we had our chat, and today he was gone, but he wasn't the kind of guy who ran. No, he took on a problem head on, he'd even said—much to my annoyance—the conversation wasn't done.

So where the hell was he?

I picked up my phone, my fingers restless on the surface as I debated calling him.

No, that was probably his plan and I wouldn't do that even if I wanted to.

Instead, I ignored the gnawing need to call and busied myself with work, the minutes ticking slower than they usually did until it was time to go home.

"You ready, Lo?" Morgan knocked at my door; last night's wine-itis making her look more tired than usual. "I'm wiped, you cool if we get takeout again tonight?"

I shut off my computer and grabbed my handbag. "I'm ready. And takeout is great, but let's skip the wine this time."

She nodded in agreement as she followed me out, my eyes snagging on Roman's open door as we left.

"He already gone for the day?" Morgan's eyebrows rose, her head tipping in the direction of Roman's office as we made our way to the elevator.

"Didn't turn up." I pressed the button and started our descent. "You don't think he would have done something, right? Eric said he was in bad shape on the weekend but . . ."

While I knew Roman was a grown man who made his own decisions—good or bad—and I was no way responsible for any of them, I wasn't a total heartless bitch.

"You want to go past his apartment and make sure he's okay?" she offered, the elevator dinging as we arrived at the lobby.

"No," I scoffed as we walked to her car.

It was ridiculous to even assume that I was the cause of his absence. How conceited did you have to be to draw that stupid conclusion? It probably had nothing to do with me.

He was probably screwing one of the multiple women in his rotation, not even giving me a second thought, and here I was concerned about his welfare.

Unless . . .

Goddamn it.

"Fine." My knuckles went white as I grabbed the door handle. "But if he's done something stupid, I'm going to kill him."

Morgan laughed, sliding into the driver's side. "I'll help you."

Anxiety filled me the closer we got to his apartment. And while I knew it could have been an elaborate plan to lure me there so we could talk, I needed to know that he was okay. Because, despite how many times I told myself I didn't trust him, didn't love him and no longer wanted to be with him—my heart knew otherwise. My heart, I'd decided, was an asshole.

"He's not here." The doorman held the phone away from his ear after buzzing him one last time. The three attempts he'd made previously I'd deemed insufficient and insisted he try again.

"Or he's hurt and unable to answer the door," I added, trying not to panic. "I think we should go up there and check."

"Ma'am, I just can't let you into someone's private residence unannounced." He lowered the phone, his impatience growing by the second. "You aren't on his list."

I didn't care about the stupid rules, or the dumb list. All I needed to know was that Roman wasn't lying in a pool of his own vomit. Or if there *was* something wrong, that I hadn't been the catalyst.

"Perhaps try calling his cell phone." The doorman gave me an unhelpful grin. "Or a family member."

His suggestion and his condescending smile just made things worse, compounded by the fact he had seen me numerous times on our way to Roman's apartment.

"Let's just go, Lo." Morgan tugged on my arm. "We'll try calling, thanks." She nodded to the doorman, probably worried he was going to call the cops.

I left under protest but not before giving the doorman the death stare. Oh, I knew he was only doing his job, but I was still not happy.

My reluctance to call Roman was over by the time we'd returned to Morgan's car. I just needed to hear he was okay, and then hang up so I could go back to being mad at him again.

The phone diverted straight to voicemail.

"I'm going to try him again when we get to the apartment." Hoping the reason his phone didn't ring was because he was on another call. "And if he still doesn't answer, I'm going to call his sister-in-law."

Using a client's phone number for unofficial business wasn't something I'd ever done before, but I would do what I had to do.

Morgan parked the car and we made our way to our front door, a wrapped box sitting in front of it.

"What is it?" Morgan asked as I dropped to my knees.

"I don't know."

I opened it and found a bottle of Macallan 18-year-old scotch with a note taped to the neck.

You hate flowers so I had to get creative.
I'm sorry.
Roman x

PS. We're not done.
PPS. Don't take it out on the scotch, it's not his fault I was an asshole.

My pulse quickened as I rolled the bottle in my hand, remembering the last few times we'd shared a drink. He'd never once asked me if I'd preferred a cocktail or some other "girlie" option like most men did. I wondered why I hadn't noticed up until now.

And it was true I hated flowers. They aggravated my sinuses and made me sneeze, but it wasn't the sort of thing we'd ever discussed. The one time I'd received flowers at work I'd discreetly given them to Stephanie, Daniel's secretary, but that had happened months ago.

"Well, I guess we can safely assume he isn't in any danger." Morgan read over my shoulder as she unlocked the door. "Nice touch with the scotch, flowers always made you sneeze."

As I clutched the bottle to my chest, I tried to call him, but again I was diverted back to voicemail.

"This doesn't change anything," I said out loud assuming it was for Morgan's benefit but it had really been for mine.

So he'd noticed I preferred single malts rather than sangrias. Or that flowers weren't really my thing. That didn't mean I'd just forgive him.

Morgan shrugged, her grin hinting otherwise. "Nope, doesn't change anything."

I didn't try calling again, deciding it was probably better to wait until tomorrow to talk to him. Then I'd hopefully have a clearer idea in my head of what I wanted to say to him.

Except the next day I arrived at work, and his office was still empty.

"Roman is still gone?" I asked Stephanie who happened to be walking past, my hand hesitating on my door.

She smiled, oblivious to how fast my pulse was racing. "Yeah, he's taken another personal day."

Great. *Another* personal day.

As I pushed open the door to my office, I almost lost my breath.

On the wall we shared that separated our offices, a huge whiteboard had been mounted, covered in his handwriting with a stack of markers sitting on my desk. There was a note taped on top.

You always preferred to see the problem laid out in front of you.

I've listed every reason you could possibly have for never speaking to me again, starting with me being a massive prick. I'd love to tell you these reasons are no longer valid, but we both know I'm a jerk and will probably continue to be.

What I can promise is that if you give me another chance, I'll never hurt you again.

I'm sorry.

Roman x

PS. The marker squeaked over every word.

PPS. I only pretended to hate it so much because it made you smile, and your smile was the highlight of my day.

PPPS. We're still not done.

The surface of the whiteboard was covered with words and sentences, like Roman's personality had bled all over it. Some of them were funny like:

I wear pretentious suits.

While others were incredibly endearing.

When I was eight I replaced the sugar with the salt and then made Nick take the blame for it.

And then there were more sobering ones.

I'm a terrible boyfriend.

I lose my temper too easily when it comes to the people I care about.

I get jealous.

I say things even if I don't believe them when I feel backed into a corner. Even if deep down I know there is no way it could be the truth, it feels easier than being vulnerable.

Until finally I saw at the very bottom.

I hurt you.

My eyes started to water as I touched the whiteboard, the words smudging under my palm.

I reached into my handbag and tried to call him but once again was diverted to voicemail. The sound of his recorded message was a small comfort as I wiped away all his faults from the surface of the board.

I didn't need to see them anymore, and I didn't want anyone else to either.

My butt sunk into my chair as I looked at the blank wall, and I knew I couldn't sit there any longer. Daniel was probably going to lose his damn mind, but I didn't care as I walked to his office and knocked on the door.

"Come in." He waved, his eyes glued to his computer screen. "What do you need?"

I cleared my throat, hoping my voice did sound like I was about to cry. "I need to take a personal day."

His head snapped up, his eyes narrowing as they focused on me. "It's Friday, Lauren, and we're already one down."

"I know." I nodded, appreciating that I was asking a lot. "And if this wasn't important, I wouldn't be asking. I'll make up the time, I promise, but I need to go."

His nostrils faired in annoyance as he leaned back in his chair. "Fine, go." He waved his hand in the air. "But on Monday I better have both of my associates or there is going to be hell to pay."

"We'll be here," I promised as I backed away toward the door. "Thank you."

I grabbed my things and left the office, my heart in my throat as I got to my car and started to drive.

I wasn't sure where I'd find Roman, but figured I'd start at his apartment.

CHAPTER 26

ROMAN'S EVIL DOORMAN was still not my biggest fan.

"Ma'am. I've told you he's not in." He lowered the phone, his displeasure of dealing with me evident after having buzzed Roman's apartment three times and me insisting he try again.

"Well, has he been home in the last two days?" I asked, giving him judgy eyes right back.

His smile tightened. "Unfortunately, I can't give out the personal information of our residents. I'm sorry, but I can't help you."

"Whatever." I slapped the desk like a child throwing a tantrum. Meanwhile, I was calculating the probability of being able to slip past him and make it to the elevator before he called security. My heels were a problem for sure, as was the detainment and possible arrest that was sure to follow.

Deciding a day in lockup wouldn't help my cause, I left Roman's apartment and headed back to mine. I assumed he had some kind of plan, so while it wasn't in my nature to wait, it was probably going to be him who made the next move.

There was a box sitting in front of my door when I got there, and beside it was Roman, who looked clearly surprised to see me.

His hair was mussed, probably from running his fingers

through it too many times, and there was a smattering of stubble across his jaw. He was also without his suit, instead wearing jeans and a T-shirt with no jacket.

"I thought you would be at work?" he said when I didn't speak, still frozen in place, his clear blue eyes widening as I looked at him.

"Personal day." The word wheezed out of me as my heart thumped. I took a step closer, desperately wanting to touch him but stopping myself all the same. "What's in the box?"

He leaned against the wall, his eyes dipping down to it. "Why don't I leave and you can open it."

I took another step. "I don't want that."

"The box?"

"You to leave."

His eyes scanned mine, but he stayed where he was. "Can we go inside and talk?"

"No," I answered quickly, knowing the minute I got him alone inside my apartment we would be doing something other than talking. And as much as I wanted to kiss him, hold him and touch him, there were things I needed to know first. "Not inside, but we can talk."

He nodded, blowing out a slow breath. "That's fair, Lauren—"

"Where have you been?" I didn't let him finish. "Why haven't you been answering you phone? And why did you see Carla on Monday? Did you want me to see her, is that why you told her to meet you at your office? And while we're talking about women you used to screw, why didn't you tell me about Anita Anderson?" I ran out of breath, but I still had questions.

"I've slept at home but spent the last few days on my bike." He answered the first question before I got to add any more. "It helps me think, and there's less chance of me doing something stupid like camping out on your doorstep like a stalker."

I tried not to smile. "I never knew you had stalking tendencies."

His mouth curled into a lopsided grin. "It was on the board, listed under *jealous son of a bitch* and *moronic asshole.*"

"Ahhh, I must have missed it."

"And my phone has been off because I knew you needed time, and I didn't want to talk to anyone unless it was you." He pulled it out of his back pocket, the screen completely black. "I checked my messages a couple of times a day but you never left me any."

I swallowed. "Every time I tried to, I couldn't think of what to say."

"You didn't have to say anything." He shook his head as he took a breath. "You could have called me cocksucker, and I'd have called you right back."

"I'll have to remember that." I bit my bottom lip, wondering how he could make me smile at a time like this.

"There's so much I should have told you, Lauren." He shook his head, blowing out a breath. "With Anita—I was stupid and didn't know she wanted a relationship. And not telling you we had a history was a dick move. That was both insensitive of me and lacked professional courtesy. But you already thought I was a whore, and I didn't want to give you more just cause, even if it was accurate. I guess I just assumed she or Chase would string you along, wasting your time like they did everyone else. Daniel knows about our history, but because Chase was originally Carter's client, it wasn't up to Daniel to cut him loose."

I'll admit it hadn't been a pleasure to hear about Roman's past, but I wasn't angry about it either. I couldn't judge him for something he did when he didn't even know me. "I would have understood."

"Maybe." He shrugged. "But I still wasn't proud of it."

I nodded silently, knowing it's not something I would want someone I worked with knowing.

"Carla was at the office on Monday because I was too drunk to see her on Sunday when I called her," he continued, answering my earlier barrage of questions. "And I'd asked her to meet me late hoping you would have already left for the day. I didn't want her to come to my house. And no, it wasn't to fuck her, even though I assume that is what you probably thought. I needed to tell her I was done, and I wanted give her the respect of saying it to her face."

"But on Monday we were still broken up, and you still assumed—"

"On Monday I had spent the weekend mourning the loss of the only woman I'd ever loved." He looked me right in the eyes, making my heart stop. "It didn't matter you were gone, it only mattered you existed at all. So whatever happens now, with you and me, I know I can't go back to that. To her, to that lifestyle—I don't want it."

"Roman." The lump in my throat made it hard to speak and I couldn't finish.

I wasn't sure if he kissed me first or I kissed him, but as my hands grabbed at his T-shirt, my only thought was why hadn't we done this inside.

"Lauren."

He said my name again and again, like he was making up for all the times he didn't say it. His lips against my skin as they moved from my mouth to my neck.

There was more of the conversation we needed to have, and the kiss didn't change what happened on the weekend, but as our mouths connected, it felt so right.

"Inside," I moaned between breaths, my hands pulling themselves away from him long enough to get my keys and open the door. "We need to be inside."

He took over, pulling me inside and shutting the door behind us, pressing his body against mine. "I want you so fucking much."

Nothing mattered.

Not anything he'd said or done, not how bad an idea it was to have sex when so much was left unresolved. I didn't care about any of it. I wanted him just as much as he wanted me and everything else would have to wait.

As weird as it sounded, I didn't want him sweet or tender, I wanted him raw and demanding like I knew he was. The anger and the emotion of the weekend spilled into a frenzy of heated lust I never knew I had.

"Get naked," I demanded, clawing at his T-shirt as I pulled it over his head. "I want to feel you."

I needed his skin, the contact of it against mine so I knew it was real. He complied, continuing to kiss me as his hands got busy blindly undressing himself in a heated rush.

Shoes, sock, pants—all discarded in a messy pile beside the door. And with only his boxer briefs left, he turned his attention to me.

"Your turn." His fingers moved agilely from unzipping my skirt to unbuttoning my blouse, each garment tossed aside to join his on the floor.

He didn't stop, snapping off my bra and replacing it with his mouth, lavishing my breasts with his greedy tongue.

My hand slid between us, feeling his hard length housed in the cotton. "Roman, please."

His arms scooped me up, carrying me to my living room, my back hitting the cushions of the couch. I watched as he ripped off his boxer briefs, standing in front of me naked as he lowered to his knees.

I loved feeling his hands and his tongue on me, but right then it wasn't what I wanted.

"Inside of me." I yanked at his arm. "You can do whatever you want later, but now I need you inside of me."

He chuckled, pulling off my underwear roughly and then spreading my knees apart. "Then that is exactly what you're going to get."

His body covered me, the weight of it pinning me to the couch as he kissed me. His hard cock pressed against my clit, hitting me in just the right spot to make me moan as he dominated my mouth.

My fingers gripped onto his broad shoulders, the muscles flexing underneath my touch as he grinded against me. The sensation made me so wet and hot, my back arched off the cushion.

"Fuck me, Roman," I begged, rocking my hips against his. "I need more."

With his lips at my throat he thrust into me hard, making me first gasp and then moan. I loved it, the feeling of him filling me as he pushed in again.

"God, you're so fucking sexy." His forehead pressed against mine. "Nothing has ever felt this good." A soft kiss landed on my nose before his mouth moved to mine, the pull of his lips growing more urgent as my fingernails dug into his back.

No matter how close he got, it just didn't seem enough. "More." The need vibrated through me as I gasped against his skin.

A growl tore from his throat, my urging, a challenge he silently accepted. A sly grin played on his lips as our eyes connected, thrusting into me a couple of times before pulling his cock all the way out.

His hands gripped my waist, taking me with him as we lifted off the couch. "On your knees, Harper," he barked in my ear as he lowered me onto the carpet. "And I will give you more."

My legs felt like jelly as I scrambled onto all fours. He pushed my knees apart, a hand sliding down between us as I turned to look over my shoulder. His fingers played with my clit as his cock once again filled me, my hips pushing against him as he went deeper.

"Yes." It spilled from my lips as he anchored himself with one hand on my hip while the other twisted against my center.

Each swing of his hips dragged his thick length out of me

before pushing it back inside, faster and more intense with each thrust.

He moved his fingers from my clit to my breast as he leaned against me and asked, "Is this what you wanted?"

God, it felt good. Everywhere he touched and kissed made my skin tingle with excitement.

"Yes, it's what I wanted," I groaned, my neck straining to look at him. "Although I remember this being better, in my office on my desk."

He laughed, pushing in harder. "You think so? Then let me prove you wrong."

My legs gave out from under me as he pulled out in a rush, his hands finding their way back around my waist as he flipped me onto my back and lifted my legs onto his shoulders.

"Look at me." He grunted as he filled me with one hard stroke. "Keep your eyes on me and tell me this isn't better."

"Jesus Christ," I gasped, every single cell primed to explode.

He chuckled, not slowing his pace. "Say *my* name, Lauren. It's not *Jesus Christ* who is fucking you."

I didn't get the chance to say *anyone*'s name, my body exploding as I came in a rush. Our eyes connected as he pumped into me again and again, his finish coming soon after mine, filling me with his load while his hands stayed wrapped around my legs.

"Fuck." He shook his head as he lowered my legs and pulled out slowly. "I'm not wearing a condom."

Ohhhhhhhhh.

Shit.

It seemed me not thinking clearly wasn't restricted to just having sex while there were unresolved issues. No, I had to have *unprotected* sex while there were unresolved issues.

No wonder it felt different.

"Okay, okay, let's not panic," I said, not taking my own advice and slightly panicking. "I'm on the pill, chances of pregnancy are slim." Which wasn't my only concern, to be honest.

Like he could read my mind, he stilled, his eyes connecting with mine. "I'm safe, Lauren, I swear."

The tension eased out of my body, hearing the words I hoped he would say. "Me too," I answered, even though he hadn't asked.

"Give me a second to clean up." He pushed off his knees, giving me the perfect view of his perfect body as he got up and walked to my bathroom. He came back a few moments later with a towel.

I'd always been too careful to have sex without a condom. Scared of STDs or an unwanted pregnancy—it was something I'd never even considered. I didn't realize it would feel so different— better, like we were more connected.

Roman carefully cleaned between my legs, leaning down and kissing my thighs gently as he did it. "I'm sorry, Lauren. I didn't plan that. *Any* of that."

"Out of everything you could have apologized for, *that* was not your fault." I shook my head. "If anything, it was probably mine."

He'd tried to slow down, but that wasn't what I'd wanted. I needed to feel him *more* than I wanted to think about what we were doing.

"Let's just take shared responsibility." He dropped the towel, grabbed the comforter that lay on the back of the couch and wrapped it around me. "I am sorry though," his lips pressed against my forehead, "about everything."

My fingers ran up his forearm. "You were—"

"Evil, horrible, a complete fucking dick?" He cut me off. "Take your pick, all of them accurate. But when you left, for some reason I panicked." He situated himself beside me, his hands locking onto mine. "It was weird, at first I was just waiting for you to come back. But the longer you were gone, the more I was left to draw my own conclusions. That the wedding had freaked you out, and you started to have second thoughts about us. About *me*."

"I sort of did, I threw up," I confessed, knowing that the initial reason I'd left was because I had been freaked out. Just not for the reasons he thought.

He tilted his head, lowering his gaze to meet mine. "You threw up because you didn't want to be with me?"

"No, because I *did* want to be with you, and I wasn't sure you wanted me."

He'd been so honest that I needed to be too. And more importantly, I wanted to be, finally giving myself permission to tell him exactly what I felt.

His arm circled my shoulders, bringing me in closer to him as he kissed me gently on my forehead. "The thought of losing you drove me so far insane, I figured it was easier to push you away. I thought it would hurt less if I walked away on my terms, but it was a million times worse knowing I hurt you. That shit I said about Chase?" He squeezed his eyes shut, shaking his head. "Unforgiveable. And I hate that I said it even though I knew there was no way it could be true. Fuck. If I could take back every single word I said to you that night, I would. In a heartbeat, Lauren, especially the part where I said I didn't care."

"So, what are we doing here?" I angled my chin, allowing my lips to brush against his. "Are we making up?"

"God, I hope so," he smirked as he kissed me back. "If not, then let's just keep doing it, anyway."

I unwrapped the comforter from my body, extending it so it covered us both. His hands immediately moved to my skin as his lips traveled up my collarbone.

My finger jabbed him in the ribs, not enough to hurt but enough to get his attention. "Are you going to quit acting like a jealous asshole?"

"Newsflash, Harper. I *am* a jealous asshole." He laughed against my skin. "But I'll be *your* jealous asshole."

I wanted that, to be his and for him to be mine. Even though I knew we'd still fight. God, I planned on it—sex after an argument with Roman was out of this world amazing.

My finger tapped my chin, deep in thought. "I guess I wouldn't know what to do with you if you suddenly turned nice."

"I may not suddenly turn nice, but I will make it up to you. I want this to work, Lauren." His fingers ghosted against my skin with no humor in his voice. "I want to be with you and I'll go through whatever hell you think I deserve to convince you of that."

"The box," I said suddenly, remembering the package I'd caught him leaving at the door when I arrived. It was the reason he'd been at my apartment and I still didn't know what was in it. "What's in it?"

It hadn't been important when I was pulling him through my doorway, trying to maul him. At that point I wasn't interested in what it was, which was why we shoved it to the side before we walked in. But now I was curious.

"So, I tell you I want to be in a relationship and you want to know what is in the box?" He chuckled, kissing my shoulder. "Way to kill my ego, Harper. I guess I had that coming."

"I'm sorry." I shook my head, realizing how it must have sounded. "I got distracted." I rested my head against his shoulder. "I thought we'd already decided we were making up, or at least that's what we are calling it until you piss me off again."

His finger tapped my nose as he untangled himself from me and the comforter and stood up. "Wait here and we'll open it together."

He picked up the discarded towel, wrapping it around his waist before opening the door and collecting the box that had been left outside.

"I didn't think I'd be sitting beside you when you opened it." He smiled, sinking to his knees in front of me. "But I'm really glad I am."

My fingers fumbled with the plain brown box as a mix of nervous and excited energy buzzed through my body. All his gifts had been so thoughtful and observant, the whole time he'd been paying such close attention.

"Oh my God." My hand flew up to my mouth as I pulled out a beautiful red heart-shaped clock that looked identical to the one given to the Tin Man in the *Wizard of Oz*. And unsurprisingly there was a note attached.

> *I took your advice, went to see the Wizard and asked him for a heart. Turns out I've had one this whole time, but I'd already given it to you. I'm sorry.*
> *Roman x*
>
> *PS It's yours even if you don't want it.*
> *PPS. I also have courage, so I need to tell you I love you.*
> *PPPS Even more shocking is I have a brain too, which means I know exactly what I lost. And I'll never stop trying to get it back.*

I held the heart-shaped clock to my ear, my eyes starting to mist. "It ticks." The words got lost in a sob.

"Of course it ticks." He took my chin in his hands and kissed my lips gently. "There's no point having a heart if it doesn't."

I kissed him back, holding tightly to the ornate chain of my new favorite thing as I wrapped my arms around him.

"I love it and I love you."

CHAPTER #27

MORGAN CAME HOME eventually and found Roman in my bed.

Which was funny because that's where I was too even though I usually would have been still at work when she got home. Even more amusing is that she wasn't all that surprised.

She did glare at him and told him if he hurt me again she'd kill him and make it look like natural causes. And that we'd already drafted his brother Eric for body disposal, which attracted a few questions that needed to be answered.

As Eric had said when he came to my apartment, Roman hadn't asked him to speak to me, or known about his visit.

He wasn't too pleased about it either. Something about him not needing anyone else fighting his battles, blah, blah, blah. I designated it something he needed to sort out with his brother. There were five of them, I'm sure they were all well versed in sibling squabbles.

And Morgan was finally going to go out with Roman, only it wasn't for reconnaissance, but because I wanted them to get to know each other better. She didn't even mind driving herself there, her eyes widening when she got a look at his Ferrari.

"Now that I know you're related, I totally see the resemblance."

Morgan tilted her head as she looked at Roman. "Do all of you look the same?" The *Larsson* connection left unspoken because we were in public.

"Dave and Nick have darker hair and eyes, but our younger brother, Alex, looks more like us." He shrugged with a goofy smile. "I don't really think about it that much."

My hand cupped his, gently rubbing it. "Morgan is just interested in the science of it all." I tried to hide my grin. "What are the chances that all the members of the family were so genetically blessed?"

"I wonder if there's a balance to all of that?" Morgan's hand rested on her chin, her brow knitting in thought. "If there is a large family of brothers somewhere else in world who are hideously unattractive."

The grin I was trying to hide could no longer be contained. "I bet they hate you all too. You would be their nemeses."

"You're enjoying this too much, Harper." He shook his head before turning his attention to Morgan. "And I assumed someone from a medical background wouldn't encourage her."

"I'm her sister first, and nurse second." Morgan grinned. "How adverse are you to me collecting your DNA and sending it away for testing?"

We all laughed, even Roman who was taking the joking about his family remarkably well. I guess he'd had lots of practice through the years, and the more I thought about it, the more sense changing his last name made.

"No DNA testing." My fingers laced with his, suddenly feeling protective. "The science will have to suffer without it."

Morgan looked at us with genuine happiness and smiled. "So are you guys going to tell your boss you're dating? Isn't it against company policy or something like that?"

I groaned knowing as much as I didn't want to, we were

probably going to have to tell Daniel. "Technically it's allowed but discouraged."

"Which translates into he can't fire us but he won't like it," Roman added.

Taking into account ideal situations, ours was far from it.

When we'd been having sex with no plans for future commitment, there had been no reason to say anything. Why bother rocking the boat for something that would probably fizzle in a couple of months. At least that was what I had assumed. Of course, I hadn't planned on developing feelings for him, or more to the point, the feelings I already had, growing into something more.

And while our rivalry had been real—both of us working harder when pushed by the other—the hatred, wasn't.

"We'll tell him on Monday," I decided, not wanting to hide it anymore. "Like you said, he can't fire us and we can keep it professional. We both owe Daniel a lot and I don't want to lie to him."

Roman nodded, giving my hand a squeeze. "You're right, first thing at our Monday meeting."

There had been so many stupid secrets throughout our relationship, I didn't want there to be anymore. Especially not now when we'd finally seemed on track.

Watching the interaction between Morgan and Roman at lunch just made me fall in love with him a little more. He was so at ease with her, he didn't try to impress her or pretend she didn't matter. And she was exactly the same way with him.

Where I'd been concerned about being in a relationship because it meant spending time with someone, now I had no desire *not* to be with him. I wanted the same things I'd wanted last month, and the month before that, but now I wanted to share them with him.

After lunch was over, we said goodbye to Morgan, and spent rest of the weekend at Roman's apartment. The two of us were in a bubble that would undoubtedly burst on Monday when we started telling people, and I wanted to stay inside of it as long as I could.

"I love you." He kissed my forehead, my skin still damp from making love.

It hadn't been sex. Roman had been slow and deliberate, taking his time as he moved inside of me. And I loved it.

My fingers traced the curves of his chest as I tilted my head to look at him. "I love you too."

He laughed, which was one of my favorite sounds, his eyes lighting up as they focused on me. "What's on your mind, Lauren?"

I'd always assumed he'd never paid attention to me, but I'd been wrong. He knew so much more than I'd ever noticed. What pizza I liked, what I liked to drink, that I didn't like flowers, my obsession with writing things on a whiteboard. Months—things that he'd seen over months, and he'd stored them away in a Lauren bank that I never knew existed.

"The first day you met me." I bit my lip, needing to know the whole truth. "When I introduced myself and tried to be friends, why were you so . . . cold?"

It had been so startling, to see a man who looked so aesthetically beautiful seem to have such hardness underneath. And it wasn't that I wasn't used to people being rude or treating me like I didn't belong, the law profession was filled with dicks. But he was different, like his frostiness was reserved just for me.

He took a deep breath and sighed, a smile creeping across his mouth. "Because I knew I was in trouble. I can deal with a beautiful woman or a sexy woman, or someone who is smart or funny. Hell, as much as you thought I was some kind of deviant, I had no problem being professional and keeping it in my pants. But you." He shook his head. "You were everything. Beautiful, sexy, smart, driven, funny, and a brilliant lawyer—I knew I wouldn't be able to keep away from you. How could I not?"

"You thought that after a five minute meeting?" I scrunched

my face up in confusion. I'd had feelings of lust at the start for sure, who didn't? He was gorgeous. But I didn't expect to find my soul mate, which is exactly how I felt about him now.

He nodded, running his hand down my body and cinching me closer. "I'd never met anyone like you. The falling in love part took me by surprise, I hadn't planned on that, but it made a lot of sense. You never took my bullshit, or anyone else's for that matter. You're strong and fucking vicious in a courtroom. I can't tell you the amount of times I got hard while you were cross-examining a witness or delivering your closing argument." He tossed his head back and laughed.

"You *are* a deviant." I elbowed him playfully in the ribs. "I just always assumed you thought I wasn't good enough, which just pissed me off. For some stupid reason, earning your respect was really important to me."

"Jesus, Lauren." He shook his head. "You always had my respect, and so much more. You're a circle, I respected and admired the hell out of you."

I jabbed him again. "What's a circle, wiseass? This better not be in reference to my body shape either."

"A circle is the strongest shape because there are no breaks." He held up his hand, connecting his forefinger and thumb to create an O. "It is just one continuous line so the beginning and the end are no longer visible. Perfect in every way, resilient, and beautiful to look at."

My heart just melted a little more, the sigh slipping from my lips. "That was the one of the sweetest things anyone has ever said to me."

"So," he kissed my temple, "now you know. I was a prick because I was trying to avoid the inevitable. I thought it would ruin one of the best partnerships I'd ever had. Or that I would screw something up, and then lose you completely. Turns out I sucked at that and fell in love with you anyway."

My lips brushed against his, my heart feeling like it was about to burst. "And I had no choice but to fall in love with you."

THERE WAS AN eerie sense of calm that washed over me on Monday morning.

I had spent the entire weekend with Roman, only returning home to collect some clothes and check in on Morgan. But it was while I was lying in bed with him—everything slowing down around us—that I really appreciated what I had.

Somehow, without even realizing it, I'd achieved the ultimate.

I was in love with a man who was powerful, smart and sexy who wasn't intimidated by me or my ambition.

And he loved me right back.

I also had an amazing job that paid well in one of the most prestigious law firms in L.A. with awesome prospects for growth, and I'd earned that honestly.

No one had handed me anything on a silver platter, there had been no lottery wins—everything I had, I'd worked hard for. And I wasn't going to give any of it up without a fight.

"Lauren, Roman." Daniel dipped his chin to the two chairs in front of him. "So nice of you both to show up. I assume you're done with *personal* time?" His voice hinted at the displeasure of losing both his associates last Friday.

"We have." Roman looked at me and nodded. "Actually, before we start, we wanted to talk to you about that."

Daniel's eyebrows rose as he leaned forward in his chair. "You better not be trying to renegotiate your contracts, you have another twelve months before your review. And if some other bastard is trying to poach you, I'll also remind you that you signed a non compete in the exact contract I'm referring to."

I smiled, almost feeling honored he valued us so much he'd sue us if we left. It was a little twisted, but I guess I liked that. "No, this isn't some joint effort to extort more money, and neither of us is leaving." I looked at Roman and took a breath. "But we need you to know we're dating."

Daniel narrowed his eyes, confused as he annunciated slowly. "Each other?"

"Crazy, I know," Roman added, his hand stretched across to touch mine, which just made Daniel's eyes widen even more. "But Lauren and I are dating. And while it doesn't violate any terms of that contract you are fond of mentioning, we know the firm doesn't look favorably on couples. Regardless, our situation isn't changing." His fingers gave mine a squeeze.

"Wait a second," Daniel rolled back from his desk. "The two of you can barely stand each other. Carter and Byrne each have a wager on which one of you was going to defect to either of them."

My mouth dropped open. "The partners have been betting on us?"

He shrugged and gave us a slow smile. "I had ten grand on you guys sticking it out, because both of you are too stubborn to give the other the satisfaction of leaving."

"Well, I guess depending on what you say next will determine who wins." Roman chuckled. "Because we're still dating, so if that's going to be a problem, we should talk about it now."

"I'm not losing ten grand, Roman." Daniel leveled him with a look. "You're both staying with me. *But* part of the reason your partnership works is because of the healthy competition you seem to have. I'd be lying if I didn't tell you I was concerned."

"Daniel." It was my turn to speak. "Being a lawyer is important to me, but being an amazing lawyer is paramount. I'm not going to suddenly be someone else because I work with someone I'm in a relationship with. That healthy competition is still going to be there because we both know out of the two of us, I'm the better associate."

Roman coughed. "What Harper means to say is." He looked at me with the same cocky grin he usually wore in our meetings. "She likes to think she is better and sometimes, she definitely brings some worthwhile arguments to the table." He straightened his tie. "But I am by far superior."

"In what universe?" I scoffed. "Showboating isn't work, Roman."

"It's not showboating if it's the truth, Harper. Don't be jealous, I just make it look better than you do." He shot me a wink.

Excitement flooded me; this was what it had always been like for us. Right here in that moment, going head to head and not pulling any punches. And I knew that he wasn't going to expect me to back down. No, he was counting on me doing exactly what we'd always done.

Daniel clapped, tenting his fingers in front of him. "I hope this display isn't just for my benefit. The enjoyment I get from watching the two of you debate a case encourages me to overlook other things, especially the stolen scotch out of my desk."

"What scotch?" Roman tilted his head looking confused. And had I not been the one to drink it with him I would have totally bought his innocent act. "Not sure what you are talking about. Harper, you know anything about this mystery?"

I rubbed my chin, deep in thought. "Can't say that I do."

"Great." Daniel laughed, "Now you guys are teaming up as well as working your solo angles, I don't know whether to be excited or concerned." His fingers rapped on the desk. "Keep it professional, give me the level of excellence I expect and we'll have no problems. But if this goes bad, the both of you are pitching in for the ten grand, and still have to live with the misery of working together."

"When are you calling in the bet?" I heard myself ask. "I can't imagine a bunch of lawyers didn't draw up terms, least of which is the end date."

Daniel turned to me surprised, but looked impressed. "End of your contract date, twelve months from now."

"And you only put down ten G's?" Roman laughed as he shook his head. "You are such a cheap bastard, we're worth twenty at least."

Daniel rolled his eyes, containing his grin. "If I've made myself understood, we're done here."

"Then we're done," I answered, because there was no way I was giving up Roman or my job.

"Good, go and I'll have Stephanie bring you your next assignment." Daniel rapped his fingers on the desk again. "Jana Cane will be in next week to go over her company's restructure. And with Anderson's ITP out of the picture, we're signing a new tech company."

I turned to Roman and shot him a grin. "Hopefully someone who's COO you don't have a history with."

"Really?" Roman cocked his head as his eyebrow rose. "You're going to go there? It was one time, Harper."

It had meant to be a joke, sort of like when I accused him of screwing all the paralegals except he didn't smile. Maybe I'd pushed it too far and broken the rule that I'd set from the beginning and made it personal.

Shit.

"Oh, so she knows?" Daniel laughed, seeming to enjoy it. "Well, that's a relief. Awesome. I have a hunch this is all going to work out. Why don't the two of you go argue about it elsewhere, I have a meeting with a client in thirty minutes."

With a wave of his hand, Daniel dismissed us, Roman getting to the door first. "After you." He held it open waiting for me to pass, his face unreadable as I walked through.

Deciding it was better to go back to his office and apologize there, I nodded and strode down the hall to his door. My fingers pushed open the door with him filling the space behind me almost immediately as he closed it.

"Roman, I'm sorry—" I couldn't finish, his mouth on mine before I could get more words out.

His firm body pushed against mine until I was a prisoner between the wall of his muscular chest and the drywall that separated our offices. I didn't resist, allowing him to kiss me as I felt him hard against me.

"Do not start doubting yourself. Not with me. Not ever." His mouth moved to my neck. "Just don't ever talk about my love life in front of a client or in a courtroom."

I gasped, loving the feel of his weight against me. "You're not mad?"

"Nope." His kisses moved back to my mouth before he pulled away. His eyes connected with mine as he looked at me so deeply a chill ran down my spine. "I *did* have history with her. I'm not proud of it, but if we're going to work together, I don't want you holding anything back. In here, you can get ugly if you need to, but we leave it here. Always, Lauren. No exceptions. And you can't bring it home and I won't either. I made that mistake one time, and I'll *never* make it again."

My hands moved up his chest. "So you want me to call you a whore like I used to do?"

"Maybe lay off the whore part since you're going to have first-hand knowledge that it's no longer true." He grinned. "But you know fighting with you turns me on, so I'm hoping we'll still play."

I pushed roughly against his chest, my effort not even moving him an inch. "Promise me, Roman. Promise me, right here and now that things won't change in the office. Because if we both can't do that then maybe one of us should go and work for the other partners."

"Not a chance I am letting you leave me, Harper." Roman laughed as he shook his head. "Not after all the time I had to wait to finally get you." He laid my flat palm against his chest, the thump-thump vibrating under my fingers. "You have my heart, Lauren. And I'll promise you whatever you want because I would never ask you to change. I love you for who you are and what you do. You make me a better lawyer, and you sure as hell make me a better man."

My hand might have been on his heart, but he had mine. "I love you, I love you so much."

I pulled him closer, my mouth finding his as he mumbled against my lips. "Now, let me screw you up against my desk. Then we can go tell Miriam we're together."

"Miriam?" I pulled back slightly confused why we'd tell someone from accounts we barely spoke to that we were now dating.

Roman's eyebrow rose as he grinned. "She's the office gossip, we tell her and everyone else will know. Means I get to spend time on important things."

"Like?" I bit my lip, excited about what his other *things* might be.

He placed his hands against the wall, the one that had separated our offices for twelve months. A wall I had glared at, hoping the power of my displeasure would penetrate it and sear him in the next room.

Now, I'd do anything to knock it down.

"Like . . ." He bent his head, his nose grazing against mine. "Planning the rest of my life with you."

And that was a plan there would be no argument over.

I didn't know if we'd always work together, or if our careers would eventually dictate we work elsewhere. But it no longer mattered because I knew two things with absolute certainty.

One. I loved Roman Pierce.
And two, he loved me back.

EPILOGUE

Twelve Months Later

THE CAR ROCKED as we pulled up to the venue. My hands had smoothed down the front of my beautiful dress at least a million times as my stomach churned uncomfortably.

"Are you sure you want to do this?" Roman asked me, looking a little nervous himself. He didn't get rattled easily which had me on edge, the energy buzzing around us.

I gazed at him, his clear blue eyes looking so amazing against his white shirt and black tux. I could barely believe we'd made it out of our apartment.

Ours.

Even all these months later it still felt weird saying it.

And while I desperately missed living with Morgan, we saw her all the time. I think secretly she liked having the apartment all to herself, especially now since she'd started dating a surgeon from the hospital she worked at.

I looked out of the blackened limo window, the crowd waiting for us to exit the vehicle. "No, I said we were doing this and we're doing this. It's not like anyone knows who we are."

Roman lifted my hand to his mouth and kissed my knuckles. "Exactly, besides they aren't here for us."

I nodded, giving him the okay to push the door open; a flurry of flashes and noise assaulting us as we stepped onto the red carpet.

"Don't step on your dress," he whispered in my ear as he lifted the hem of the amazing Valentino gown I was wearing. "And if I haven't told you tonight, you look beautiful."

My lips spread into a grin, ignoring the crowd who was quickly losing interest when they didn't recognize us. "You have, but I like hearing it." His arm moved around my waist as we slowly walked the red carpet.

"Now who's got the big ego?" He laughed, guiding me through the mayhem to the quieter foyer of the theatre.

He was definitely a little off, wanting to be away from the crowd even though we both knew what we were getting into.

I turned, the privacy we were now afforded allowing me to speak more freely. "Well, if what the critics say is true, I think it's going to be your brother who has the big ego. The words *Academy Award* have been tossed around more than just a few times."

Roman grinned. "If anyone deserves it, he does. But if you repeat that, Harper, I will deny it." He showed our tickets to an usher. "Someone needs to keep him grounded."

We were led to our seats, the theatre still largely empty, and sat down. Almost everyone was still outside. They were either waiting for the stars of the latest blockbuster to show up or hoping to get noticed, which was why we preferred to be away from the noise, happy to just be here to support Eric.

After his wedding to Tia and a short honeymoon, Eric had spent three months training and then a further four months shooting in the remote Canadian wilderness. He played an explorer abandoned by his expedition crew in Antarctica. Who not only survived the harsh wilderness with almost no supplies, but also managed to stay alive long enough until the next crew arrived and rescued him.

I didn't have to see it to know it was going to be good.

Naturally, Eric wanted all his family to be there on opening night, even Roman who up until this point had safely flown under the radar.

And as we arrived, no one suspected a thing. Choosing to ignore what was a startling resemblance to the main star, to focus on one of the smaller costars who'd arrived around the same time.

It was still pretty cool to be at the premiere of huge movie, even if I did feel slightly out of my depth. I was glad Roman had wanted to get off the carpet sooner than later. I think deep down he might have been worried the longer we were out there, the greater the chance of someone making the connection.

"Wow, they're just letting anyone into these things." Nick took the seat next to Roman. "I guess now that you have a beautiful woman on your arm, they just let you go where you want." He treated me to the famous Larsson charm as he flashed me a grin. "Lauren, always a pleasure. Let me know when you're ready to upgrade to a better model."

"Stop hitting on my girlfriend, asshole." Roman discreetly flipped off his brother, his usual grin missing in action. "Have some class."

"Who doesn't have class?" We were joined by Dave, who flashed his own sexy Larsson grin as he took the seat next to me. "Lauren, you're looking beautiful. You could do so much better than Roman." His arm playfully draped along the back of my chair.

"Tell me, Dave." Roman leaned forward, his voice surprisingly calm considering the tightness of his jaw. "Is there a lot of work for armless actors these days? I'd hate for you to be unemployed."

"Relax." His brother grinned as he moved his hands away from me and into his lap. "I'm just yanking your chain, and you make it way too easy."

Roman gave them both a stern look before interlocking his

fingers with mine. "Our parents should have stopped at two children."

Even though our relationship was no longer new, the Larsson
men took great joy in giving Roman hell. It was all in good fun,
and for the most part he took it all in stride. But every once in a
while it made me nervous. The memory of Eric's wedding, and the
things they had probably said to him in jest, still not distant enough.

"I love you." I squeezed Roman's hand tightly as I leaned in
and kissed him. "Help me find a bathroom."

He nodded, lifting out of his chair then holding out his hand
to help me out of mine. I smiled as I stood, my fingers curling
around his arm as he led me away from his brothers in the direction of the bathrooms.

"I didn't really need to go." I pulled him into a quiet corner.
"I just wanted a minute with you before it gets crazy. As soon as
Eric shows up it's going to be a circus. And you know I love Dave
and Nick, but their joking around . . . you just seem tense tonight."
He looked a little confused as I ran my hands along the front of his
lapels. "I just needed to tell you how much I love you, how amazing
my life is with you and how lucky I am to have you in my life."

The words didn't seem enough, didn't seem to do justice to
how blessed I felt. But I wanted to tell him anyway, even though
we were in the middle of the Dolby Theater waiting for a bunch
of famous people who we mostly didn't know.

"You were worried about me?" He tilted his head, his lips
twitching at the edges. "Because of Dave and Nick? Lauren, nothing
those losers say tonight is going to change the way I feel."

Shit, maybe I had read it wrong? "I just thought . . . you
seemed . . ." I couldn't put my finger on it.

In the car I had assumed it had only been nervous energy but it
was more than that. "Roman, please tell me there's nothing wrong."

"Nothing's wrong." He brushed his lips against my forehead.

"This just isn't my scene."

He sounded convincing, and if I hadn't seen him work a court-room like a virtuoso so many times I'd lost count, I might have believed him.

But crowds had never bothered him, and while he wasn't crazy about hanging with famous people, he'd never been uncomfortable with it.

I'd been the one who had found the adjustment to having a boyfriend with a famous brother a little awkward at the start, not the other way around. So, I was either imagining the weird vibe between us or there was something he wasn't telling me. And after a year of *no more secrets*, there was no way I was going back to that.

"Please, just tell me." I took a deep breath, the churning in my gut getting worse. "I know there is something you aren't telling me."

His hand raked through his hair roughly, the way he did when he was nervous or upset. And now I knew there was something wrong as he looked at me. "Jesus, Lauren. It's not what you think."

I hated those words.

"Then tell me, because what I'm thinking isn't good." I wasn't even pretending I wasn't worried, because I was.

He looked around, his eyes darting around at the people in the distance. We had maybe ten minutes before the space was filled with an audience and we'd be directed back to our seats. And if I was going to find out what was bothering him, I needed it to be now.

"I promise you, I will not freak out. You can tell me anything." I tried to reason even though I was basically promising something I had no idea I was going to be able to keep.

He'd had a private meeting with Daniel on Friday that he said was about some new account, but what if he'd decided to resign? Our contracts were up next week so anything was possible.

His head tilted to the side, watching me with interest. "You have no idea, do you?"

My eyes widened as the uneasy feeling started to grow. "No idea about what?"

"It wasn't supposed to be here. I was going to do it later tonight when it was just the two of us." He took a deep breath. "I should have just done it before we left."

"Roman, now I'm starting to freak out."

He cupped my chin in his hands and kissed me, gently brushing my lips with his. "I have a ring in my pocket, Lauren. I'm going to ask you to marry me."

"What?" I said a little too loudly, the socialite in the tight red body stocking turning around to look at us with judgment. "You were going to propose? We haven't even talked about marriage. You said it wasn't your thing, that you hated it."

Or at least that's what I thought he'd said, my memory was foggy thinking back to his stance on marriage. It hadn't been favorable, I did remember that. Of all the things I thought he was going to suggest, marriage was the last thing I'd have picked. And I was okay with that, just happy to have what we had. I didn't need a piece of paper if he didn't want it.

"Things change," he said, the smile I'd been desperate to see all night spreading across his lips. His first genuine smile. "And I want you as my wife, if you'll have me."

I couldn't speak, my eyes starting to water as every single word I wanted to say got lost on the way out of my mouth.

"I had this plan to take you to Heart and Vine, and then I was going to—"

"Yes." I didn't bother letting him finish. "Yes, I want to marry you and I don't need a fancy proposal. Oh my God, Roman." I wrapped my arms around him and laid my head against his chest. "A million times yes."

He chuckled, his laugh vibrating under my cheek. "I would have gotten on my knees, Harper. You sure you want to give that up?"

I hugged him tighter. "I'm not giving anything up and that includes you."

His hand disappeared into his pocket and he pulled out a small teal box, inside was a gorgeous platinum solitaire. A perfect round band with a perfect round stone—simple, elegant, and exactly what I would have chosen for myself.

He lifted my left hand from his chest and slipped the ring on my finger. "Marriage never made sense to me before because I couldn't imagine loving anyone forever. But now I have you, and there isn't a future without you in it. Now I understand why people do it, and nothing makes more sense than asking you to be my wife."

Any hope I had of not crying was lost as a tear ran down my cheek. I couldn't even speak, too emotional to say something equally as beautiful to him. So I nodded and then kissed him, and it seemed to be enough. The tension in his shoulders eased as he kissed me back, wrapping his arms around me as the noise inside the theatre got louder, Eric and Tia having recently made their arrival.

"You want to go back to our seats?" He kissed my hand, ignoring his older brother moving to the front of the theater as the crowd applauded.

I nodded, clearing my throat. "I'll go anywhere with you." My answer making him grin.

With the ring he'd given me less than a few minutes ago on my finger, he led us back to our seats, and my cheeks hurt from smiling.

I didn't care if it wasn't a traditional proposal, or it hadn't been the way he'd planned, or that he hadn't gotten down on one knee. None of that would have been us anyway.

Dave and Nick both smirked when they noticed my hand,

trying to offer their congratulations discreetly while the director spoke about the movie. I was sure they had more to say about it, but we were probably going to have to wait for that. In truth, I didn't care what they said, or what anyone else said for that matter.

A man who had once been my biggest rival was now my number one love.

Life was nothing but awesome.

THE END

ACKNOWLEDGEMENTS

THIS BOOK NEEDS extra special thank yous, because without the love and support of some amazing people, I might not have made it through. For every single one of you beautiful angels who checked in on me, visited, sent flowers, messages, emails, smoke signals—I love and appreciate you more than words. You are my heart when mine was in pieces.

Gep, Jenna, Liam and Woodley—without you I am lost. I have the best family in the world. You are perfect.

To my mum—all those times I needed help and you never complained or turned me down. Thank you a million times. I need to call you more, and I will.

To my brothers, the amazing sister-in-laws they've given me and their families. You're awesome and we're all okay.

Thank you to my friends. LORD, how did I get so lucky? You are rock stars; I love you and I thank you for understanding me and accepting me as I am.

To my amazing "person" at Social Butterfly PR- Emily Smith-Kidman. I have no idea how I would have gotten through #1 Player's release and moved onto this one. I will never be able to thank you enough for your kindness, understanding, love and support. I adore you.

My agents, Kimberly Brower and Jess Dallow from Brower Literary and Management—Thank you.

To my amazing betas, MK and Danielle. Your insight and keen eyes are the bomb. I love your feedback, and so glad you enjoy my books.

To Hang Le—So much love. You have gone beyond being a cover designer, you are a friend and someone I'd be lost without. BUT your covers continue to defy my expectations.

Thank you to Nichole Strauss—my editor at Insight Editing. You were so gracious and patient with me, moving our schedule when I fell into a heap. I know we both keep each other on our toes, and I drive you crazy sometimes, but it works. Thank you for helping me through this, even though editing was the last thing I wanted to do.

To Christine Borgford from Type A Formatting, it's a constant pleasure to work with you. Not only do you make everything beautiful, but you are a wonderful soul as well. Sorry for the date changes, and thank you for your patience.

Special thanks to my proofreaders MK and Rosa—your sharp eyes help make my books super awesome.

To all the authors who are in my world. Big, small, near or far—every single one of you has meant everything to me. The kindness you have shown me goes beyond words. No words. Literally none. Thank you doesn't seem enough.

To all the bloggers and reviewers! I know I don't always see your posts, reviews, comments, shares but I feel your love. I feel it and I appreciate it. Thank you for your tireless and often thankless work. Rock on!!

Thanks to the T Gephart entourage, you are awesome!!! I love "hanging" out with you. Thanks for everything you do.

Last but not least, thank YOU. To the person who bought this book, read it, possibly reviewed it or told someone about it. Whether you fit into one of those categories or all of them, I thank you. As long as you want to read my crazy, I'll keep writing.

ABOUT THE AUTHOR

T GEPHART IS a USA Today and International bestselling author from Melbourne, Australia.

With an approach to life that is somewhat unconventional, she prefers to fly by the seat of her pants rather than adhere to some rigid roadmap. Her lack of "plan" has resulted in a rather interesting and eclectic resume, which reads more like the fiction she writes than an actual employment history. She'd tell you all about it, but the statute of limitations hasn't expired yet. But all those crazy twists and turns have led her to a career she loves—writing romantic comedy.

When she isn't filling pages with sassy and sexy characters with attitude, she's living her own reality show in the 'burbs of Melbourne with her American husband, two teenage children, and her fur child—Woodley.

She loves adventure, to laugh, travel, and strives to live her life to the fullest.

CONNECT WITH T

www.tgephart.com
Facebook
Goodreads
Twitter

BOOKS BY THIS AUTHOR

The Lexi Series

Lexi

A Twist of Fate

Twisted Views: Fate's Companion

A Leap of Faith

A Time for Hope

The Power Station Series

High Strung

Crash Ride

Back Stage

The Black Addiction Series

Slide

Sticks

Stand

#1 Series

#1 Crush

#1 Player

#1 Rival

#1 Lie

#1 Muse

#1 Love (coming 2019)

Collision Series

Train Wreck

Car Crash (coming soon)

Standalones

The Fall